Angel Of Fate

The Fate Trilogy

L.J. Kentowski

More books by L.J. Kentowski

Fate Trilogy:

Guardian of Fate (Book 1)
Seeker of Fate (Book 2)
Angel of Fate (Book 3)

Lexie Pearce Series:
Descended in Vengeance (Book 1)

Heart of Seeton Series:
Love Owned (Book 1)
Full Potential (Book 2)

Learn more about these books at
http://www.laurakentowski.com/

<u>Get a FREE Urban Fantasy Short Story!</u>
When you sign up for my VIP Newsletter, you'll receive access to release news, upcoming events, and exclusive content and giveaways!
As a thank you for joining, you'll also receive a FREE bonus short story companion to the Lexie Pearce Series!
Get started here:
https://preview.mailerlite.io/forms/1675703/160480288834586588/share

ACKNOWLEDGEMENTS

To my loyal fans: Oh my god. You guys are amazing! I've made you wait so long for this final installment of the Fate Trilogy, but you stuck by me, and I am eternally thankful for you. You are the ones who kept me writing. You are the ones who brought my dreams to reality. There are no words for how you've shaped my world. Books are about dreams and fantasy worlds. You've brought mine to life.

To my wonderful husband: I can't even find the words to tell you how much your support of this journey means to me. Without it, the color in my life wouldn't be as brilliant. Thank you for pushing me to continue and realize my dreams aren't as far away as I believed. We got this.

To my friends and family: All of the support, belief, and motivation you've given me have pushed me beyond what I ever thought I could accomplish. You're confidence in me is amazing and inspiring. Darcy, you've been my rock when I didn't think I'd be solid enough. I love you, sassy girlfriend. Keep pushing me, and I'll keep your glass full and your reading hot ;) Loni, you've been by me through this whole journey, and I'll always be thankful. Rainbows are ahead, always ahead, never behind, making the future bright and colorful. If we look that way, we'll always see the sun shining on our path.

To my editor, Kathy Lapeyre: It was by chance we met, but I feel like an angel granted you to me. You've taught me so much already, and made this novel shine for me. I'm so grateful we connected, because I know this book wouldn't be half of what it's become without you. I can't wait to tell more stories with you.

To my beta readers (Tif Thordal, Sherry Lynn Wolfe, Kathleen Bergeron, & Holly Elizabeth): You guys freaking rock! I can't thank you enough for your help making Angel Of Fate the best it can be. You've gone above and beyond for my story, and me. I couldn't ask for better friends than you.

CHAPTER ONE

"I have a surprise for you," I whispered into Hunter's ear as I lay over his naked torso.

A rumbling moan echoed from deep within his throat, and he hardened even more beneath me.

"Do you, now?" his low, seductive voice purred back.

Straddling him, I sat up on my knees and grinned as his mouth lifted on one side in a sexy smile, blue eyes glowing with passion. Sweat glistened on his muscled chest from heat radiating within, causing his scent to invade me like a pheromone.

So many times before, my insides would have melted from a mere glance at him like this. Even without looking, the energy pulsating from him would have drawn me in.

Not this time.

"Stay right there," I told him, meeting his sexy smile with one of my own.

I reached over the side of the bed, my hip movement causing him to moan again. Knowing the effect I had on him always brought a smile to my face.

Complete control.

Reaching between the mattress and box springs, my fingers slid across until I felt metal brush against my fingertips. I leaned over the edge of the bed, grasped the hilt of the Sword, and pulled it out.

Energy hit me like a jolt of electricity, sending currents up my arms, around my shoulders and into my chest, where they zoned in on my heart, deadening it with every shock. Completely transfixed by the beauty of the Sword in my hands, I sat for a moment, reveling in the fact it was a part of me, the source of my whole being.

And now together, the Sword and I would clear the way for absolute power and domination.

The man before me who thought himself my soul mate for the last year had given up the very essence of his being to stay with me, to save me from my own evil fate. But Fate couldn't be molded or shaped. It was unyielding, fixed. I had become who I was meant to be, and there was nothing or no one who could change that.

I had no soul mate because I no longer had a soul.

Hunter would never concede to Fate, so this would be his.

Raising the Sword and tilting the tip forward, I aimed it for Hunter's heart. Our gazes locked over the shiny steel of the blade. His eyes narrowed, no longer blazed with passion. A muscle twitched near his jaw, but the rest of his gorgeous body remained motionless. Surely he was fighting every instinct to defend himself. Or did he know he didn't stand a chance? That was the beauty of Hunter—his demeanor never gave him away. His enemies never noticed him coming. It was a valuable lesson I'd learned from him.

I gripped the Sword tighter and inched it closer to his skin. Hunter's eyes never wavered from mine.

"Fight it, Cassandra."

"You can't fight destiny," I told him.

"Your destiny is with me."

Stilling the Sword above him, I said, "My destiny is where you should have left me."

His gaze intensified as if it were trying to penetrate my soul even though he no longer had that luxury. Time stood still and what might have been hours was only a few moments. In lazy defiance, he added, "I have no regrets."

One edge of my upper lip eased into a grin. My eyes burned with new luminosity, flares of light reaching out like sparks spitting from an open wire. I was in my true form.

"Neither do I." My words echoed with finality.

Before his eyes closed, he inhaled, cutting off the connection between us as if he were already at peace with his Final Death. That's when I plunged the blade straight into his heart.

***

I jolted up in bed from a resounding scream that had penetrated my sleep. As I scanned the room, images from my nightmare returned in waves. The scream had been my own, and my body shook, but it wasn't enough to rid the dread of what had happened and how it consumed my thoughts.

Past experience told me my recurring nightmares weren't like everyone else's. It wasn't merely my mind's way of playing creative genius with random pieces of my day while I slept. No, mine were warnings. Premonitions.

Fingers lightly brushed my arm, and I quivered from the touch. Gentle lips kissed my bare shoulder, and I exhaled the breath I didn't realize I was holding. The combination released tension throughout my body, urging it to relax. Everything appeared as it should be. Hunter was there... alive... and I loved him. These thoughts had become routine every time I woke from the nightmare. Groping at scattered beliefs to confirm it could never happen, no matter what the past had taught me, I told myself, not this time, not this one. *This time*, I wouldn't let it happen.

"Another one?" he asked, still at my shoulder.

I couldn't look at him. Not yet. Dreams or not, it was too difficult to meet his eyes knowing I'd just killed him. Instead, I simply nodded.

He kissed my shoulder again, this time with more tenderness than usual, but I still couldn't shake the imprint from my mind.

Lately, more kisses were required to provide enough relief for me to completely warm back up. We'd played out this same scene too many times during the last month. Each time the emotions from my nightmare appeared closer to the surface, more powerful, lingering longer.

And still, I wouldn't tell him the truth.

"Do you remember anything more?"

I shook my head. "No. They're just more... intense."

"It's going to take time, Cassandra. Your mind is only trying to deal with what you've been through. Who knows what that monster did to you down there. But you're safe now. I'm here."

Hunter thought my dreams were about Nergal holding me captive in Hell. I'd blacked out during most of that ordeal, losing all track of the time, but almost wished the nightmares *were* about that. It might make looking him in the eye each morning much easier. I continued letting him believe I was reliving that nightmare, choosing my own secret hell instead.

How could I tell him I dreamt about killing him every night? He understood my dreams always ended up being some whacked out form of a prophecy, so what would I say? "I think I'm going to kill you soon because every night I stab you through the heart with the Sword of Final Death"? No way. We were finally able to be together. *Together*, really together. No one blocking our path. Neither of us chained to something in Hell. Free to sleep every night in each other's arms. It was wonderful, except for the terrifying nightmares that invaded the bliss while I slept, or when the occasional image popped into my head when we were together. But my time with him was precious, and I wasn't about to change that.

I finally got the nerve to look back at him over my shoulder. Our gazes locked instantly as if they were connected to an invisible beam magnetically drawing them to one another. We stayed that way, taking each other in.

God, he was beautiful. This man, who to everyone else was a feral predator, a lion who only needed to look at you to cause you to unravel, was a pussycat when it came to me. But it hadn't always been that way with us. First, he wanted to kill me, and then he wanted to claim me. Now, he only wanted to love and protect me.

I'd been as bad in the beginning, trying to fight the draw between us, afraid of what he was and what he might make me. But eventually we both realized when it came to the heart, there were no sides. Black and white, good and evil, they all melded together until neither of us cared what it was anymore as long as it was by our side at night.

Of course, I understood I was riding a thin line lying to him, and eventually it would reach a breaking point. Most of the time, Hunter was able to read my mind, but so far, there were no telltale signs he knew. That meant he was either playing along or his telepathic abilities were on the fritz. More than likely, his mind-reading skills were temporarily down. Based on my previous experience with him, Hunter didn't *play along* with anything or anyone. He was a blatant kind of guy, and by blatant, I mean unrepentant, audacious, cocky, fearless, pretty much in-your-face. Hunter got what he wanted, no matter the cost or consequences. Heaven help me if he thought for a minute I was lying to him.

I wondered why he didn't have all his powers, though, but assumed it was because he was a demon living under the roof of the angels. Maybe Hadraniel snuffed out Hunter's power to avoid a war every time an angel had bad thoughts about us, which was pretty much every time they set eyes on us.

Lying wasn't my strong suit. Avoiding was another story. Avoiding, I did well.

"I just want all this over with because I hate living here. The way they look at me every time I enter a room, I feel like I need to check my shoes for shit." By they, I meant the angels... but he knew that.

"You know, I'd be more than happy to take care of that for you," he said with a sparkle in his eyes. "Just say the word. I'm only here for you, you know. If it were up to me, I'd take you away from all of this, somewhere where it's just you and me." He brought his lips to my shoulder again and proceeded to trail a luscious line of kisses across it and then up my neck. A new kind of shiver overtook me. "Where I'd ravish you all day." He gave me a solitary kiss. "Every day." Wow. Another mind-blowing kiss.

A moan escaped my lips. Hunter also had a delectable way of taking my mind off everything—nightmares, monsters—the world.

"Hmmm... if Caleb doesn't show up soon, I may take you up on tha—"

A loud knock on the door interrupted me. Hunter growled his distaste. I was about to get up, but he ignored whoever was there and started feasting on my neck again. Apparently, whoever was at the door didn't warrant acknowledgment. With the pure pleasure he was dishing out, he left me no choice but to agree.

Two more loud knocks boomed, echoing through the room, but Hunter still couldn't be distracted.

"Hunter, we should probably see who it is."

His tongue started on my ear.

"Hunter... really," I released on a breath.

He growled again, this time a long, low one, reminiscent of defeat instead of rebellion.

I silently cried over the loss of his lips on me as he shouted across the room, "I'll be right there, Eric. Meet me in the foyer downstairs."

"You knew who it was all along?"

He pulled me onto his lap to face him, a sexy smirk playing on his lips. "I know everything."

"Oh yeah, smart guy?" I laughed. "Then when is Caleb going to show up so we can finally get on with our lives?"

I'd meant it to be playful, but Hunter's smile quickly disappeared. He placed his finger underneath my chin, easing my face up so I'd look him in the eyes. "I'll find Caleb," he said, his tone leaving no doubt this was nothing more than fact. "I'm going to find him, and I'm going to kill him. And then we'll go far away from all of this where I can fill your world with everything you've ever fantasized about, leaving no room for nightmares. I promise you, Cassandra."

He melted me. He did. Hunter was the only one in the world who had the power to change my fate. My nightmares didn't stand a chance as long as I had him. I loved him beyond words, beyond actions. It was a love that could only be experienced to be believed. The emotional side was so intense and sometimes it held me paralyzed, unable to move or utter a word. I could only gaze upon him and let the feelings pulse within me like a racing heartbeat trying to return to a steady tempo.

His thumb slid over my bottom lip, bringing my attention back. I kissed the tip of it.

"I believe you," I whispered.

He smiled. "Too bad. I was hoping I needed to convince you." His gaze raced down my neck to my bare chest. His finger followed.

My eyes closed of their own accord, and I moaned, leaning into his hand, as it cupped one of my breasts.

"Isn't Eric waiting for you?" I said on a pant.

"Yes." His lips were at my neck again. I could feel he was more than ready for me as I moved my hips against him.

"Is it important?"

"We have a lead on Caleb."

It took a moment for the words to sink in since they were muffled against my neck. I snapped back, grabbing his busy hands at the same time.

"Hunter."

While trying to make eye contact with him, his still heavy with passion and focused on my other body parts, I took his hands and shoved them hard against his chest. "Hunter."

Finally, I got his attention. He read the look on my face and sighed as he leaned his forehead against mine. "Caleb is going to experience pain like he's never felt. Only then will I let him die," he said, and then gently lifted me off his lap. As he got off the bed, I covered myself with a sheet.

Watching him dress, I asked, "What's this lead?"

He sat on the bed to put his boots on. "Some rogue the angels captured. Supposedly, he worked with Caleb and knows where he is. Same shit, different demon. We'll see if he's legit."

Word had made it out months ago the angels were looking for Caleb and would pay dearly to get him, something the demons banked on when they were captured. Every one of them claimed they knew where he was, but up to this point, none of the leads had panned out. The demons were merely using desperate attempts to escape their demise.

Hunter insisted that he, Eric, and a few other loyal demons were present when the angels questioned those captured. The angels had a tendency to be a little trigger-happy when it came to demons. Hadraniel refused to have his angels bring any demons back to the Sanctuary to be questioned, so Hunter and the group had to go out whenever one popped up.

"How long will you be gone?"

"Not long. I'll be back by dinner."

I almost laughed at the unintentional normalcy of his answer, as if we were some old married couple. He was going out for bowling and beers with the boys, instead of reading the mind of some demon from Hell who allegedly had knowledge of the self-proclaimed king of the Underworld. The truth was, I was getting tired of being the little woman stuck at home, waiting for the men of the house to get back from taking care of business.

"Let me go this time," I said.

One look at his face and I immediately knew the answer. I'd seen it so many times in the last few months, words no longer needed to follow it. I rolled my eyes and turned away from him.

"We talked about this, Cassandra."

"Yeah, yeah. I know. It could be a trap. They might be waiting for me... blah, blah, blah." I faced him again, bracing myself on the bed with one hand while holding the sheet against me with the other. A tirade didn't produce the desired results while body parts jiggled. And a rant was exactly what I was about to let loose on him. "Maybe that's what we need. It's probably the only way we are going to get to Caleb. Did you guys ever think of that? It's obvious he's not coming to the Sanctuary. He's been gone three months. Ninety days that I've been cooped up in this godforsaken place to do nothing but sit here like some lamb roped up to a pole in the ground. It's not fair, Hunter." Yeah, I knew I sounded like a spoiled child, but if they were going to treat me like one, I might as well give them the full treatment.

"You're safer here."

God, sometimes I hated his simplicity.

"I'm safe with you. You said so three months ago."

"And at that time, I believed it. But now, I don't know that I'm enough to keep you safe."

"What are you talking about? Of course, you are."

"Caleb is building an army, Cassandra. It's not just the few demons I believed were stupid enough to follow him. He promises rogues the chance to rule the world with him if they help recover two things—the Sword and you. One of those things I'm not willing to lose for pride. I may be one of the strongest demons, but I can't fight off an army. And I'm no good to you if they get to me. Here, I have an army to fight with... one that has the same goal. Regardless of our hatred for the angels, we have the same goals right now."

"But we don't even know if Caleb still wants me. Maybe he's moved on and found a new queen. Maybe—"

Hunter jumped up from the bed and glared down at me. "I'm not willing to take a chance with you on *maybes*. Ever. You're to stay here where I can keep you safe. Is that understood?"

I clenched my teeth and mimicked his glare. He was the stubbornest man I'd ever known, but I also understood I'd never win this fight. We'd had the discussion before. His resolve hadn't budged an inch. Especially with everyone else siding with him. Not one person under this roof would see my side of it. Not my mom, dad, or even Nora.

"Fine," I yelled, turning my back on him. "Go save the world while I sit here and learn to knit or something."

The mattress lowered near me, and before I knew what was happening, Hunter spun me around by the shoulders to look at him. His face was inches from mine as he held me in place.

"My only care in this world is you. The rest of it can go to Hell. I don't give a shit. But I will not lose you, Cassandra."

His kiss was demanding, possessive, harsh against my lips until I melted into it. Then it turned soft and sweet, a mark of love.

I knew it was his love for me making him obstinate about this. Caleb had promised he would come for the Sword and me. He wasn't one to forget his demented goals, regardless of how much I tried to convince myself and everyone else otherwise. But none of that changed the fact I was going stir-crazy being stuck day after day, not knowing when or if anything would ever happen. It also didn't stop the moments of resentment I frequently had toward everyone in the Sanctuary. A passing reaction? Maybe, but I couldn't seem to control it anymore. After

Hunter left, I decided to burn off some of that pent-up frustration by beating the shit out of something.

CHAPTER TWO

The Sanctuary's training facility could have been used for Olympians. It was the size of a football stadium on the inside alone. Fluorescent beams of light shone down from the cathedral ceiling to light the room up like a sports arena night game. The entire floor was constructed of a hard padding, making it sturdy enough to maintain footing, but soft enough for a tough landing.

Steel glistened from the lights reflecting on the far wall, showcasing swords resting on perfectly aligned pegs from top to bottom. Next to them various shields were lined up, all with the same emblem depicting two angels, their wings spread out creating a barrier to the sun, as if to guard it. The display symbolized the army of the angels, and the insignia was on everything inside and outside the Sanctuary, twisted in wrought iron on the entrance gates, sculpted in the architecture over the entrance doors, as big as the sun itself. Angels' clothing, armor, and even the angels themselves displayed the mark on their skin. I wasn't sure if the tats were a branding ritual or just the cool angel thing to do, but they all wore it. I vowed to ask one of them if they had anything in a half-angel look, but I had yet to get that personal with any of them.

A set of double glass doors in the middle of one wall led to a huge outdoor training area. About the same size as the indoor facility, it was cordoned off by a tall, thick, hedge of bushes and paved with smooth concrete that felt like glass under bare feet. A small opening in the hedges revealed a path to a huge underground pool. The water was crystal clear, allowing a translucent view of the decline in depth from one end to the other. There'd been a few times after a hard training session when I'd been tempted to take a dip, but I never acted on it. I didn't have swim apparel, and if Hunter found out I had skinny dipped within a ten-mile radius of anyone else, it would have started a war.

A couple of freestanding kickboxing bags were located on the far side of the room, which really sucked because they were my targets. Two angels were battling it out on the floor in front of them. No secret, I'd come to hate the angels. I probably should have been struck down by a bolt of lightning for even thinking that, but I couldn't help it... they'd made me this way. I'd been like the girl with cooties during school. Every time I entered a room, they'd turn their noses up at me and leave unless Hadraniel forced them to stay. I wasn't welcomed into the Sanctuary. I was tolerated. Sometimes I wanted to scream at them that my veins pumped the same blood as theirs, but I knew they wouldn't see it that way. They were blinded by the darkness that dimmed the light of my pure blood. I guess taking down the devil had no bearing with them. So, to hell with all of them, was my motto. I was way past defending who and what I was to anyone.

I grabbed a towel from the racks by the door and with my spine straight and chin up, I made my way to the bags. I hadn't even made it to the middle of the room before the two angels noticed and stopped to watch me walk across the mat. I recognized Aviar, the shorter, stockier of the two. We'd run into each other a couple of times in the Sanctuary, and now, similar to all the other times I'd seen him, his lip curled up in disgust at the sight of me. His opponent, however, I'd never seen before. Evidently, he didn't know who I was either because he watched me with fascinated curiosity rather than blatant scorn.

Continuing my walk of shame with style, I winked in their direction and said, "Boys," in acknowledgment.

Aviar's lip somehow found its way even further up his face, while he leaned over and whispered to the other guy. *Had he forgotten I could hear everything he said, or did he simply not care?* "That's her," he said. "The Demon Lover. I'm outta here. I suddenly have a need to shower."

"Good call, Aviar," I said as I walked past them and set my towel down near one of the bags. "You smell like shit. I was fighting my gag reflex way back there."

I deliberately turned my back on the pair and took off the T-shirt I had on over my sports bra, knowing the silence from behind me probably included a couple distasteful gestures from Aviar.

"You coming, man?" Aviar asked his friend.

I sat on the floor and started to stretch, my back still to them. The clang of metal echoed in the room, as they unceremoniously put away the sparring swords, or so I guessed. A few seconds later, I heard one of the glass doors leading to the outdoor training area open and close. I exhaled in relief as I stretched, relaying my hatred for the angels over and over again in my head. The animosity always gave me a motivational boost in training.

Standing, straight and tall, I threw a roundhouse kick at the bag, my foot connecting with a solid smack.

"Good form," a voice behind said, startling me. No, honestly, it scared the shit out of me. On instinct, I swung around, fists ready. The guy who had been sparring with Aviar raised his hands in surrender. "Whoa. Sorry about that. I didn't mean to freak you out."

I eyed him suspiciously. "What are you doing here?"

His eyebrows rose at the question. "Uh... I was here first."

"Yeah, I'm not blind. I thought you left with Aviar. Aren't you afraid you're going to catch something from me?"

"Are you planning on throwing things at me?" he asked with a smile.

"Why? Are you going to give me a reason?"

"Not unless you want me to," he said with a chuckle. With hand extended, he stepped toward me. "Hi," he said, "I'm Braydon."

I took a step back and deliberately ignored the gesture.

"Seriously, why are you still here, Braydon? I know you know who I am, and I also realize the angels would rather cut off their wings than make nice with me, so what's the deal?"

He dropped his hand, finally recognizing I wasn't going to shake it, crossed his arms, and leaned his shoulder against the bag next to him, all without taking his eyes off me. "Well, I guess I'm not like the others."

It was my turn to laugh. "Oh, really? So what are you, like Rebel Angel? The Troublemaker of Saintdom?" Without realizing it, I mimicked his stance, now leaning against the bag behind me with my arms crossed over my chest.

"Depends on what you consider trouble." The smile was gone as he spoke, and I wondered exactly what point he was trying to make. His eyes glinted green, and it almost seemed as if they were twinkling directly at me, confirming his mischievous ways. I didn't need that to tell me this angel was trouble. His whole appearance screamed rogue, from his messy, chin-length chocolate waves and five o'clock shadow, to his lean, muscular build that seemed to swagger even when stationary. I had to admit, he was very attractive, but he had the look of one of those guys your mom warned you about and your dad refused to let in the house. He wore *dangerous* like a neon sign across his chest. I *so* shouldn't be thinking that was sexy as hell.

Our gazes met, and I realized I was blatantly checking him out as if he were a sculpture in an art museum. Braydon smiled in an I-got-your-number sort of way, and I knew I'd been caught. My cheeks warmed. *What was happening? Was I some kind of schoolgirl?*

"I've never seen you around. Are you new here?" I asked, trying to regain my composure.

"No, I've been at the Sanctuary for years. Until today, I was on day shift guard duty. They just switched me to nights."

"Oh yeah? Guarding what?"

"Ahhh, that's top secret angel stuff, Cassie," he said with a smile. "If I tell you, I'd have to kill you."

I rolled my eyes at his dramatics. "Oh, please."

"You want to know, don't you," he teased as he pushed away from the bag and took a step toward me.

"No," I lied.

"Yes, you do." He came even closer and said conspiratorially, "I'll tell you what. If you can take me in a sparring match, I'll reveal the secret."

I giggled... couldn't help it. Something about this guy made me relaxed and comfortable with him, despite only having met him. *Too* comfortable. Maybe it was curiosity, or just plain excitement, a break from the droning days of my life the last few months.

"I told you, I don't want to know." Maybe if I didn't have the cheesy smile still plastered on my face, it would have been more believable.

"Yeah, I guess it wouldn't be much of a fight anyway."

He was goading me. I knew he was, but it didn't stop my pride from jumping out of my mouth. "Oh, really?"

"Well, yeah, I mean little ol' you, taking me on? You wouldn't have a chance."

"Oh, really?"

"You said that already."

Okay, if this guy wanted to play, I was going to give him a game he'd never forget. Dropping the smile, I narrowed my eyes and flashed my own set of blues. "You really are trouble, aren't you, Braydon?" He granted me a cocky arch of his brow. "You know the best way to deal with a troublemaker?" I hinted.

"How's that?"

I made him disappear, a nifty little demon power I'd perfected during my last two months of boredom. Positioning myself in back of where his shoulder had been, I made him reappear. Before he had a chance to get his bearings, I whispered up to his ear, "Kick his ass."

And I did. Using only a portion of the power within me, I connected the bottom of my foot with Braydon's ass, which happened to be nice and firm, I noted. Then, I launched him across the room until the wall broke his momentum. He hit so hard, he slid to the ground in a comical sort of way.

For a few moments, he lay in a crumpled heap on the floor, and I almost thought he was down for the count, but then he shook his head and glimpsed over his shoulder at me. The gleam in his eyes brightened as a smile crept across his lips. "You fight dirty."

I smiled back. "I'm half demon. Or haven't you heard? That's what we do."

"Oh, no, I've heard. I think it's sexy."

I rolled my eyes.

He chuckled. "Okay, you proved your point. You're much more powerful than you look. Can you help me up? I think you actually sprained my ankle." He winced as he turned toward me, holding his ankle.

"Seriously?" I laughed at him. "You're weaker than I thought."

"Now that's just mean," he said, faking a pained expression. "C'mon, give me a hand, Cassie."

"No."

"No? Really?"

"I think you owe me something first."

He looked at me for a minute, before it dawned on him. Once it did, he laughed. "I thought you didn't want to know?"

"I don't, but a deal's a deal." I crossed my arms and leaned back on the bag in the same place as we'd both done before.

"Principled. I like that in a woman." When I didn't react to his flirting, he said, "And tenacious obviously." He sighed. "I guard the Sword. Now will you help me up?"

I don't know why, but his revelation hit me like a vat of ice water over my head. My heart jolted into overdrive, and I couldn't catch my breath fast enough to keep up. I lowered my arm, holding it against the bag behind me, anchoring my body to keep me upright. The word Sword repeated in my head as if it were bouncing off my skull like an echo.

"*The* Sword?" I asked in a breathy whisper.

Braydon eyed me closely. "The Sword of Final Death, yes. You okay?"

"Yes." *No. God, what was wrong with me?* "Can I see it?" The words flew out of my mouth before I even knew why I was asking. It's not as though I didn't know what it looked like. I'd held the damn thing enough to know what it looked *and* felt like. I hadn't seen it, other than in my dreams, since the angels took it from me to lock it away after I'd come from Hell, but all of a sudden I needed to see it and touch it.

"If you don't help me up, I won't be able to see it either because I'll be stuck here for all eternity, crouched by the training room wall, crying like a baby."

I stared at him until I was finally able to shake my obsessive thoughts about the Sword. "As much as I'd like to see a grown angel cry," I said as I approached, "this might be the ammunition the others were begging for to pin my wings to a cork board."

"You have wings?"

"No," I said while crouching on the floor next to him, reaching my arm around his back. "But I think they'd find a way to improvise."

One minute I was stooped next to Braydon, helping him to his feet, the next I was lying on my back, the wind knocked out of me. He hovered over me, pinning me to the mat.

"What the fuck?" I said, once I'd caught my breath. Braydon's cheesy smile above me was enough explanation.

"You're not the only one who knows how to play dirty, beautiful," he said.

"You are *so* going to Hell."

He laughed. Hard. I couldn't help but crack a smile, even as I shook my head. I wanted to be mad at him, but if anything, I should have been furious at myself for letting my guard down. That's no fun.

"Your ankle's not even sprained, is it?" I asked.

"Nope."

"Nice." I pushed at his chest. "Okay, you can let me up now."

He didn't move. "Why go for the demon?"

"Excuse me?"

"Hunter. Why'd you choose to be with a demon instead of being with an angel?"

He was serious. No more smiles. Braydon stared at me with such intensity, I thought he might be soul-searching for an answer. The comfort level I'd had before with him vanished as quickly as it had come.

"Get off me, Braydon." I squirmed beneath him. I didn't want to use my power on him again, but I would if it came down to it. "I'm serious."

"Just tell me, and I'll get up. It's a simple question."

"No. It's not. Besides, I never planned on being with Hunter, *the Demon*. I had no idea what he was. Hell, I didn't even know what I was. We just sort of ended up together. Also, it wasn't as if I had angels knocking down my door either, for God's sake." I don't know why his question bothered me as much as it did. I'd never had to try to explain my feelings for Hunter before. Not to anyone. The only people I associated with knew the story and accepted it. Well, except for Hadraniel, but he didn't accept anything. "This is stupid. Get off me."

"What if you did?"

"What if I did what?"

"What if you had angels knocking down your door? Would you open it?"

"You have two seconds to remove yourself from her before I do it for you." Hunter's voice thundered from across the room.

My eyes widened in horror. I didn't even have time to catch Braydon's reaction before he was suddenly ripped off me and flying through the air.

"Time's up," Hunter growled. In a blink, he was standing next to me.

The noise was deafening. A bang followed by a grunt, and then a loud crash of metal.

I sat up, leaning on my elbows, and gaped at Hunter. He was glaring at the wall by the swords, his eyes aglow with blue fire. His features were taut. He was in kill mode. I followed his gaze and spotted Braydon lying on the floor with several swords and shields piled on top of him. Luckily, none of them seemed to have pierced him, at least that I could see. He was lying so still, he might have been dead for all I knew. Wait... no... his chest was rising and falling.

Don't move. Don't move. Don't move, I chanted to myself. Hunter was like a lion, waiting for his prey to twitch an eyelash so he could strike again. If Braydon continued to play dead, he had a chance Hunter would leave him alone.

Just as I thought it, Braydon opened his eyes and pushed himself up to sit.

"Wait." I struggled to stand. "Hunter... just... wait..." The tension emanating from him was amazing as his muscles pulsed, sending shock waves into the air around them. I finally gained my footing and grabbed onto one of his wrists. "Hunter, don't," I said in a sort of forceful plea. He spun his head toward me and peered into my eyes. I softened my voice as I added, "Please."

For a moment, he held my gaze, and I thought I actually might have convinced him to leave well enough alone. The clatter of metal from Braydon scrambling to get up broke the spell. Hunter turned back to face him, and I tightened my grip on his wrist but knew it was pointless.

"It was only a matter of time before I killed one of them, Cassandra. I think we both knew that," Hunter said.

I didn't want to look in Braydon's direction. In fact, I didn't want to see any of it. So I closed my eyes and held on to Hunter for dear life.

CHAPTER THREE

A sound to my left rallied my attention, and I realized a waft of air hit me when the door to the outside training area opened.

Oh Lord, I thought. My eyes stayed closed as I continued to hang onto Hunter's wrist. More angels were coming to Braydon's aid and Hunter was planning to try and fight them all.

"There will be no killing of angels today," Hadraniel shouted, his voice booming as if canceling a training session instead of a death match.

When I opened my eyes, Hadraniel had positioned himself an equal distance between Hunter and Braydon. Aviar lingered off to the side, eyes darting back and forth nervously.

"Come now, Hadraniel," Hunter said in a low, even tone. "With as many as you have here, you won't even miss him."

I stole a glance at Braydon, expecting him to look, I don't know, terrified because that's what Hunter's wrath usually did to people. Instead, he seemed extremely calm, maybe even some cockiness showing through. He caught my gaze, and I quickly turned back to Hadraniel.

"As much as I know Braydon needs punishing for his troublesome ways, it will be at my hands, not yours. This..." he said, spreading his arms out, indicating Hunter and Braydon, "will not be tolerated within the walls of the Sanctuary."

"Neither will your angels touching what is mine," Hunter said.

Braydon scoffed at that, and I almost voiced my own opinion about being treated like a favorite dog toy. Choosing to take the high road, I figured now was probably not a good time to lay out the *I am woman, hear me roar* speech. Hunter was kind of old school that way. *Very* old school. I hadn't had the proper opportunity to bring him up to speed on the times yet.

"We have to work together here, Hunter," Hadraniel said. "Braydon is one of my best soldiers, and he plays a big role in our plan to take down Caleb. I will have a talk with him about what's appropriate and professional, but I won't relieve him of his duty."

"Not good enough," Hunter said, in a calm but steely voice.

"Who the hell do you think you are?" Braydon shouted.

"Braydon, shut up," Hadraniel's reprimand was swift.

This was going nowhere fast.

"Hunter," I said, pulling at his wrist so he'd look at me. It took a couple times, but he finally turned his face toward mine. "It's not what you thought."

"It looked like he was molesting you," he said, his tone now blunt and not as calm.

"It's *definitely* not what it looked like then. We were sparring. He got the better of me. It's my fault. I dropped my guard. You need to let this one go." I held his gaze, silently trying to convince him. Hunter was a stubborn man. Once he believed in something or someone, he became steadfast in his fight for it. I knew that for a fact because our love was something he fought for in more ways than anyone I'd ever known. In order to get him to walk away from this, I was counting on that. "Believe me," I said.

His jaw tensed, the muscles pulsing like a heartbeat, and I knew he was fighting hard to resist acting on his protective instincts. I hoped Braydon listened to Hadraniel's order and kept his mouth shut. One word, and I'd lose my grip on Hunter. And it would be messy.

He turned away from me and glared at Braydon. I braced myself, practically digging my nails into his arm in the process. Hunter didn't seem to notice.

"You better pray you don't even dream about her at night because I'll be there when you wake up. And if I ever hear her name cross your lips, I'll tear them off with my bare hands."

It wasn't a white flag, but at least he was still standing next to me and no blood was involved. Yet, at least. Braydon appeared ready to shed some of Hunter's. Maybe it was exactly what Hunter was hoping for. My relief was short-lived as I held my breath waiting for Braydon's reaction.

Hadraniel didn't give him the chance. The second Braydon's mouth opened, Hadraniel rushed him, firmly placing a hand on his shoulder. I hadn't heard Hadraniel say anything, but something must have passed between them because Braydon turned and walked away with Aviar at his heels.

"I expect there won't be any more problems between the two of you," Hadraniel said. It was said as a statement, but he waited for acknowledgment.

"As long as you keep him on his leash," Hunter answered.

Hadraniel's face pinched. Anyone in the room could see how much he hated being challenged by someone he deemed a lesser being. These battles of wills between the two of them had become common since we'd been at the Sanctuary. If they both only realized how much alike they truly were.

"I won't thank you," Hadraniel stated.

Hunter smirked. "And I won't say you're welcome."

With that, Hadraniel left. Hunter continued staring at the door long after he'd departed. His tension had ebbed, but it was definitely not gone.

"Well, that went better than I thought," I said, trying to break the uncomfortable silence. Now that everyone was gone, I started to feel like a kid who was bailed out of jail by mom or dad. The threat of public humiliation was gone, but the parental doom remained.

Hunter took a deep breath and turned toward me. His features were tight again, only this time, his anger was directed squarely at me. His eyes seemed to pierce my skin as if sharpened icicles froze me in place. "Did it?" he said in full sarcasm mode. "I was thinking of an outcome altogether different."

"Killing off angels isn't going to help our situation, Hunter. It'll only make it worse. Don't you think it's bad enough we walk around like lepers here? You start taking angels out on your jealous whims and we'll be voted off this island before you can say, 'Me, Tarzan.'"

When he narrowed his eyes, I knew my little tirade wasn't taken well.

"Maybe if you didn't do things to put me in a jealous whim state-of-mind, *Jane*, we wouldn't have a problem," he shot back.

My mouth hung open for a moment before I could even respond. The blood rush finally settled on my cheeks as adrenaline started to pick up. "You're blaming me for this?"

"No. I blame the piece of shit who took the liberty of laying his hands, among other things, on you. However, that opportunity would not have existed had you simply stayed away from him in the first place."

I was speechless. I mean, I knew Hunter was archaic when it came to the whole relationship principles, but this was downright caveman-ish. Closing my gaping mouth yet again, I put my hands on my hips while glaring at him.

"I'm sorry. Am I not allowed to talk to anyone around here? Maybe I should just be the good little woman and stay in our room all day while you go off and do your manly thing. Should I wait naked in the bed for you so you can—"

"Don't be ridiculous, Cassandra. I'm merely saying the angels here do not respect us, and you're better off avoiding them.

There are plenty of people here for you to talk to, other than the angels—Nora and Eric, your mom and dad, Anael."

"You're as bad as they are, Hunter. You blanket them into a category, just as they have done with us. So where do I fit in?"

That hit a nerve. He snarled as he grabbed my upper arm and pulled me to him. "You know that's not true. If it were, I wouldn't have put my life on the line for your family and Nora, as I have for you."

He had a point, but I was still pissed. I was sick of being told what to do, alienated. The truth was, I didn't know where I fit in. I wanted to live life, but what life? Where did I really belong? Being a third wheel everywhere I went, always on the outskirts, never truly connecting with anyone, was getting old. Maybe it was just me, knowing I would never really be like any of them. They all had choices of what they wanted to be, even Eric, who was planning to have me turn him as soon as we got Caleb. I didn't have that choice. I would always be stuck in the middle.

"You will never be like them," Hunter said as if he could read my thoughts once again. He released my arm and gently raised my chin until I looked up at him. With softened features, his gaze swept over my face, his thumbs tracing its path. "I never want you to be. You're my soul, Cassandra. That's where you belong. With me. Forever. Nothing or no one else matters."

His words radiated, a light penetrating the fog of my awareness. His touch, like a sculptor's caress, defining the beauty of his art. I closed my eyes for a moment, reveling in the warmth he evoked in me, knowing he would always be the anchor I needed to stay afloat. I opened my eyes and locked them onto his.

"Thank you," I whispered.

He kissed me on the lips with caution, before pulling back to look at me again.

"Don't ever thank me for loving you."

I ran my palms over his chest and smirked up at him. "Are you sure? There are many ways to say thank you." I wanted us to feel normal again because I was tired of always fighting. It seemed the only time we didn't argue was when we were intimate.

He put his hand over mine and guided it farther down, where he had already grown hard. "Come to think of it, I did like that part you said about waiting naked for me when I was done with all my manly duties."

I snatched my hand away from his and pushed at his chest in a playful manner that made him smile. "You're horrible."

He laughed, pulling me into his embrace. "Yes, I am. But you love it."

I grinned against his chest. He was right. I cherished everything about him, especially since he was the one who kept me grounded after all the mysteries surrounding my life unraveled in the last year or so. If it weren't for him, I might be living as a servant to the king of the Underworld. Hunter had saved me from an eternity of Hell, physically and mentally. Way too often lately, my selfishness clouded the memory of who and what was important. It was no wonder I seemed so alone. My own fault, brought on by self-centered tantrums.

I kissed him lightly on the chest, the heat of his body emanating from the T-shirt he wore and warming my lips. He squeezed me tighter.

"Hey," I said, pulling back and staring up at him. "I thought you were going with Eric to question a demon? You couldn't have gone that fast. What happened?"

"One of the angels accidentally cut off his head before I even made it down to meet Eric." His sarcastic tone on the word *accidentally* was intentional.

"They're getting impatient," I said, more as a thought out loud.

"*I'm* getting impatient," Hunter retorted.

This waiting business was taking its toll on everyone. None of us would have ever guessed Caleb had the patience to refrain from attempting to at least steal the Sword for this long. If we had known, I'm not sure any of us would have agreed to the arrangements we were living with now.

"I'm telling you, we need to up our game, Hunter. Raise the stakes." I grabbed his hands in mine, squeezing them from my excitement. "Let me go out there. Better yet, let me go out there with the Sword. If that doesn't draw him out, he's not coming. And if that's the case, this charade is over, and we can go on with our lives."

He was looking directly at me, but I could tell he was deep in thought. Was I finally getting through to him? I held my breath, waiting for his answer as if the next words from his mouth would make or break me.

And break me they did.

"No."

I stared at him for a long time as the tension started webbing its way through my body. How quickly he could swing my emotional control. When had I let everyone else dictate my life? I signed off on being bait but didn't agree to be a puppet whose strings were so tightly wound it merely hung there, lifeless. As much as I loved Hunter, he was one of my puppet masters, and he wasn't immune to the anger and resentment that were building deep within me. I couldn't temper them much longer. They had reached the brim of containment, and I was ready to explode.

I dropped his hands and shoved them away from me, let out a short chuckle, and fixed him with a haughty glare. "You know what? Forget I asked. I just remembered, you don't own me, so I don't need your permission. In fact, I don't need anyone's permission. I left my chains back in Hell."

His face hardened and his eyes narrowed on me. "You're comparing me to Nergal?"

"All I'm saying is I'm trying to put Hell behind me, but all everyone wants to do is keep me chained down. *Including* you. I'm done with being told what I can and cannot do. I'll make those decisions from here on out."

A long stretch of silence followed as he pinned me in place with his eyes. I wasn't used to his heated energy being directed at me, but I fought the urge to fidget under his gaze. Hunter was a predator by nature and a very intimidating one. He honed in on weakness. I was hoping my anger would be enough to overpower any weakness he might sense from me. But damn those eyes of his. They burrowed into my soul.

"Didn't you try that once before?" he said, his tone bitter. "Tell me, how did that work out for you?"

He was referring to the times I had put my trust in Caleb, only to be deceived by him in the end, not once but twice. The first time, Hunter was sent back to Hell to be tortured daily, and I nearly got my best friend, Nora, turned into a demon. The second time, I was the one who ended up a prisoner of Hell. So my track record wasn't great in the decision-making department, but I was a different person now. I'd survived Hell and helped bring down the devil. An experience such as that changes a person, makes them smarter and stronger.

"You don't need to stick my face in it. Nergal already took care of that back in Hell. I think I've learned my lesson, but thanks anyway."

A muscle in his jaw pulsed while he studied me as if seeing me for the first time.

"No, Cassandra, I don't think you have."

After one last penetrating look, he turned his back on me and walked out of the room, leaving me pent up with a comeback I had yet to form, breathless from the adrenaline pumping through my body, and worst of all, questioning what in the hell I'd just done.

CHAPTER FOUR

I went down the hallway outside the training room with no particular destination in mind. The fight with Hunter was still heavy on my mind. It wasn't so much the fact we fought, we seemed to do that a lot lately, but this one seemed more final than the rest. The look on his face before he had walked out haunted me. The pain in his eyes weighed on me. My words, my actions, they caused that pain. For the first time, I'd mentioned my suffering in Hell during one of our fights, and I knew he blamed himself for taking so long to rescue me. I also knew it couldn't be helped, but apparently that hadn't stopped me from using it as a hit to the gut in the heat of the moment.

The more I thought about it, the more awful I felt. I wanted to take it all back, yet I didn't. What I really wanted was for him to realize I wasn't the fragile little flower he'd stalked so many months ago. Hell had changed me. I was ready to fight for our freedom. My resolve was stronger on instinct now. I'd been training for months, perfecting the skills borne by angels and demons, and honing in on the abilities only I possessed. There had been a time I would have settled for just being protected, but not anymore. I'd been through too much. Maybe it was revenge that made me want to be an active part of this war, that baseless motivator capable of destroying civilizations. But hadn't I earned that right?

Whatever it was, it was causing me to lash out at the people I loved more often and dealing out apologies like Halloween candy. I was going to have to add a special treat in Hunter's bag for this latest outburst. Then I could hit him with a few negotiations. *Nicely.* He'd need time to cool off, though, so I decided to wait until I saw him at dinner.

Feeling satisfied with my best course of action, I realized I'd walked to the entrance of the gardens. It was one of my favorite places in the Sanctuary. The vibrant colors, smells, and peacefulness balanced me. Every step in the gardens seemed to wash away more and more of the negative energy that had festered within me since coming to the Sanctuary.

I was about to open the door to enter the gardens when I heard another one open behind me.

"Trouble in paradise?" a deep voice asked.

I turned to see Braydon standing in the hallway. His hair was wet and glistening as if he'd just stepped out of the shower. My breath caught at the sight of him, barefoot and bare-chested, clad only in a pair of worn, faded jeans. *Trouble indeed.*

"More like trouble lurking in the shadows, wouldn't you say?" I asked, eyeing him with distrust.

"I wouldn't call it lurking. It's more like a low-level stalking. Lurking sounds so creepy."

A small chuckle escaped my lips before I could contain it. I didn't want to encourage him after what just happened with Hunter. Dead angels didn't quite fit in with the whole make-up session I'd had in mind a moment ago.

"Oh no, you're definitely a creepy lurker. Were you eavesdropping on us?"

"Me?" he asked, all fake innocence and smiles. "No way. You just have that *trouble in paradise* look on your face. It's pretty obvious. And eavesdropping is way beneath me."

"Really? You don't seem like much is beneath you."

"Ooooo. Yeah, well, not much has been beneath me lately... sadly."

Damn, he was a bold one. That carnal bit of information was meant for nothing but provocation. Even without Hunter's warning, I knew it would be best to keep my distance from that fire, which wasn't as easy as it sounded. The guy was smokin' hot, with the charisma of an ancient god, luring you in before you knew your feet were no longer on the ground. The heat alone was enough to make me sweat from the ten feet we were standing apart.

"With that lurky nature of yours, I can't say it surprises me."

"Ouch," he said, placing his hand on his chest, drawing my eyes to the clearly defined muscles.

After realizing I'd allowed myself to gawk too long, I raised my eyes back up to his. He smiled at me, undoubtedly enjoying my blatant examination.

"Did you want something, Braydon?" I asked, needing to cut this conversation short before someone, namely Hunter, caught me talking to a half-naked god... I mean, angel.

His eyebrows shot up, most likely because of my curtness.

"Actually, it's something *you* want." He pushed away from the wall he'd been leaning against and started toward me. I quickly glanced behind me, instinctively looking for an escape route should it come to that, and realized my back was already against the glass door to the gardens. I should have turned and walked out, but curiosity, and maybe a bit of something else, kept my feet rooted to the spot.

"Excuse me?" I breathed out when he'd gotten so close I could see the flecks of gold glinting in his emerald eyes.

He leaned in so his lips were close to my ear. As wrong as I knew the position was, I didn't move away.

"The Sword," he whispered. A shiver ran through my entire body from the heat of his breath on my ear. Or was it the object he'd referred to because the same obsessive thoughts chanted in my head just as they had in the training room when he'd mentioned the Sword. I couldn't breathe. I couldn't move. I felt paralyzed by the single word as if it had been spoken by a hypnotist. "Meet me tonight. I'll show you anything you want to see."

While my brain screamed *No,* something deep inside me demanded I go. Whatever it was didn't want to wait until tonight. It needed immediate fulfillment, and I had no idea where it was coming from or why it was so compelling. That scared the hell out of me. Suddenly, I'd become this psychotic nut job, who secretly argued with herself. I had to get out. This place was making me crazy.

"No." I blurted out, more forcefully than I'd meant, at least not toward Braydon. The little psycho in my head, on the other hand, needed to listen up.

Braydon took a step away at my outburst, looking confused and more than taken aback.

"I mean, no," I said in a softer voice. "I have plans tonight."

He studied me a moment, then his composure loosened up.

"All right then," he said, pronouncing each word slow and steady. "Maybe some other time. I'm there almost every night, but Hadraniel wouldn't appreciate me having guests, so let me know when you want to, and I'll figure something out. It'll be our little secret." He winked, and a sly smile formed his lips, making him appear dangerous but sexy as hell.

"Okay, sure," I rushed out, my brain starting to overpower psycho with thoughts of getting as far away and as soon as possible. "I... I gotta go, Braydon." I turned toward the door and proceeded to blindly fumble for the handle.

An arm calmly reached over me and grabbed the handle. I jerked my head over my shoulder to look at him. He smiled and held me with his eyes as I heard the door open. "Talk to you soon, Cassie."

It took me a moment to gain control of myself, captivated by this angel who had somehow managed to unbalance me with a mere smile, flirtation, and promise. When I finally did, I scrambled out the door spurting out something incoherent even to my own ears and ran through the gardens until I could breathe again.

Clearing my head, I glanced around. I was in the middle of the gardens, a sprinkling fountain marking its centricity. A decorative, red brick walkway surrounded the water feature and branched out into four directional paths. I knew exactly where each path led because I'd been to all of them multiple times, each bringing me comfort in different ways from their deliberately landscaped coloring and scents. Various vibrant flowers lined the paths, creating a symmetrical mosaic that, from the air, must look like a beautiful, aesthetic art piece.

I sat on a cushioned park bench a few feet from the fountain and closed my eyes, letting the sweet, aromatic fragrance permeate the air. Soft, steady pinging of the water fountain calmed my rampant emotions. I had no idea what was going on with me, but I had to get whatever it was under control. I felt like a hormonal teenager in the midst of a monumental puberty phase. Not really the frame of mind I wanted to be in when and if Caleb decided to show.

Maybe it all stemmed from feeling so imprisoned in the Sanctuary. When I first agreed we would stay here to bait Caleb, I figured I'd be free to come and go as I pleased. Free to go out on searches with Hunter for information, on guardian missions, or simply to get away. After all, we were doing the angels a favor by helping get rid of the competition. For the first few weeks, it was exactly what I thought it would be. But all that changed after I was almost captured by a demon while out on a mission with Hunter and a few others. I hadn't seen him coming. None of us had. He laid in wait while a whole group of demons attacked our group, and then sprang out and grabbed me. The minute Hunter saw what was happening, he came to my rescue. I was shaken, but safe. We found out that day, Caleb had put a price on my head, promising any demon a place by his side as king if they captured me and brought me to him alive. That was the last day I was allowed out of the Sanctuary, and quite possibly the day I started going bat-shit crazy.

Or maybe my mental state simply had to do with too many sleepless nights. Scientific evidence proved a lack of sleep could lead to a diminished mental capacity. Whether it affected those of the angel/demon variety was probably not a researched statistic, but I still had human attributes, and maybe that was enough. The problem wasn't that I didn't sleep, it was just my dreams of killing Hunter made it a restless kind, which left me more exhausted than when I hit the pillow. My previous experience with nightmares made it more horrifying, but I'd learned a few very important lessons about the prophecies of my dreams—I had the power to change their outcome—and fate is a path you create, one step at a time. My immediate plan was to tiptoe through it because every step I took seemed to trip a different land mine.

The nightmare of killing Hunter hit me on such a deep emotional level, more than any of the others. He was the love of my life. My soul mate. The mere thought of holding the Sword to him made me physically ill, which was why the strong reactions I'd been having at the simple mention of the Sword scared the hell out of me. I knew, as much as I wanted to deny it, the nightmare was trying to press its way into my reality, and I had to take control before it was too late.

If Hunter couldn't be convinced, I'd have to take matters into my own hands. *Again*. Maybe that's what Caleb was waiting for anyway. A string dangling from the tightly woven fabric of the angel army might be enough for him to stick his hand out and give it a tug. Becoming that string would be next to impossible, though, as everyone was dead set against me leaving the protection of the Sanctuary. Nora, Eric, Mom, Dad—none of them would help me. They were even worse than Hunter, wanting to keep me under constant supervision. I loved them all, but the situation was almost as if I couldn't even shower without one of them showing up in the stall with me if I took too long.

Braydon. His name popped into my head from out of nowhere.

Maybe if I got friendlier...

No. No, that was insane. I could never do that. Where did that even come from? Not happening. I'd find a way to convince Hunter to work with me, come up with a plan to tempt Caleb out of hiding once and for all.

But if he didn't, I just might have a backup plan.

CHAPTER FIVE

I entered the dining room feeling more relaxed and balanced than I had earlier in the day. Sitting in the gardens for two full hours and contemplating the what-ifs, I'd gone over what I would say to Hunter when we talked. Then I wandered along the paths, simply taking in the beauty around me, letting it seep into my soul to lighten the darkness, which seemed to have grown within me. The heaviness had lifted, but I still felt a small lump attached to my heart threatening to build back up again. It had been there since I'd gotten back from Hell… a scar I'd earned, flaring up when I became frustrated or hurt and making me much more cognizant of my emotions. Regardless, it seemed I had little control of them lately.

The normal dinner crowd was seated at the long, hardwood table, only half-filling it as usual. Angels didn't dine with our group, and we were more than okay with that. Who wanted to eat with people who thought you deserved nothing more than a bowl on the floor for scraps?

A quick glance around the table and I smiled back at Nora, Eric, my mom and dad, and a few other demons, who had become part of our group due to their allegiance to Hunter. Nora and Eric always sat together at one corner of the table, as did my mom and dad on the opposite side. Others filled in alongside them. The head of the table had been designated for Hunter, which he refused at first, claiming my dad's seniority was more deserving of the honor, but my dad wouldn't allow it. He told Hunter it was his strength and endurance that had led to his daughter's safe return from Hell, and for that he deserved the honorable position. Of course, Hunter was adamant I sit by his side since that area was big enough for two. It seemed silly to me. They were just chairs, for crying out loud. We sat, we ate, we left. It was all too old-fashioned for my taste, but who was I to argue? I couldn't even leave the property *with* an armed guard.

At the moment, the head of the table was a gaping hole. Hunter hadn't shown up yet. At least, that's what I told myself, but the niggling feeling in my gut twitched as I walked the length of the table to my chair. Once I sat down, maids started bringing in covered dishes and setting them on various parts of the table. One maid, Trina, who often came to our rooms to change out the bedding and towels, filled my glass with water. That's when I noticed there was no table setting for Hunter.

"Trina," I said, "it looks like someone forgot to set a spot for Hunter."

"No, ma'am," she said. "Hunter will not be dining in the hall tonight."

"What?" Hunter always came to dinner with me.

Eric cleared his throat, louder than necessary, and I jerked my head to look at him.

"She's right," he said. "Hunter's not coming. He said to eat without him tonight."

My stomach dropped. It was stupid, I know, but this was the first time since we'd been at the Sanctuary he wasn't here with me. Even in all the times we'd had our tiffs, he'd come to dinner. It was a staple in our lives. If they weren't on a search mission, they came... *he* came. Something was definitely wrong.

I searched each face for answers, but they all put their heads down when my gaze fell on them. It was as if they knew his absence was as monumental as I was making it out to be, and I was certain they were uncomfortable being caught in the middle of something.

"But why? Where is he?" I asked Eric.

"I don't know, Cassie. He said he needed a break." Eric paused a moment, and then added, "Alone."

A break. Alone.

Coming from anyone else, those words were simple, innocent. Knowing they came from Hunter and were said because of me, was crushing.

The lump in my chest began to grow, playing havoc on my emotions. It was my fault he was staying away, and I knew that, but knowing it didn't make the pain any less cutting. Another dark emotion latched itself onto that pain, barely at the edge of it, as if feeding on it until it was nourished enough to detach itself and become its own entity. I was losing control.

"*He* needs a break?" I asked, unable to keep the bite from my tone. "*He* does?" I stood and braced my arms on the table. "Well, that must be nice for him. Anyone else need a break?" I glanced around the table. "How about you, Nora? Mom? Dad?" Anael entered the room, and I stood straight and motioned toward her. "What about you, Anael?"

She stopped in her tracks as her eyebrows shot up. "What about me?" she asked scanning the room, searching for clues to what she'd done.

"Cassie," my dad whispered as he reached over to put his hand on my arm, to pacify my building tantrum.

I pulled my arm away. "Don't you need a break?" I asked Anael. "Oh wait. You're free to take as many breaks from this place as you want. In fact, all of you are. How stupid of me."

"Cassie," my dad said again, not as gracious as before. He stood and came around the table. "Obviously, you're upset with Hunter, but that's no reason to take it out on all of us. What's gotten into you?"

I turned and studied the expression on his face, a condescending look one would give a crazed person in the middle of an episode. It made my blood boil.

"What's gotten into me? You're all just like him. You all wave and tell me to have a nice day as you walk through the swinging doors of this place and let them slap me in the face at your back. None of you give a shit about me being stuck here day after day."

"Cassie, you know that's not true," my mom frowned and yelled as she came to her feet. Nora said something similar and started toward me, but I held out a hand to ward her off.

"Really?" I said. "I thought that came out loud and clear when you all agreed I shouldn't leave."

"That is for your own protection," Eric chimed in.

I glared at him. "Yeah, because I can't take care of myself." Sarcasm dripped from my words. "Maybe I should remind all of you I recently took on the devil in Hell, was tortured for months, and managed to survive it all. I won't even mention I was the main reason Nergal is dead and the Sword is snuggled safely away here with the angels. Or better yet, why don't I remind each of you of how I saved your ass?"

No one moved. Not one word was said. The silence became like thick fog in the room, and I was choking on it.

Shaking with rage, I regarded each of them in turn and saw the shock on their faces. I'd gone too far. But the darkness had consumed me so quickly, and I couldn't think straight. I was seeing the faces of the closest people in my heart, but treating them as if they were my enemies.

What the hell was wrong with me? I wanted to scream. I wanted to cry. I wanted to take each one of them in my arms and hug them close like a protective blanket. I wanted to throw every one of them across the room.

Instead, I ran.

***

Slamming the door behind me, my breathing was heavy from running all the way to my quarters. I half expected Hunter to be there, but he wasn't, and it hitched my adrenaline level another notch. As much as I wanted to throw myself on the bed and bawl my eyes out, I was too jacked up to lie down, or even sit, for that matter.

I paced the room, trying to get hold of my racing emotions. The expressions on the faces of my friends and family flashed in my head like a staccato light, one by one, haunting me, as the hated words I had spewed at them echoed along with them. It wouldn't have surprised me if each and every one of them told me to go back to Hell. Surely, I couldn't blame them. I'd become this horrible, evil person even *I* would cast out. No apology could take everything I'd just said to them back. I wouldn't know how to try and couldn't even explain it to myself.

One thing was for sure—I was about to know how it felt to be completely alone. The thought was enough for me to finally throw myself on the sofa and let it all out, in a torrential downpour. My chest heaved as I cried into one of the throw pillows, only coming up occasionally to gasp for air.

Time escaped my conscious mind because I had no idea how long I continued on that way before I heard a timid knock at the door. At first I wasn't even sure I'd heard it, so I held my breath to listen. I heard it again. It could have been the first or the hundredth knock, for all I knew.

At first, I thought about not answering it. It could only be one of the people I'd just said the most god-awful things to, and I didn't know if I was ready to face that yet. The guilt got the better of me. Wiping my face with my hands, I went and opened the door.

Nora stood, studying me from the other side of the threshold. Even a blind man could tell I'd been bawling my eyes out. Tilting her head to the side, she said, "Hi," in a very gentle tone of voice. I couldn't stand to see the pity in her eyes. Not with what I had just done to her, to all of them.

I lowered my eyes to the floor and whispered, "Hi" back.

"Can I come in?"

I nodded and shuffled aside.

"Those were some pretty harsh words you dished out tonight," she said as I closed the door and faced her.

She was standing next to the sofa, watching her own hand as she played with the fabric. I was glad she didn't meet my gaze. At the moment, I had a handle on my own emotions, but one look from her could change that in a heartbeat.

"I know, and I'm sorry. I've—"

"Why?" she asked. She watched me as I stood awkwardly in the middle of the room.

I knew the question was coming but wasn't prepared to answer it, probably because there *was* no answer, at least not a logical one.

"I don't know," I said, my eyes focused on the floor again as I did my best to answer her. "I wish I did. I feel like I've been body-snatched or something. One minute I'm fine and the nex—"

"No," she interrupted.

I scrutinized her, confused, as she approached and took my fidgeting hands in hers.

"I mean, why are you sorry? You were right. Obviously, I can't speak for the others, but you were dead on about me. When I agreed you should stay within the Sanctuary... after you were almost captured... I didn't think about what that would do to you. It's no excuse, but I really thought it wouldn't be long before this was all over with anyway."

I shook my head. "You couldn't have known how long this would go on, Nora. You can't blame yourself for that. I was wrong to say the things I did."

"It doesn't matter if I knew it or not. What matters is so much time has gone by and I haven't bothered to see what kind of an effect it had on my best friend. God, Cassie, you're even more than that to me. You're family." She sighed and squeezed my hands. "I'm so sorry. I feel terrible. You've been here suffering, and it seems all I've been worried about for the last few months is my love life. How petty am I?"

Not long ago, I was apologizing to her for completely missing that she and Eric had hooked up in the first place. Now, here she was apologizing to me for being so wrapped up in that very relationship that she'd missed out on what I was going through. It was the irony of life. Karma at its finest.

I pulled her into a hug. "You're not petty, just living your life as best you can." I leaned back but kept her at arm's length so I could peer into her eyes. "You shouldn't be sorry for that. I'm just going stir-crazy here, and apparently I want to take everyone down with me."

"So what you're saying is, it's not me it's you?" She grinned.

"Ha ha. I guess you could say that."

"No, I don't think so. We're in this together. It takes two to tango. I'm the Jekyll to your Hyde. You're rubber, I'm—"

"Okay, okay. I get it. Enough with the one-liners." I laughed. Nora could always make me chuckle and it seemed like old times before our lives spun into a whirlwind of chaos. It was what I needed to bring me back from the low, dark place where I'd been dwelling.

She jumped and grabbed my arms, scaring the bejeebus out of me. "That gives me a great idea."

"What does?"

"One-liners," she cried out as if it were obvious. "It's cheesy, but let's have a movie night like we used to. They have an awesome theater room here. We'll get some greasy pizza, make some popcorn, drink some beers, and watch the tackiest horror movies we can find. What do you think?"

The idea alone sounded like a full-blown fiesta to my doom and gloom world. She had me at cheesy. Even if the thought of having a *seems like old times* night with my best friend didn't convince me, the sparkle of anticipation and excitement in her eyes would have.

"I would love that," I said. "When?"

"Are you free at all tomorrow?" she asked, and I knew she was goading me now like she used to. It was refreshing.

"I don't know." I pretended to think about it. "I'm going to have to cancel all the exhilarating plans I had." After a pause for dramatic effect, I said, "Oh, all right, but I want all the juicy details about you and Eric."

"*All* of them?"

"Hell, yeah. You can't give me cake without the frosting, girlfriend."

We both erupted in laughter like a couple of schoolgirls whose lives hadn't been corrupted by the life and death situations we dealt with.

"Oh, I'm totally excited now," she said. "Okay, let's start early, make it a whole day thing. We have a lot of catching up to do. Say noon?"

"Sounds great."

"Cool. All right, well, I'm going to go and get a really good night's sleep then. You better do the same. I'm going to paint your face with pizza toppings if you fall asleep on me."

"No worries there. This is going to be one of the most exciting days I've had since I've been here. There's no way I'm going to miss it by falling asleep." I saw a quick flash of pity come over her expression. It was the last thing I wanted, so I steered her away from it. "I just hope they have some good horror movies here, being an angel sanctuary and all. I mean good by our standards."

"If they don't, I'll send Eric out and get some for us," she said with a wink. We stood there smiling at each other for a moment without a word, but then she sighed and her expression turned serious. "Come here, you." She pulled me into a hug. "Things are going to be different from here on out. I promise."

I believed her. When Nora was conscious of something and made a commitment, she was solid with it. I loved her for wanting to make me feel better under the circumstances, but all I really needed was for the circumstances to be over.

"Thank you," I said, squeezing her tight.

CHAPTER SIX

After Nora had left, my spirit felt lighter knowing I'd cleared the air with at least one of the people I'd completely alienated. But I was also exhausted, run down from the spikes and plummets of my emotions. I decided I'd wait until tomorrow to talk to my mom and dad. My dad, of all people, would understand what I was going through, and mom... mom would always forgive me, the same as I would do for her. We had that unconditional love a mother and daughter share, probably more so than others because of all we'd been through together.

For now, nothing seemed more right than a long, hot bath to ease away any lingering tension. I grabbed a few candles and made my way to the bathroom, on a mission to forget everything that had transpired during the day.

It was liquid heaven in an insanely large, claw foot tub, with the sweet calming scents of jasmine and chamomile. Exactly what I needed. All of my anxiety, all of my anger, seemed to drift away as if the steam rising from the water was taking it all and evaporating into nothingness.

My eyes popped open when I heard a knock at my front door. Feeling lethargic, I slowly eased up from the tub when I heard the door open and then close. Had I forgotten to lock the door?

"Hello?" I called out while reaching for a towel and stepping out of the tub.

Hunter suddenly filled the bathroom doorway, and I jumped, nearly slipping back into the tub. In the panic to right myself, the towel slipped from my hands, but I quickly swiped it back up, holding it in front.

"Need some help?" Hunter asked, checking me out with a raised eyebrow.

I met his gaze with a deadpan look as I wrapped the towel around me and tied it. "When did you come in?" I asked in my most casual voice while sitting on the edge of the tub. Trying to avoid looking at him, I reached over to drain the water. I didn't want to seem too eager to talk since I was still pretty mad at him. Regardless, my heart was racing from being caught off guard. At least I told myself that was why. It was definitely *not* because I was half-naked, and his eyes had just raked over my body as if they physically touched every inch of skin as they went.

"About an hour ago," he said.

"Holy shit. How long have I been in here?"

"I imagine longer than an hour."

That got him another deadpan look.

"Why didn't you come and get me out?"

"You looked peaceful."

"So you let me sleep in the tub? You know that's dangerous. I could have drowned."

"You were under constant observation."

His eyes made another sweep over me, and his meaning sank in as his focus came back up and locked onto mine.

"You... you watched me the whole time?"

"Not the whole time. Someone knocked on the door and I answered it."

He was leaning against the doorframe, his arms crossed over his chest. His expression was classic Hunter, no telling signs of what he was thinking or feeling. Well, except for the sultry look in his eyes. I'd seen those enough times to know exactly what was going on behind them. But they couldn't sway me this time. I was still pissed at his little disappearing act during dinner. As petty as it was, he still owed me an explanation. He knew I'd take offense to him not being at the table without me knowing he wasn't coming. I was certain that's why he did it.

"Oh? Who was it?" I asked.

Breaking eye contact, because quite frankly, those eyes had a way of making me forget everything, and I didn't want to just yet, I got up and opened the cabinet under the sink. After grabbing the lotion, I sat on the marble vanity bench and squeezed some of it into my palm. Deliberately slow, I smoothed the lotion onto one of my legs, from my ankle up to my thigh. There had been a time he would have been the one applying it. I hoped to refresh that memory, but only to torture him. *A smart girl has more than one way to get retribution.* My payback was a tease.

After I let the silence linger for a while, I peeked up to find Hunter watching my hands, his eyes zeroed in on each movement. His jaw tensed. He breathed deep when he realized I was watching him. I stilled my hands and raised my eyebrows, letting him know I was waiting for an answer.

Straightening, he uncrossed his arms, widened his legs, and hung his thumbs from his jean pockets. *God*, the man was sexy, and he didn't even *need* to be half-naked rubbing himself to make me all gooey inside. At the moment, that sucked. I had the ball. It was in *my* court. I went back to massaging the lotion on my legs... massaging the *hell* out of them.

"Anael," he said, his voice a bit raspier than it had been a minute ago. "She came to tell you that as soon as Hadraniel came back from his mission she'd talk to him about letting you out."

I snapped my head up. "Really?"

A muscle twitched on the side of his face. I knew he was clenching his teeth.

"Yes," he said. "Apparently your tantrum at dinner worked."

While it was true, it was most definitely a tantrum, in a moment when I was trying to be a tempting seductress, he made me feel like a child.

I stood up, grabbed the lotion, and put it back in the cabinet, closing the cabinet door more forcefully than necessary.

As I walked past him, deliberately rubbing against his arm, I said, "How would you know? It's not as if you were there or anything. You were on your *break*."

My back to Hunter, I scrunched up my face and walked into the bedroom, mentally chastising myself for the immature comeback. Nothing like feeding into the childish persona he'd already tacked on me.

"Did my not being at dinner make you that mad?"

He knew it did. I was sure he got the whole sordid scenario painted for him by any one of the people unfortunate enough to witness my breakdown. I chuckled an extremely fake snicker.

"Not at all," I said while continuing my path to the dresser. "You're free to do whatever the hell you want, whenever the hell you want, apparently. Lucky you." I added the last part under my breath.

"So that's the way of it now?" His voice came from right behind me. When had he moved? "You've resorted to lies and pouting to get what you want?"

I swung around. "Lie... pou... wait just a—"

He stood there, straighter than normal, all pompous and snooty, with his arms folded across his chest and his eyebrows up on his forehead, as if to say, "Go ahead and prove me right."

I took a breath and said, "I haven't lied to anyone."

"So, you weren't mad that I didn't come to dinner? You didn't flip out on everyone there after you found out I wasn't coming?"

"I didn't *flip* out. I simply asked if they all might need the same kind of break you obviously needed."

He narrowed his eyes, making me squirm from the truth I was avoiding.

"Okay, fine. I flipped out. But it was really shitty of you to stand me up like that. Where were you anyway?"

He smiled, and it melted my heart at the same time it boiled my blood. "So, what you're saying is, it was really just an inflated case of missing me."

"What? No."

Laughing, he said, "C'mon, admit it. You missed me."

He inched in my direction, and I backed up, but I didn't get far since the dresser was at my back. When he closed in on me, I stood straight and raised my chin.

"No, I didn't," I said with complete petulance.

"You didn't?" He brushed the backs of his fingers across my chest, above the swell of skin the towel had created. I stood as still as possible, trying my damnedest not to moan out loud when they moved up to my shoulder and slowly down my arm until his touch reached the inside of my wrist. The wall I'd created in anger seemed to be breaking away, brick by brick. His eyes transfixed me as they followed the trail his fingers were making. I sucked in a breath when his tongue darted out to lick his bottom lip and then retreated back into his mouth.

When his eyes connected with mine once again, I realized he was waiting for an answer.

"What's the question?" I asked, breathless.

"You already answered it."

His hands cupped the back of my head, tilting it just so before his mouth descended on mine like a predator capturing its prey. The familiar taste, like a heady, red wine, sent explosions of desire throughout my body, flirting with every one of my senses. His heavy breathing flooded my ears, while his clean, woodsy scent, hinted with musk, permeated the air all around me. The incandescence of his blue eyes bathed me in a shower of glowing brilliance.

It was Hunter's most powerful weapon, at least with me. I fell easily into his seductive trance, my anger suddenly a distant emotion, buried beneath the pleasure his kiss promised to fulfill. I melted in his arms as he took his time untying my towel and letting it drop to the floor.

When Hunter's mouth left mine, I tried desperately to catch my breath, but it was even harder to breathe when his kisses continued across my jaw and down my neck, his lips and tongue devouring my skin.

"I'm still mad at you," I moaned.

He nipped at my earlobe, and I let out a squeak.

"Hold that thought," he whispered, his hot breath soothing my lobe and sending hot waves of pleasure to my core.

One of his hands came around and grabbed the back of my hair, tugging my head back, exposing my neck to his torturous mouth. His other hand slid up my waist and found a hardened nipple. He brushed his fingers across it ever so lightly, and I sucked in a breath as I arched into him. I needed more. Much more. More of his mouth, more of his hands, more of... him... everywhere.

"Hunter." His name crossed my lips on a half moan, half plea.

Freeing my hair, both his hands went to my breasts, cupping them, molding them, roughly positioning them so he could toy with their peaks. Painful tugs with his teeth were followed by soft, fleshy massages from his tongue and lips. Every touch, every lick, seemed to be directly linked to the growing pressure between my legs. My body had betrayed me, and I couldn't stop pulsing from his touch. His appreciative groans against my skin only made it race faster.

A hand slipped down my body and reached between my legs. Bracing myself against the dresser, I couldn't help but lean into the palm he was using to rub against my most sensitive spot.

"I knew you'd be wet for me," he said in a low, raspy breath. "You're always wet for me, aren't you, Cassandra?"

I couldn't speak. I couldn't even think. He made me crazy with want.

"Tell me," he demanded as his fingers teased the very place I was dying for him to touch.

"Yes," I managed on a pant, barely able to breathe.

"Open your eyes, Cassandra. Look at me."

I did, and his blue orbs burned into mine with a fire that demanded my complete submission, simultaneously promising absolute ecstasy in return.

"Yes, what?" he asked.

My body had taken over my mind and complete control of everything, making me a slave to his mandates without question. "Yes, you make me wet. Please, Hunter."

"Tell me what you want."

"I want you." He continued staring, demanding more. "I want you inside me."

He kissed me hard, claiming me with his mouth. I reached for him and tried to wrap my fingers around his large, hard length through his jeans, but the denim was too thick, too restrictive. Wanting to feel his skin against mine, my clumsy hands tackled the button on his jeans, but he pulled away.

I cried out in frustration.

"Still mad, baby?"

I lifted my heavy, passion-leaded lids and caught him looking down at me with a sexy smirk.

"Seriously? You're going to play that?" I glared.

His fingers stopped their magical antics and the hand that had been at my breast fell to my hip.

"Oh, yeah," he said, his smirk now a cocky grin.

I narrowed my eyes and crossed both arms over my chest. "Well, then, yes, I guess I am." My voice almost cracked from the strain of trying to suppress my over-anxious libido. I braced myself, knowing damn well all it would take was one flick of the finger he still had between my legs and I'd jump him. Hell, as jacked up as I was for him, even a come-hither look would probably do the trick.

He smiled. *Shit.*

Before I even knew what happened, my feet were off the ground. Hunter's arms clamped around my thighs, and I wrapped my arms around his neck as he hoisted me up onto the dresser.

I looked up at him as he stood between my legs. One side of his mouth lifted slowly. Cocky. Smug. Sexy.

"I was hoping you'd say that." His tone was dangerous... exotically dangerous, and the ache between my legs intensified from it.

Slowly, he reached back and unclasped my hands from his neck. To my surprise, he placed them on his head. I looked at him questioningly, until he began to lower himself, keeping those piercing blue eyes on mine as he dropped, inch by inch. Torture.

"Yell my name when I'm forgiven."

The minute his lips touched the inside of my thigh, I wanted to scream his name, but I didn't dare stop what they were promising. I wanted... no, *needed*... release from the almost unbearable tension at my core. When he touched my sex with his tongue... *dear God*, I had to bite down on my lip to keep it back, it felt so good.

I couldn't hold back the moaning though. It came from deep in my throat, a place I had no control of and seemingly connected to the thorough loving of his mouth. The moans grew louder as I felt myself on the brink of complete ecstasy. Pulling his hair as my body writhed against his mouth was all I could do to hold on, until his own groan against my sex, made a low vibratory sound that pierced through the pressure point, causing an explosion of bliss. The ecstasy reached every single inch of my body.

I yelled his name... over and over again with every wave of orgasmic pleasure that swept through me.

When the euphoria started subsiding, I gazed down at Hunter, who looked at me from between my legs, a satisfied smile on his face. Not one that boasted accomplishment over me. Instead, it said how much he loved seeing me in such a state as if he lived for it. The act wasn't about sex and pleasure to get out of a bitch session, but it was about love conquering all. As cheesy as the adage was, it fit us. At that moment, with that look, I knew it didn't matter about the hell we'd gone through, were *going* through. Together, we could get through anything as long as we held on to the love we had.

"God, I love you," I said in a breathy whisper.

He stood and pushed a hair from my face, his gaze locked on mine. His eyes were passion-filled as he leaned in and brushed my lips with his. "And you always will. I'll make sure of that."

"We still need to talk, Hunter. I feel—"

His finger pressed against my lips, silencing me. "You're still upset. I understand. In fact, I'm glad you're not giving up that easy." Without another word, he lifted me up from the dresser and carried me to the bed, where he laid me down and settled over the top of me.

"Hunt—" I started to protest.

"Shhhh. We'll talk as much as you want after, I promise. Right now I want your mouth for something else, and I can't wait."

My breath hitched and he used the opportunity to close in on my mouth. His need was desperate as his tongue frantically sought mine. No matter that I'd been fully satiated, my body responded in an instant to him, arching against touch, grinding against his erection. I was still writhing when his body left mine. He stood and looked down at me as he removed his shirt, revealing a muscled chest and perfect abs. A sheen of sweat glistened in the light and made my mouth water with the urge to lick it off. I was practically panting when he pulled down his jeans and his sex was released in all of its thick, veined glory.

Any arguments vanished. At the moment, there was only Hunter. Hunter as he lay back on me. Hunter as he entered me, filling me completely. Hunter as he made love to me over and over again throughout the night until my senses were numbed, leaving an erogenous tingling of my body. He'd become a drug in my veins, pulling me deeper into the depths of a calm, blissful serenity.

I spooned against him, and he pulled me in closer, wrapping his body around me like a warm blanket. Sighing, I closed my eyes.

"Dream of this tonight, baby. Only this." Hunter's whisper was accompanied by a kiss on my temple.

A smile covered my face as I drifted off, praying my subconscious followed his orders.

***

The smell of burnt flesh invaded my nostrils and my eyes snapped open. A bright glare blinded me, and it took me a moment to realize I was standing near a large hearth, flames snapping out at my skin like striking snakes. I jumped back, instinctively rubbing my arms where the fire had reached, but my back hit something large and solid that caused a gasping breath from the impact.

Slowly I turned, careful not to step near the fire. Strangely, the heat at my back wasn't as unbearable as it should be, but I didn't have time to ponder that oddity, because, in front of me, Hunter was strung up, spread-eagle and naked, manacled to floor-to-ceiling columns. I was the only thing standing between him and the smoldering fire, but the burns on his skin were evidence the flames had no problem bridging the distance in my absence.

I studied Hunter's situation in confusion. His head hung limp against his chest, his hair soaked and dripping beads of sweat on the floor at his feet. Blood and charred flesh covered his entire body, marring its statuesque perfection. I should have been horrified by the sight of my love so tortured, but that wasn't the emotion drumming through me. I felt... relief. Relief and excitement.

When I started to grasp my reality in the strange situation, I smiled, an arrogant smile that reached all the way to the corners of my eyes, which was the expression Hunter saw when he lifted his head. If he was surprised by it, it didn't show. His eyes were dead, showing no sign of the light they usually held when he looked at me. They were pale, cloudy blue, an indication he might be losing his sight altogether.

While gazing into those eyes, the last piece of the puzzle locked into place, and I knew exactly why I was there, why I couldn't feel the heat of the very same flames now torturing my lover. I *was* the fire and controlled the flames that singed his skin. I'd made them dance for me against his body until he no longer had the strength to cry out. Not that he'd show its effects on him anyway. His pride and resolve were too strong to show such a weak state. Too bad for him. Pride and resolve didn't stand a chance against my power.

"Do I make you hot, baby?" I taunted, swiping at the sweat on his chest, arms, and back with a finger as I circled him.

"You can still fight, Cassandra," he said, his voice gravelly and low. "You can escape it."

I laughed. "I think you're confused." I stood directly in front of him once again. His eyes met mine, and he searched their depths for something I knew was not there. With a sardonic grin, I added, "You're the one who should be looking for escape." I reached up and shook the chains that bound him. "But don't bother because there is none."

"Don't fool yourself, Cassandra. You're more prisoner than me. Hell has drawn you in with its promise of power and darkened your heart, but your soul can still fight it. You already have more strength than anything Hell can give you. Fight, Cassandra. Fight for us."

Something inside of me, deep in my chest, thumped. Not a big movement, more of a small jolt, but it was enough to make me lose myself for a moment, similar to when you forget what you were doing or why you were in a place at a given time.

I stood there, facing Hunter, staring without really seeing, waiting for my mind to catch up to the reason I was in this place. Then I saw it. My purpose throbbed with illumination against the wall, just behind Hunter. I zoned in on it, feeling the power once again pulsing through my veins, my hands itching to wrap my fingers around it.

Fixing my gaze back on Hunter, our eyes locked, hope evident in his, until I smiled. Then his chest rose from a deep breath before slowly closing his eyes, hanging his head.

"You're really pathetic, you know," I told him as I walked over and picked up the Sword. "To think, you were supposed to be king of the Underworld. Look at you now… so weak. You're not worthy to wipe the king's ass." I stood behind him and ran the flat side of the blade across his back. "You disgust me."

"You think Caleb has what it takes to be king of the Underworld?" He let out a short laugh. "He's too stupid to rule over anything. Those he believes he controls… will overtake him the minute he turns his back."

I leaned in close to his ear and whispered, "I already have."

With the Sword pressed against his back, I placed a kiss on his neck and slid my free hand around his waist until I reached his shaft. He was hard. I knew he would be. Wrapping my fingers around it, I said, "It's too bad you're the only one left in my way. I'm going to miss you... well, parts of you." I stroked him and smiled to myself when I heard the hiss of his breath. His jaw clenched. Even standing behind him, I could see the muscles drumming against his jaw. The smell of his arousal mixed with sweat filled the air. I really *was* going to miss the power I had over him.

"Fight for me, Cassandra," he said through clenched teeth.

Another thump in my chest caught me off guard. My hand dropped from his sex, and I stepped back from him.

"You love me," he continued. "I love you. We can beat this. Together."

A white light radiated from the Sword and it warmed in my hands. I let out the breath I didn't realize I'd been holding and looked upon its glow, a beacon showing me the way. The Sword always brought me back where I was supposed to be. I loved it for that. Nothing would come between us. I knew what I had to do.

"I do love you, Hunter," I said, still behind him. I raised the Sword and aimed it at his back. "Just not enough."

"Then why don't you face me when you kill me?"

His question caught me off guard, and I even contemplated it for a minute, confused why it might affect me. But then the answer came to me. "Because you deserve to be stabbed in the back like the coward you are."

His torso arched, and he strained forward against the chains as the blade slid easily through his flesh.

CHAPTER SEVEN

I woke with a start, lying on my side, clutching a pillow against my sweat-soaked body. The last remnants of my dream dissipated, like fog lifting at sunrise. Reality slowly came into focus. I uncurled my cramped fingers from the pillow and noticed I'd shredded a portion of the cloth confining the down within. Throwing it aside, I sat up.

Hunter was gone from the bed, and I realized it was his pillow I'd shredded. Listening for any sign he was still in our chambers, revealed nothing. I was disappointed he was gone but relieved he hadn't witnessed my reaction to the nightmare. Would he have been the victim of that violence if he'd been there? I was afraid if I didn't get control of my nightmares, it was exactly what might happen.

Forcing myself to get up and make my way around the bed, heading for the bathroom, I spotted a piece of paper lying on the floor near Hunter's side of the bed. I recognized Hunter's scrawl.

Cassandra,

As much as I hate leaving you lying naked in our bed, my help is needed by the Army early this morning. I didn't want to wake you. You looked like you were getting some much-needed rest, not to mention, it afforded me a voyeuristic view of all your delicious parts. Now that I've tortured myself, I'll try to make this as quick as possible in order to come back and have a taste. Stay naked for me.

Yours,

Hunter

His words lightened the last bits of darkness that lingered from my dream, and I smiled on my way to the bathroom. As much as I complained about being the little woman lying in wait for her man to come back and please him, right then, I wanted nothing more than that. First, I needed to wash off the sweat that had nothing to do with our previous night's lovemaking.

As I stepped out of the shower, I heard a knock on the door. Covering up with a robe, I approached where I could hear the voice on the other side.

"Cassie? You there?" Nora asked.

"I know you wanted to start early, but it's only ten, Nora," I said as I opened the door.

She stood there, eyes wide, mouth agape.

"What?" I asked.

"I can't believe you're so calm right now. I would have thought you'd be bouncing off the walls. Hell, I half expected you not to be here." She rushed into the room, leaving me standing at the open door.

"What are you talking about?"

"Hunter didn't tell you?"

"He was already gone when I woke up. What's going on?"

"Oh. Uh..." Her thoughtful cringe caused me to immediately take offense. I was about to tell her that when she stalked back to the door, checked the hallway, and then shut it.

"They brought a demon here," she whispered.

"In the Sanctuary?"

"Yes."

"Who did? Hadraniel?"

"No, no. A team of seekers. They have him locked down in a room underground."

The Sanctuary had a level kept exclusively for enemies of the angels. It was a prison of sorts, but without barred cells. Several small rooms lined a long hallway, not much different than a hotel floor, only the rooms held the bare essentials and nothing more.

"Eric and Hunter are with him now," she continued. "Supposedly the demon was sent by Caleb to steal the Sword. They caught him outside the gates."

"Outside the gates?"

My blood was pumping. I wanted to be excited that we might be one step closer to ending this nightmare, but I was confused. After months of silence from Caleb, I couldn't believe he would send an incompetent demon to get caught at the gates of the Sanctuary. It had to be some kind of trap. Now my blood was really boiling. Hunter would have known it was a trap, but instead of waking me up to let me in on this major turn of events, he left me unconscious and wrote a cutesy love letter. I was far beyond pissed.

"I'm getting dressed and going down there," I said, already making my way toward the bedroom.

Nora grabbed my arm. "Cassie, wait. I don't think we should... I mean... they might not want you there." Before the words left her mouth, my anger had sparked to a level off the charts. "For your own safety, I'm sure," she quickly threw in.

I narrowed my eyes. "We're really going to do this again, Nora?"

She cast her gaze to the floor. "I'm sorry. I know. It's just..."

"I get it, okay? You don't want anything to happen to me. But I'm just going to check it out. They won't let me go out to help, so this is my only chance to feel like I'm doing something constructive. Maybe I can even turn him. If I do that, the demon might be more willing to help us. Don't you think that's worth letting them pout over me being there?"

Nora mulled it over, chewing her bottom lip as she did. I gave her a second to think she had some say in the decision. Whatever conclusion she came to didn't really matter. I was going. I actually thought she was starting to see things my way until she pursed her lips together and shook her head.

"Yeah, but—"

"Look, I'm going. Whether you like it or not. I don't need you to go with me."

With that, I spun and left her in the room, heading to the bedroom to change. I had no idea if she would stay. I didn't really know where her loyalty was anymore. Come to think of it, I never really knew. All those years I thought we were friends simply by fate, she'd been watching over me for Hadraniel all along. Now our friendship was up against her love for Eric, whose loyalty was with Hunter. If she went with me, they'd know she told me. I couldn't imagine she'd take that chance.

That's why I was surprised when I came out and she was leaning against the door, waiting for me. Unless...

"You're not going to stop me, Nora. I'm doing this."

"I know I can't stop you. I just want to make sure you think about this before you go barreling down there. Hunter will probably be pissed if you—"

"I don't care if—"

"Hear me out, Cassie. What I was going to say is that this could end up far worse than pissing off Hunter. I highly doubt Caleb would send someone stupid enough to get caught so easily stealing the Sword. More than likely it's some kind of decoy. Caleb is as devious as they come. We both know this. You could be falling right into whatever trap he may have set, and I don't know if I'd ever forgive myself if something happened to you because of me."

"Nora..." I didn't really know what to say. I knew her words were true. Hunter probably thought the same way she did. They didn't want me exposed, but I was already trapped in the Sanctuary, and I'd be damned if I would also be a prisoner in my own chambers too. I could handle myself, but I had to prove that, if for nothing other than my own self-preservation. "I have to do this."

"I know," she said as she opened the door. "But I'm going with you."

"You don't have to. I know Eric will be—"

"Eric will just have to get over it. Now let's go while I'm feeling all rebellious and shit."

***

Both Nora's rebellious intentions and mine were nothing more than skid mark dreams when Eric met us at the door leading down to the underground level. As we approached the hallway, the seeker originally standing guard ducked out like a coward. By the time we reached the door, Eric was hulking before us.

He gave Nora a look before he turned his attention to me and said, "Not going to happen, Cassie."

"Eric, get out of my way. I have just as much right to be down there as you do. And don't blame Nora, she had no idea Hunter wouldn't tell me. Most people who claim to be in love share life-changing events. Like you and Nora, for example."

I watched them exchange a look, one Hunter and I had shared so many times, but what seemed ages ago now that so much smoke had clouded up between us.

"Just let me through, Eric. Don't make this any messier than it is. I'll deal with Hunter."

"Messy is the only way you're getting through this door," he said turning back to me, poised and ready for me to get physical. I narrowed my eyes at him and automatically tightened up. "Hunter isn't the only who doesn't want you down there. It's too dangerous."

"Give me a fucking break," I shouted, fisting my hands at my sides to keep me from doing what I wanted to with them. "It's just a demon, for chrissakes. I've taken on bigger and badder than that, and you know it." When he looked as if he wouldn't be swayed, I scrambled for a different approach. "Did you ever think this was exactly what Caleb was counting on? That Hunter would put all his efforts into getting what he could from the demon while I was kept locked somewhere far away from it? Alone? Unguarded?"

Eric didn't show any more reaction to that angle, but a flash of concern crossed his face. He was adept at hiding his emotions, however, and it was gone in an instant. Hunter and Eric were very much alike. Nora had her work cut out for her, although, she didn't have to worry about being left out of everything... or having a demented psychopath coming for her.

"You were supposed to remain in your chambers," he said. "You're safe there."

"How do you know that?"

Eric didn't answer, pretending he hadn't heard my question. He simply looked back at me in the same statuesque manner that made me want to throw him across the room. Instead, I let out a loud growl-like noise and turned to pace. "*God.* I am so *sick* of this." I twirled back around to him. "I swear I am this close to forcing you out of my way, Eric."

The hand I held up to show him trembled so bad I could barely keep it up. My whole body was shaking, and I sensed my eyes glowing as they glared up at him. I was ready to explode. Nora placed a hand on my arm, and I nearly detonated.

"Cassie, let's just... let's just go. I'm sure Hunter will get the information out of the guy. He'll tell you everything when they're done."

I threw her hand off me and turned my glare on her. "No. I'm not leav—"

The door behind Eric opened and he stepped aside as Hunter came out. "Yes, you are, Cassandra," he said as he grabbed my upper arm, spun me around, and started walking me down the hallway.

I managed to wrench myself free and faced him. "So this is how you're going to treat me now? You don't even have the balls to tell me what's going on? You just sneak off and leave me love letters to keep me put?"

A muscle ticked on the side of his jaw as his eyes locked on mine. Enough heat radiated in them that told me there was only a sliver of patience left in him. "If it means keeping you safe, then *yes*."

"This is bullshit, Hunter. I can help. I can try and turn him, maybe he'll—"

"If he knows something, I'll get it out of him. I don't want you anywhere near this guy."

"What could possibly happen with you right there?"

I could see in his eyes the moment he snapped, even before he grabbed me again, this time by both arms, practically lifting me off the floor. "Dammit, Cassandra. Anything can happen. *Anything*. With or without me there. I have no idea what Caleb is capable of anymore, and I'm not willing to take chances when it comes to you. Why can't you just do what you're told?"

I stared at him, eyes wide, mouth open. "Do what I'm told? Are you serious? What am I, a child now? I can't believe you just said that to me."

"If you're going to act like one, I'm going to treat you that way. Your tantrums are getting tiresome, Cassandra, but they won't change my mind. I love you and will protect you at all costs."

His words burned and I stood there, tense under his grasp, unable to do anything but stare back at him. A shadow seemed to pass over my heart at that moment, darkening the overwhelming happiness I felt mere hours ago when we made love. It splintered the connection I was once sure could never be severed, like a rope pulled taut and shredding under too much strain.

I wrenched my arms free of his grasp, and without another look, I turned my back on him and walked away.

"Cassandra," he yelled. When I didn't answer, he shouted, "Where are you going?"

I spun around. "I'm going to pout. That's what children do when they don't get their way, isn't it?" I was seething and didn't care if he saw it. He'd already revealed what he really thought of me. It seemed I was becoming more of a burden. A burden with benefits.

"Don't bother coming back to our room when you're done. There won't be anything naked waiting for you."

"Cassandra," he growled.

But I didn't pause to hear the rest. I kept walking. And he didn't bother coming after me.

I waited for the pain to set in, but it never did. With every step I took, I felt a slow fire of anger burning that rope that had kept us together.

And with it... a strange sense of relief.

***

I had every intention of going back to our room... *my* room, not because that was where Hunter wanted me, but because I really was pouting, and it wasn't something I wanted any of the asshole angels to get their rocks off seeing. As I neared the training facility, I heard male grunting coming from within, and it drew me in. I tiptoed near and crept in, so as not to alert whoever was inside.

Unconsciously, I drew a breath at the sight of Braydon, bare-chested, steeling himself in a prone position above the floor, then slowly lowering himself down, biceps bulging, back muscles working, as he held his own weight. The sweat glistened on his whole body. He was definitely a sight for pained, sore eyes.

I stood silently, content on watching him. When he rose back up with another grunt, the sound pulled at something low in my belly, and my breath became heavy.

"I'm going to have to charge you admission if you stand there much longer, unless you want to spot me," he said without moving.

Guilt should have overcome me for so blatantly ogling another man, but after what had just happened with Hunter, I was feeling spiteful, and I-don't-give-a-shit-ish,

"What's the going rate?" I asked, picking up a towel and sauntering over to him.

He raised up, looking at me, still poised in the push-up, muscles taut as they strained to keep him in position. "For you?" He smirked. "It'll be pretty costly."

"Why? Because I can kick your ass?" I grinned and threw the towel down next to him as I approached.

He leaned his weight on one arm. While I was admiring the view, he used his other arm to sweep my legs out from under me. My ass landed hard on the mat, and I let out a loud *oomph*.

"No." He laughed, grabbed the towel and stood. Looking down at me, he offered his hand to help me up. "Because you think you can."

I eyed him for a moment or two, checking for signs that he wasn't just playing the helpful Samaritan only to set me up for another fall.

He chuckled and waved the white towel when he realized I was leery. "You can trust me."

"I don't trust anyone," I said but took his hand anyway.

Pulling me up, he said, "That must be lonely."

Once I was on my feet, his hand lingered on mine longer than necessary as our eyes locked. Little twitters of excitement fluttered underneath my skin, making me uncomfortable, so I pulled my hand away and took a step back.

"I have my circle of friends," I said in defense.

"And you trust them?"

His question hit home like a spotlight shining on my heart. He'd managed to hone in on the one aspect of my life I believed was slipping away and killing me inside. I thought about the few people in my life whom I trusted, and how each one of them had taken that trust and burned me with it. *How could I be any more alone?*

While deep in my thoughts, I didn't realize he'd encroached on my space until his hand cupped the side of my neck, brushing his thumb across my cheek. His touch was so gentle; I wasn't sure it happened. "I'd like to be your friend, Cassie," he whispered.

His eyes were soft and sincere as I gazed into them. Every part of me wanted to trust them if only to find someone who would be open and honest with me. No secrets, no lies, no prisons. But my heart had a dark shell formed around it now and even thoughts of letting someone else in bounced off it.

I put my hand around his wrist, stopping the caress. "You mean, you want to get in my pants."

He arched an eyebrow and smiled. "I won't deny I've fantasized about playdates with you. You're a gorgeous woman, Cassie. I'd have to be dead not to want you lying naked beneath me."

With my hand still on his wrist, he raised his thumb to my mouth, and I watched as his tongue darted out to lick his bottom lip, his teeth capturing it, before slowly letting it out. At that moment, I wanted nothing more than to have those lips on mine, his tongue in my mouth, his body flush against mine, working to put out the fire that had just flared within me.

I knew I couldn't allow myself to act on my emotions. The consequences would be disastrous. "Braydon, I can't—"

He brought a finger to my lips. "No, don't say anything." Ducking his head so he could look directly into my eyes, he said, "You don't need to make any decisions right now, Cassie. Just let this be. Do what makes you happy." His other hand came up to cup the other side of my neck and both of his thumbs caressed my cheeks again as his face drew in closer. "Does this feel good to you?"

I couldn't keep my eyes off his lips. Without thinking, I said, "Yes," on a breath.

"It feels like heaven to me," he whispered, and his lips gently touched mine.

Alarms went off in my head and lightning flashed from the contact, and suddenly I couldn't breathe at all. It felt so good... but so wrong at the same time. Carefully placing my hands on his chest, I leaned back and sucked in a deep breath. "Braydon, stop."

His lids were heavy over his eyes, but the green in them blazed with passion from underneath. He studied me before whispering, "I'm won't say I'm sorry because I'm not." He grabbed my hands and held them in his. "Now that I've gotten a taste, I want more. Don't fight it, Cassie." His hands slid up my arms, rounded my shoulders, and then made their way down my back until they finally rested on my hips. Shivers followed the entire wake of their path.

My emotions skittered all over the place. I was attracted to Braydon, extremely so, but something within me was repelling me away from him. Was it my love for Hunter? Even though I despised him at the moment, was the devotion I'd held for him so deep and strong it acted on its own, as a guardian of my heart?

"If I don't fight it, someone else will," I told him. It was true. Regardless of whether Hunter and I were together, I knew my being with Braydon would cause a war.

"I'm not afraid of Hunter."

"Well, you should be because he's going to kick your ass... and then he'll kill you. Get your hands off her, Braydon."

I jerked in Braydon's arms, my heart practically jumping out of my chest at the unexpected sound of Nora's voice. She was standing at the entrance of the training room, hands folded across her chest, eyes narrowed in on Braydon.

"Like... now," she added.

From the expression on Braydon's face, Nora's outburst hadn't concerned him in the least. In fact, he seemed bored by it, maybe even amused if the smirk on his face was any indication. I broke from his arms and pushed him back before I faced Nora. A range of emotions swept through me—shock, embarrassment, guilt. But more than anything... anger.

"You're spying on me?" I asked. "Oh, wait. That shouldn't even surprise me, should it? That's what you do. It's what you all do."

She was floored at my words. The hurt expression on her face was instant, and I'd meant it. I was done bowing to everyone's beliefs about how I was supposed to act, or feel, for that matter. Maybe it was time for the whole group of them to understand how I really felt.

"No, I wasn't spying on you," she said, her voice full of disdain. "I was looking for you... to make sure you were okay. Obviously, you are. What the hell are you doing, Cassie? Kissing Braydon because you're pissed at Hunter? I don't get it. That's not you. What's happened to you?"

We were about ten feet away from each other, but it could have been double that and I'd still see the clear contempt on her face. It pissed me off even more.

"You may have watched me all these years, but you don't know me, Nora. No one does. Yet, you all sit on your thrones and shake your heads at me as if you're better than me."

"That's not—" she started, but I wouldn't allow her to finish.

"You want to know what's happened to me? I woke up and decided I just don't give a damn what any of you think anymore. Go chase away your own demons. Let me deal with mine."

Her gasp echoed throughout the room. I continued to glare at her while my heart raced and my hands trembled. Silence followed like spidered glass no one dared touch for fear the impact would lead to a shattering end.

After minutes of silence ticked by, Braydon's hand touched on my arm, sending a searing flash of heat through my skin. "Cassie, I'll go." His voice was serious but soft.

"No," I shouted, and I swiped at his hand, shaking it off my arm. I whirled around to face him, but before I could say more, a wave of dizziness hit me, and the room faded to black.

CHAPTER EIGHT

Standing on the sidewalk in the city's busy commercial district, I was surrounded by office buildings and parking structures. People bustled around me, heels and loafers clicking on the concrete, fast-paced and determined to reach their destinations. Some people carried paper bags and coffees from nearby delis, others lugged leather briefcases or satchels. All of them were oblivious to the impending doom in my heart.

Blue skies peeked around the rooftops. The sun was blocked out from the height of the buildings around me, casting shadows along the lengths of the streets. A bustle of activity filled my ears—cell phones singing, car horns blaring, people chattering. It all seemed to melt together into one single hum until the wind carried with it distinct clapping and clanging noises from up the block.

My body reacted to the sounds like sonar, drawing me to their origin. My skin tingled, and the hairs on my arms stood on end as I started that direction. About midway down the block, I spotted a huge crane across the street and one block up. From what I could see, a building was in the process of being erected. Moving closer, it appeared as if the concrete framework for four or five floors had already been set, and workers were beginning to add the next. Crews of men and women, donned in hard hats and fluorescent vests, carried out their duties, heaving, drilling, pounding, operating machinery, or simply supervising.

Making my way to the site, another crane grabbed my notice. While the first one I'd seen from down the block sat dormant, the other was hauling a huge slab of concrete toward the building. In an instant, a shout came from inside the structure and a man appeared at the opening in the wall. He looked angry, his hands waving erratically as more shouting ensued. The crane stopped, the concrete still dangling from its grapples. My eyes were drawn to that slab of concrete, slowly swaying back and forth in the air, like a medallion at the end of a hypnotist's chain.

"Miss, you're not allowed on the site without a hard hat," a man said. He stood directly in front of me, although I hadn't even noticed I'd walked so close to the area. I'd been mesmerized by watching the crane's activity. "Are you looking for someone?"

Over the man's shoulder, I noticed the crane had started to reverse its direction, moving away from the building. Its neck began to spin around, and as it passed the operator's station, dark movements beneath caught my breath. A single shadow lurked in the small compartment with the operator, looming over the controls.

"Miss?" the man in front of me tried regaining my attention. I was about to explain myself to him, how I didn't know, but several shouts drew our combined attention back to the crane. The operator was panicking inside the compartment, frantically pulling and pushing on levers. The crane neck jerked back and forth swinging the concrete violently in the air. People were running away from the machine, crouching as they went with arms over their hard hats, as if the crane might launch the slab at any moment.

One man stood oblivious to it all. He wore huge earphones that resembled something that might deafen the sound of a nuclear blast. His back was turned as he studied something in his hands. He had no idea when that slab of concrete spun around until it was directly above him, escaping the crane's grapples. No screams of fear were heard, at least not from him, before he was crushed beneath the thick weight. Lifeless fingers peeking out the side of the heavy stone was the only sign he had ever been there.

I stared at those fingers, waiting to feel... something. No. I was numb. Or maybe I was simply dead inside. For a while, I stood there, coming to terms with that fact as I let the darkness bleed out of my blackened heart and overtake me.

***

I tried to open my eyes, but white light hit them like a shockwave to my senses. Through rapid blinking and hardcore squinting, I saw the bright lights of the training room on the ceiling above me.

"Cassie," someone close whispered to me.

My body was jostled, and I realized I was cradled in a lap.

"Hey, welcome back. You okay?" Braydon gazed down at me.

Confused, I scanned my surroundings the best I could. We were on the floor in the middle of the training room.

Nora ran over and kneeled down near us, eyebrows furrowed over concerned eyes. "How're you doing, sweetie?" She pushed a strand of hair away from my face and tucked it behind my ear.

Thoughts, images, and a myriad of emotions battled for control of my head, leaving me confused and clueless. "What happened?"

"You fainted," Braydon said.

"Fainted?"

"Yes, you were arguing with Nor—"

"It looked like you went into a vision," Nora interrupted.

Suddenly, all the pieces fell into place. The construction site, the crane, the man underneath it... *oh God.*

"I have to go," I said so loud it hurt my head. When I attempted to stand, I faltered.

Braydon was right there. "Whoa, hold on there. You just came to, Cassie. Take some time to get your bearings."

"There is no time. I have to go." With as much power as I could gather, I pushed at him, but it wasn't enough. "I'm fine." While I met his gaze, I made sure my voice remained even, smooth.

He must have believed me because he released me.

I stood, but before I'd made it more than five feet, Nora blocked my path.

"Cassie, wait. Just tell me what happened, and I'll go for you."

Tightening my fists at my sides, I glared at her. "No freaking way, Nora." My tone was low, tight. "I'm going. Don't try and stop me. I won't warn you again."

Nora flinched. We stood for what seemed an eternity face to face, her gaping, me glowering. Finally, she shook her head in a gesture of defeat. "You're threatening me now? That's what we've come to?"

"That's what you've brought us to. I don't have time to talk about relationships right now, Nora. You know this. Or maybe you just don't care about what it really means to be a guardian anymore."

Her face reddened.

Good, I thought, maybe I pissed her off enough to finally leave me the hell alone.

"Nora, let her go," a voice behind me echoed. Hadraniel.

I stiffened. He took me by surprise, not only had I not known he was in the room, but also because he was willing to let me go. I whirled around to face him.

"You're letting me leave?"

"In your state, I don't see that any of us have much of a choice, but I agree, you should go."

Arms crossed over my chest, I studied him. "What's the catch?"

Hadraniel shot me with a soft, friendly smile. "No catch. I talked with Anael. She convinced me you've grown in your abilities since you were nearly captured the last time you were out. I trust you won't prove her wrong." The threat in his words was subtle. So much so, it would have been missed by most, but there it was, not only in his words but also in the piercing gaze he leveled on me.

"I'll be fine."

"Hunter won't like her leaving," Nora piped in, bursting my freedom bubble.

I gave her a fierce stare.

She ignored me and kept her focus on Hadraniel.

I was about to give her my uncensored opinion, but Hadraniel stole my thunder, only in a calm-before-the-storm kind of way. "You and Braydon can accompany Cassandra, along with a team of angels. All of you will watch for any threats to her while she does her job."

Unsure how I felt about that, I wasn't going to argue. I guess it wasn't a bad thing to have someone watching my back. Out there, I was fair game. Caleb's minions had come after me before, and it could happen again. While I felt more powerful and sure of my abilities now, it didn't hurt to have extra ammo.

"Hunter would definitely not agree," Nora argued. *Again.* I wanted to punch her.

"*Jesus*, Nora," I said. "Cut the Team Hunter bullshit or go find his ass so you can kiss it in person."

She swung her gaze at me, nostrils flaring, eyes practically bulging out of their sockets. "Dammit, Cassie. I've had it with your little temper tantrums. I'm only trying to help you."

"You want to help me?"

"Yes. If you weren't so damn stubborn—"

"If you want to help me, then *help* me. Come with me. Don't stand in the way of what little freedom I have here. Let me worry about Hunter later. He's my problem anyway, not yours."

"I'll deal with Hunter," Hadraniel said as he stepped between us. He turned his attention to Nora. "You will go with Cassandra. That wasn't a request."

Whatever look he gave her caused her to bow her head.

"Now all of you, go." He dismissed us with the swipe of one hand. "Before the poor soul is lost because his guardians can't play nice."

"C'mon, Cassie." Braydon urged me forward with a gentle touch on my lower back.

We made our way toward the entrance of the training room where I noticed a group of angels already waiting in the hallway. I didn't bother to check over my shoulder to see if Nora followed.

To be honest, I really didn't care.

***

Most people would feel blessed to have a group of angels watching over them. I wasn't most people. It might have had something to do with the fact I'd been snubbed by them for the last few months, or simply that my blood pumped to the beat of a darker drum. Needless to say, I didn't offer them a cheery welcome when our group joined them in the hallway, nor did I get one in return. Geared up and ready for battle, they were military statues with stoic expressions, there to do a job, nothing more.

Nora joined us as I was giving a quick summary of my vision. I glanced in her direction, but she quickly turned to talk with one of the angels. It was deliberate avoidance, and I knew then our relationship had changed. The new tension between us seemed irreversible. No time to deal with it now.

Being with the angels did have its advantages. Travel was... well, instantaneous. It was a power both angels and demons held, but somehow I hadn't inherited it. Command of my powers was still developing, however, so I had hope it would yet transpire. I also hadn't dismissed the possibility Hadraniel was blocking me from using that particular one to keep me under his watchful eye. Nothing surprised me anymore.

We arrived at the construction site, on the outskirts of the fenced area. No one around us seemed to think it strange we appeared out of nowhere, but I imagined the angels had something to do with that too. People continued to mill around, going about their normal, daily bustling lives, walking around us as we stood in the middle of the sidewalk staring at the workings inside the fence.

The site was exactly as it had appeared in my vision. Workers shouted over the drone of machines to one another, clouds of dust billowed all around and sparks flew as metal clanked against metal. The shell of the building was growing piece by constructive piece. Each worker seemed to know exactly what he or she needed to do, but every one of them was oblivious to the fact someone was about to die.

My plan was to find the victim and get him out of the way of the crane before it had a chance to crush him. How I was going to do that had yet to be determined. Nothing new there. Nora had volunteered to go with me. At first I wanted to argue, but I realized it was just out of spite, and it wouldn't hurt to have someone close by. Regardless of what had transpired between us, I knew she wouldn't let anything happen to me.

While Nora and I searched out the victim, the angels went to scout out any threats in the area. To the mortal eye, they'd appear as normal Joes, blending into a society that barely noticed their surroundings anyway. Their weapons, armor, and undeniable beauty were veiled so as not to draw any attention.

"Do you see him?" Nora asked when we walked through the opening in the fence.

I scanned the area and spotted the crane. The operator was inside, but the man with the earphones wasn't around.

"No." I pointed. "But that's the crane."

"Okay, let's go over there. Maybe you can distract the operator before the guy even gets close."

I nodded, and we set off but didn't get far. A big bulk of a man came out of nowhere and blocked our way.

My heart jumped out of my chest at the same time I heard Nora gasp.

"You two can't be here," he shouted.

"They're here for routine inspections." Braydon had come up from behind us to stand in front of the man with us at his back.

Frowning, the man looked up at Braydon. The guy was at least a head shorter than the angel. He rubbed the back of his neck and opened his mouth to say something, but whatever it was never came out. Mouth still agape, his gaze was transfixed on Braydon.

"They're on your itinerary for the day." Braydon nodded in the direction of the clipboard the man had tucked underneath his arm. "You can check."

The man seemed in a trance for a moment, as if processing the information Braydon had just given him. He blinked once and pulled out the clipboard.

I held my breath, knowing we couldn't have been listed on his itinerary.

Opening the metal cover, he examined the contents and nodded. "Yes, okay, that's right." He shook his head. "Don't know how I missed that. Where would you like to start?" His gaze darted back and forth between the three of us.

Braydon spoke up, "Actually, I have some paperwork I'll need you to look over with me. The ladies know what they need to do. Do you have a mobile office we could go to?"

The man hesitated, and for a moment I thought he might argue, but Braydon grabbed his upper arm and the man stared up at him again.

"Mr. Bilcron, your office?"

The man bobbed his head. "Yeah, okay."

Braydon urged me on with a nod as he led Mr. Bilcron away.

The tension released from my body, and I glanced at Nora. She let out a whoosh of breath. After finding our break, we turned towards the crane.

"Wait," the foreman called out.

I froze.

"Mr. Bilcron," I heard Braydon say, his voice smooth, but demanding at the same time.

I thought about continuing to walk but froze when the man approached, fast. I turned to face him.

"You'll both need to wear hard hats. It's mandatory for anyone on site." He tapped his own yellow, battered one.

"Of course," I said to him. "Where can we get them?"

"There's a barrel of extras over there." He pointed to a fluorescent orange barrel off to the side of the entrance. "You can pick one from there."

I thanked him, and Nora and I set off to get a couple hardhats from the barrel. He watched us, a confused expression on his face until Braydon approached, capturing his attention once again. With a clear path to the crane in sight, I made a beeline to it with Nora in tow.

My eyes were focused on the crane, trying to key in on any distinctive shadows inside with the operator, but I couldn't make anything out. I turned to the building and spotted the man from my vision walking around the structure checking various areas of the floor and ceiling braces. He wasn't paying attention to the crane.

The operator was distracted with the load he was maneuvering so he didn't see Nora and I come around the back and over to the other side of the crane.

"Anything?" Nora whispered.

I looked into the elongated window but still couldn't see any shadows that didn't belong.

"No," I said over my shoulder.

We had to walk alongside the crane as it crept toward the building. I peeked in frequently. As we drew close to the building, the man in the structure began to shout and wave his hands. The actions had been the same in my vision. My heart raced, adrenaline pumping again for what I knew was coming, but when I glanced into the crane, there was still no sign of the shadow.

What the hell?

The crane stopped.

"Isn't this when—" Nora started.

With a curse from the operator, the crane began to reverse.

"Shit. Something's wrong." I spun around in search of the worker with the earphones, and spotted him about twenty feet behind, his back to us, completely unaware of what was taking place. Without concern for our covert positions, I grabbed the handle of the crane door, swung it open and jumped inside.

The operator jumped in his seat as he faced me, eyes wide eyes, mouth open. The crane jerked to a halt.

"What the hell do you think you're doing?"

I wasn't prepared to answer him. I wasn't prepared for anything. Every move I'd made so far came from pure adrenaline.

"I... uh..."

I glanced out the back window to see that we'd stopped about ten feet away from the man with the earphones. He'd turned to face the crane, narrowing his eyes in our direction, no doubt trying to figure out what was going on. His gaze strayed to one side, and I glanced over my other shoulder. He was watching Nora, who stood next to the crane, anxiously darting her eyes between him and me.

It took me a moment to realize this was the first time I'd seen his face, and I looked directly at him. In the vision, I'd never had the chance.

Wait a minute. He'd seen the crane. Would that be enough to change his fate? Was my job here done?

"Hey," the operator shouted to me.

I turned to him with every intention of spitting out some half-assed apology and getting the hell out, but his hand was resting on one of the levers attached to the console, and I couldn't seem to take my eyes from it. Darkness descended over me, like a thick blanket being laid upon my soul, smothering it. A shiver passed down my spine. I closed my eyes and worked my neck, silently waiting for a coherent thought to tell me what was happening. A tiny voice inside my head kept telling me this body wasn't mine, while another, deeper, more powerful one demanded my job was not yet done here.

"I asked what the hell you're doing in here?"

The angry words from the operator quieted the voices in my head like a whistle in a crowded room. They fused together inside, binding into one echoing call of duty.

With a sweet smile aimed at him, I quietly locked the door behind my back.

"I'm going to have to ask you to leave, sir."

He shook his head. "What?"

"I'm taking over."

His eyebrows furrowed. "The hell you are."

"Exactly."

After a quick wave goodbye, I made him disappear.

With him gone I took to his seat and started working the controls of the crane. I'd never manned one before, but somehow I knew exactly what each lever, button, and pedal did. I hit the lever for reverse and put my foot on the gas.

The crane inched backward. Out of nowhere, Nora was at the passenger door, slapping her hand on the window, yelling through the Plexiglas. My head spun and I checked over my shoulder, careful not to meet her gaze when I saw the man was backing away. The crane lurched to a stop when I hit the brake.

"Cassie, what are you doing?" Nora yelled once she got her footing back.

Our gazes met through the window for a split second, and in that brief moment, something within me cried out as if in pain. It paralyzed me, and for a few flashes in time, I could do nothing but stare at one large button on the dash of the crane, my hand hovering over it.

"Cassie, no."

Nora's cry broke the spell, and my hand dropped down on the button.

CHAPTER NINE

A loud crash and several screams sounded near me, and I jerked in the seat of the heavy equipment. My hand hovered over a button on the dash, and I snatched it back as if I'd been burned. Relief washed over me when I snapped my head up and saw a slab of cement dangling from the crane clasps above, but utter confusion remained.

What the hell had happened?

A rustling noise caught my attention off to the side, and I had to strain my eyes to see through the cloud of dust, but eventually I spotted Nora's form standing and helping someone else up. I rotated in the seat and moved to the passenger's side window to get a better view.

Nora's glare over her shoulder burned into me through the glass, but with her sideways stance, I was able to see the man standing behind her. Bending down, he picked up the earphones. No doubt in my mind who he was.

So, I hadn't killed him, but how close had I come? Pushing that button to release the block of concrete over the man was so clear in my mind, but it hadn't actually happened. Thank God it hadn't happened, but the act of doing it had obviously run through my head. In my mind, I'd killed the man. Not the shadow... *me*. And I'd liked it. No, I *thrived* on it. The memory created a heavy darkness in my heart I wasn't sure I'd ever shed.

I opened the door of the crane and took a step down when Nora stalked toward me, fire in her eyes.

"Is he okay?" I asked.

"Stay the fuck away from him, Cassie." She jabbed a finger in my direction as she stepped closer.

I froze next to the crane... staring at her in disbelief.

"I mean it." Her jaw clenched. "Don't go anywhere near him," she hissed.

With arms out and palms up, I shook my head in defeat. "Nora, I didn't..."

"I saw you. I saw what you were going to do."

"I didn't know what I was doing. Something just came over me... I don't know..."

Nora closed her eyes for a moment and when she opened them back up, I witnessed the sadness in their depths. "There's something wrong with you, Cassie. You've changed, and I don't know what it is. Ever since you got back from Hell, you haven't been the same. I'm actually afraid of you now. Afraid of what you're becoming, and scared for who you'll hurt in the process." Her eyes filled with tears threatening to brim over. "I can't help you anymore. I just... I just can't."

She turned away from me but was stopped short by Braydon and the other angels when they all approached on the run.

"What happened?" Braydon asked.

All I could do was stand there, frozen by my thoughts and fears. Nora had been my friend through everything, by my side for every shocking thing that had transpired in my life during the last few years. And now, because of actions I seemed to have no control over, I'd lost her. I'd lost Hunter, and after what happened here, I was sure to lose my parents. Whatever was inside of me, eating away at my soul, was making damn sure I'd face it all alone.

I had no idea how to stop it.

"It's over," Nora said. She motioned toward the man, who was now standing about twenty feet away, rubbing the back of his neck and shaking his head as another man questioned him. "He's safe. We're done here."

I'd held my breath, waiting for her to explain my part in the whole incident to the angels. Instead, she marched toward the entrance of the site without another word. My breath came out in a slow, steady stream. I had no idea if she was giving me a temporary reprieve, but I wasn't about to ask.

Braydon's questioning gaze fell on me and I nodded.

He came close and cupped my cheek with his hand. "You're okay?"

I let my head fall to his chest, unable to look him in the eyes. "Yeah."

His arms wrapped around me. "You're shaking."

I took another deep breath to try and steady my nerves. "It's just... It's been awhile since I've done this. I need rest to come down from it all."

"Well, then let's get you home." He kept one arm around me as he steered me toward the entrance.

Home. I knew I had no place in the home he was referring to. I didn't deserve to share space with the angels. Not after this. What home I was meant for, I had no idea anymore, but I let him take me anyway. I had nowhere else to go.

On the way to the entrance, it dawned on me that I'd made the crane operator disappear. I stopped and looked back to the site to see him sitting in the driver's seat, looking dazed. I wasn't surprised to see him there but relished in the sense of total control over my powers of making someone vanish and reappear.

The poor man was surprised to see me. When our gaze met, recognition set in and he stumbled out of the crane walking toward us with an awkward and unsteady, but determined, gait.

"You. Wait, stop right there."

My heart sped up, and the slow burn in my veins began to build again.

"We gotta go, Braydon." I faced the entrance and urged him that direction.

Braydon caught a quick glimpse of the man but didn't change course.

Without turning around, I heard the operator's fast approach, but it was too late. We'd reached the entrance, where Nora and the other angels were waiting for us.

Once outside the gate, I eyed the operator. His face was red, his breathing heavy.

I had an incredible urge to wave goodbye.

So, I did... with a wicked smile and a wink.

And then we were gone.

***

We appeared in front of the gates of the Sanctuary. Within a moment, the giant metal barriers slid open. The angels weren't taking any chances even with their own kind. No one was allowed to just poof onto the grounds, and especially not within the Sanctuary walls until those in charge had inspected and approved. The inspection was done by a divine intervention type of satellite... no video cams to stare into.

Braydon continued walking with his arm around me as we all made our way toward the Sanctuary. The group was silent, but it wasn't a tension-filled silence, more of a satisfied victory kind of calmness. Well, except for Nora, who was like a live wire marching next to me. No way I dared look at her. Didn't need to. I could feel her.

Nora aside, for the first time since I'd been at the Sanctuary, the angels seemed to show some respect for me. It was something about the way they made eye contact with me when I happened to glance up at them. Normally, any eye contact came with a grimace of sorts or a full on look of disgust. Now that they believed my angelic side had prevailed, their icy facades were melting.

If they knew what had really happened at the construction site, they would be burning me at the stake, and I had no idea how long my secret would keep. It felt wrong deceiving everyone, but I didn't believe I had a lot of options, nor did I have a chance to think anything through. So for now, I'd have to remain at Nora's mercy. At this point, I had no idea what her intentions were, but I'd deal with it, if and when the time came.

As we got closer to the Sanctuary, I picked up on raised voices coming from near the entrance. We were still a full fifty feet away, but when I turned toward the sound, I could see a big group of angels gathered at the bottom of the entrance steps.

My ears picked up on Hunter's raged voice. He wasn't shouting, he rarely did. He didn't need to. When he was angry, his tone was menacing enough to make someone hunker down in terror. I couldn't see him, but it was obvious he was at the center of the crowd's attention.

"If anything happens to her, I will show you what hell is really like. I should kill you just for letting her go."

The group of angels drew into a tighter circle. They were anxious, nervous. Several of them shifted their weight from one foot to the other in anticipation.

"Your threats are irrelevant." Hadraniel's voice came from the middle of the group. "They have already arrived back and Cassandra is no worse than when she left. I believe your greatest concern should be whether she really wants to see you, should it not?"

The whole crowd seemed to part as it turned toward our group, giving Hunter an unobstructed view. Our gazes met across the fifteen or twenty feet still between us, and I got that warm, familiar sensation at the sight of him. That was, until his jaw clenched and his eyes glowed bright, like laser beams aimed at me... or at least something attached to me.

I'd been so wrapped up in the drama playing out with the group around him, I hadn't realized Braydon's arm still hung over my shoulder as we walked. Hunter hadn't missed it as his gaze locked in on it. He prowled forward like a predatory cat, slow and deliberate, at first, but gaining speed at every step, steely eyes trained on his prey—Braydon.

I flung Braydon's arm aside and stepped in front of him. I was no match to stop Hunter, but I might slow him enough to allow Braydon a chance to get away.

"Go, Braydon," I said over my shoulder without taking my gape from Hunter. He was almost upon us. I heard no movement behind me. "Braydon, go now."

"I'm not going anywhere." The resolve in his tone was a perfect match to Hunter's doggedness.

"That's too bad." Hunter stopped in front of me, but the glare in his eyes was over my head. "I like a good hunt before a kill." Without taking his eyes off of Braydon, he added, "Cassandra, go inside."

After the last few days, his order shouldn't have surprised me, but my jaw dropped anyway. I snapped it shut, lest my pride fly out and run away with my backbone. "I don't take orders from you, Hunter. But you know what? If you two want to beat the shit out of each other, have at it." I stepped aside, shrugged my shoulders and spread my arms out. "I'm tired of being in the middle of testosterone pissing matches. Let me know who's got the bigger dick when you're done. Maybe you'll find out neither of you does."

With that, I walked away. No second glance, until I heard a loud crack followed by a thump. Apparently, Hunter didn't care about my disdain for his chauvinistic actions because he had Braydon on his back. Leaning over him, Hunter fisted Braydon's shirt and lifted him up from the ground. He wasn't going to just beat the shit out of Braydon, his mindset was to kill. But just as that thought crossed my mind, Braydon shot his leg out, entangling it around Hunter's to take him off balance. Hunter hit the ground... hard.

The group of angels started to descend upon the two, and I knew they wouldn't hesitate to jump on Hunter, given the incentive. With the way Hunter threw Braydon off him and about ten feet into the air, they had plenty of it. Hunter glared back at them. He knew it too but obviously didn't care.

"Dammit, Hunter. Stop this. You can't fight the whole freakin' army."

His gaze locked onto mine with a fierce deadliness sparking in their depths. "Watch me."

Just then, Eric and a group of demons filtered into the crowd, ready to stand their ground for Hunter.

I couldn't believe a war was brewing right in front of my eyes. It was asinine. But the men in my life seemed born for situations such as this. Including Hadraniel, who stood on the outskirts of the group, obviously intent on watching the melee.

Making sure I was in between Hunter and Braydon, I got in Hunter's face. "This wasn't their fault. I wanted to go. I *needed* to go. You need to accept that, Hunter." I threw my arms out. "They have. Why can't you?"

He narrowed his eyes at me. "Because I'm the only one who cares about you."

"You think none of them care about me? Nora? My mom and dad?"

"Not the way I do."

"Then it's too much. You're smothering me."

He lunged at me, grabbing my upper arms and yanking me close. "I'm keeping you alive, dammit."

I struggled to free myself from his grasp, but that just made him squeeze my arms harder. I cried out in pain. "Hunter, you're hurting me."

He twisted around to stand beside me but continued to hold one of my arms. "Then stop fighting me." He pulled me forward toward the house.

Braydon hurried to the other side and grabbed my wrist. "Cassie, you don't have to go with him if you don't want to."

I didn't have time to answer. Hunter sprang forward and grabbed Braydon by the throat.

"Hunter, no." I tried my best to get between them and pushed at Hunter's chest, but it was no use. "I'll go, okay? I'll go. Just please leave him alone."

He acted as if he hadn't heard my pleas, and I saw his arm flex as he tightened the hold on Braydon's neck even more.

I placed my hand on his forearm, digging nails into flesh. "Hunter."

His gaze finally dropped to mine, and I let my features soften as he took them in. Something sparked within the depths of his eyes... a connection with my very soul... and it seemed to melt away any resentment I had towards him and fill it back up with all his love for me.

"Go inside. I promise you I won't kill him," he said.

"Let him go, and come with me," I countered.

He loosened his grip on Braydon's neck but didn't let go.

"I said I wouldn't kill him, Cassandra, but we still have unfinished business. Go inside. I'll be in to talk with you when I'm done here."

Unsure of what else to do and thinking someone must see reason, I searched the crowd. Nora turned her cheek when my gaze fell on her. I'd lost any chance of her siding with me. Then I spotted Hadraniel.

"You're going to let this happen?" I asked him. "I can't believe you are standing by while they beat on each other."

He shrugged. *Shrugged.* "I won't let it get out of hand. You have my word."

"Are you serious? I can't believe you." I scanned the crowd. "Any of you? This is completely senseless."

"It was bound to happen, Cassandra."

I spun my head to glare back at Hadraniel. "Really? Is that what your good book tells you? Maybe your blood's not as clean as you let on."

Without letting him respond, I turned back to face Hunter. "Don't bother looking for me when you're done. I'm going in, but I have nothing to say to you."

"I'll find you. And we *will* talk."

I turned my back on them all and stormed toward the entrance without another word.

CHAPTER TEN

Walking into the Sanctuary, I was in a daze. Each step had nowhere to go. Heading back to our room wasn't an option. It would be the first place Hunter would look for me, and I didn't want to deal with him just yet. I also knew I'd drive myself crazy trying to figure out what the hell was going on with me.

Surely, I was going insane. The voices, the evil thoughts, the uncontrolled actions, there could be no other explanation. But why now? Did it really have something to do with my ordeal in Hell? Had Nergal done things to me that would forever alter my spirit? Would my subconscious somehow purge it out of me if he had?

No one had the answers. How could they? My friends and family had no idea what went down in that cell with Nergal. Only he knew, and he wasn't talking.

I wandered the halls of the Sanctuary, deep in my own thoughts when I realized I'd reached the door to the basement, the one leading to the imprisoned demon Hunter was interrogating. No guard stationed at the door. That was strange, but odd seemed to follow me everywhere lately.

Call it a sign, or blatant stupidity, but I felt compelled to go down there. If the demon was still around, I had no idea what I'd do—stare, talk to it, maybe even kill it. No plan. I was going with my gut.

Expecting the door to be locked, I was surprised when the knob turned easily in my hand. The old wood creaked as it slid open, and I checked over my shoulder on instinct, but no one had followed. I hurried inside the dark stairwell and quickly shut the door behind me.

My breaths picked up as my heart rate accelerated, bringing with it the dank smell of humidity and mold, and maybe a hint of blood and sweat. I opened my mouth to lessen the impact on my senses, but that only helped in taking the moist air into my lungs, causing me to breathe heavier.

The chill in the air, or maybe the basement's eerie similarity to the corridors of Hell, dimly lit and lined with several closed doors, sent shivers across my skin. While the silence should have been a comfort to someone sneaking around, it filled my head with thoughts of maddened souls plotting death, hanging in the shadows for just the right moment to strike.

"I've been waiting for you."

The voice cut through the silence, and I jumped. It had come from farther down the corridor, but as much as I strained my eyes against the dimness, I saw no one. The sound had to have come from behind one of the closed doors.

"I know you're there, Cassandra. I have a message for you."

Curiosity urged me forward, and I made my way down the corridor with caution. Metal slats on the doors could be pulled aside to look inside without completely opening the door. I didn't bother with the first few I passed. The voice had come from the end of the hallway.

As I walked farther that direction, I started to have second thoughts about being down there all alone, confronting whomever, whatever, was calling me out. I'd come down there with adrenaline pumping, pride suffering, and a need for rebellion. Now that I was there, my instincts for self-preservation started to beat down all of those reactive emotions. Especially knowing whoever was behind that door expected me. But the fact they knew I'd be there at all—that they had some message for me—wouldn't allow me to turn away. This might be what we were waiting for, our chance to put this whole damn nightmare to rest.

"What message?" I called out in a raspy whisper.

For a few moments, no one responded, and I almost thought I'd imagined the voice until it actually answered, "Come in and we'll talk."

Now at least I knew it was two doors down, but I didn't make a move.

"You feel the pull. I know you do, Cassandra. It won't let you turn away. I could help you understand it."

I wanted to scream that he knew nothing about me, but I couldn't deny the draw, something strong.

Pissed again that I seemed to be at the mercy of someone else's will, I marched up to the door and slammed the slat aside. Grey-blue eyes inches from the door stared back at me.

"Talk," I demanded.

"I thought we could enjoy a nice visit." The fair-haired man stepped away and opened his arms in a welcoming gesture. He was attractive, strong, and handsome... seductive, as all demons were meant to be. Their primary weapon. "Won't you come join me?" He waggled a finger between his eyes and mine. "This seems so impersonal."

"If your message is so important, this will do."

He moved closer again and the skin at the corners of his eyes crinkled up. "Very well. How are you, Cassandra?"

I glared back at him with my own set of glowing blues. "Don't waste my time, or I'll make sure yours runs out fast. The message."

"The darkness rising within you is almost complete. When it is, he will be ready to guide you."

"What the hell are you talking about?"

"You know. You feel it. You try to fight it, but it's inevitable."

"What? My demon blood? I've fought it this long. What's so different now?"

"When you're ready, he'll guide you."

"Who? Who'll guide me? Guide me where? You're not making any sense. This is all a bunch of bullshit. What, did Caleb send you here to confuse me? Make me think I'm going crazy? Where is he?"

"That was the message I was sent here to give you. That's all I'll give."

"Well, what the hell am I supposed to do with that?"

"You'll know when the time comes."

His evasiveness was making me crazy. Crazier than I already seemed.

I slammed my hand against the door and practically smashed my face against it so he wouldn't miss the anger in my eyes. "I should kill you for wasting my time."

He stepped back from the door so I could see all of him. The move wasn't done out of fear from me because his movements were slow and nonchalant. With a shrug of his shoulders, he said, "If you don't, your boyfriend will, but I knew that before I even came. If given the choice, however, I'd much rather meet my final death by the hands of one of our own."

"Hunter *is* one of your own. More so than me."

"No, he's not. Not anymore. He may have the same blood, but it flows toward a different end now. But you... your blood is like a beacon to us. It's so strong."

"What are you talking about?"

With a smile, he shook his head.

"Tell me."

My scream echoed off the walls at the same time the basement door slammed open.

"Cassandra," Hunter's voice boomed down the corridor as he stalked toward me. "Get away from that door."

I ignored him and urged the demon with my eyes to continue, but he stared at the floor in front of him. He'd already shut down.

Hunter grabbed my upper arm and yanked me away from the door, spinning me to face him. "What the hell are you doing?"

"I'm trying to get out of him what you apparently can't."

"And how did that work out for you?"

I was about to blurt out everything the demon had told me, to shove it in his face. He wasn't giving me credit or acknowledging that I could help in ways he couldn't, but something inside stopped me. I didn't want him to know. Instead, I wanted to keep it to myself. Part of the reasoning was because I wanted to make sense of it all first, but also because finally... *finally*... I was the one with information no one else had.

I put my head down. "It didn't. He wouldn't talk."

"He said nothing to you?"

I looked up at his face, afraid he might have heard everything and just caught me in a lie, but his features told me nothing.

Choosing my words carefully, I said, "Just their normal *I belong to them* kind of crap."

Hunter's stare made me uneasy. It was as though he was peeling away layers of me until he found what he was looking for. I forced myself to remain calm under the intensity, relaxing my face, even giving him a show of disappointment, as if I'd tried and failed. It wasn't far from the truth. I hadn't exactly gotten anything useful out of the demon.

"Why, Cassandra?"

At his pause, I scrambled with how to answer the open question, but he didn't give me a chance anyway.

"Why are you doing these things? Do you want to die?"

"What? No. Of course not."

"Then why do you continuously put yourself in situations where you could?"

I met his gaze, not in defiance, but with a plea for understanding. "I'm trying to help. I just want to get out of here."

"Then let's go."

His answer took me by surprise. "What?"

"Let's leave the Sanctuary. I'm done chasing my tail here. And I'd rather have you with me than rebelling against me, putting yourself in danger... alone."

"Where will we go? Back to our old life? Can we even do that? You said you couldn't handle Caleb and his new army alone."

"We can go wherever you want. My crew will come with us. I'll talk with Hadraniel. We've played his way long enough. He'll have to play ours now. In the meantime, I'll make sure the others stay on alert, ready to fight for us if and when we need them. I'll put it in terms he won't be able to refuse."

I didn't know what to say. At the very least, I wasn't expecting this. He'd been so adamant lately that we couldn't possibly survive without the angel army. I should have been happy. Hell, I should have been ecstatic with his change of heart, but it only made me leery. Would I be leaving a prison only to live life with a shadow underfoot, guarding my every movement, watching my every breath? At least in the Sanctuary I had some privacy. Hunter felt safer with an army around, so he didn't pursue the need to be at my side every minute. Without them, would I be smothered by his protective nature? I couldn't handle that, especially with the uncontrollable changes that had been taking over me lately. I didn't even understand it, so how could I expect him to?

His hand raised and cupped the back of my neck, his thumb stroking my cheek. "I won't let anything happen to you, Cassandra. You know that."

He must have taken my contemplation for fear. His eyes were tender, full of love and devotion to keeping me safe, telling me he would forever be my guardian. I had never doubted that. I was more afraid that might change if he saw what was happening to me.

I leaned my face into his hand, closing my eyes so he couldn't see into my heart and of the real fear within.

"I do. I just... I don't know what the right thing to do is anymore. Shit, what am I talking about? I *never* did. I know I've driven you to make this decision, but I don't want to get anyone killed either. I do know we still need to find Caleb though, Hunter."

"We will. I'll keep sending guys out, the angel army will keep going out. None of that will change."

"But not you?" I asked.

"Having you safe with me is my only concern." He lowered his head, and his lips hovered over mine. "That's all I've ever wanted."

My eyes closed, and I shut out everything else in my head except the feel of his mouth as it brushed against mine, teasing me with its tenderness. I pressed into him, wanting more, taking more from his mouth, overzealously covering up my sense of deception with physical worship.

"How touching," the demon said from behind the door.

We both stepped back, and I leaned over to glare at him through the slat in the door.

Hunter turned and slid the slat closed. He was very calm about it. Too calm.

Facing me again, he used a finger under my chin to bring my gaze to his. "Go and pack your things. We'll leave tomorrow morning. I'll use tonight to tie up a few loose ends and will meet you in our room in a few hours. Then we'll go to dinner."

I knew exactly what loose end he would start with, but I didn't mind. The demon's life was of no consequence to me, and he had come here to die anyway. I was afraid of the things he'd told me and maybe, as impossible as it was, knowing he was gone would make them less true. It was my rationalization.

"Okay," I told Hunter. "You'll talk to Hadraniel?"

"Yes. I'll talk with everyone. They will all know by the time you see them at dinner."

"Do you want me to pack for you, as well?"

"Yes, that would give me more time to make sure everything is in place before we leave."

"Okay, then. I'll see you in a few hours."

I started to walk away, but Hunter grabbed my hand.

"We're going to be okay, Cassandra. I promise you."

I caught a glimpse of him over my shoulder, and he turned back to face me. He didn't even need words to make me feel safe. Just the way he looked at me was enough. I believed him.

"I love you," I said with everything that was true in my heart.

"I love you too, Cassandra."

"Thank you."

He nodded and kissed my hand before letting it go. I smiled at him and then headed to the basement door. Looking back, I expected to see Hunter enter the cell, but he stood in front of the door, intent on watching me leave the area, and I waved before walking out and closing the basement door behind me. I didn't even want to think about what would happen after I'd left them alone.

CHAPTER ELEVEN

Heading straight back to our room, I didn't waste time, getting more excited about our decision to leave with every step. Finally, I would be rid of this place. No more hostility, tension, and anxiety. Well, maybe still some anxiety since Caleb was still out there, but at least I didn't have to feel like a pariah amongst a bunch of saints anymore. Of course, fear of the whole, I'm-going-to-be-evil-thing the demon had foretold would be in the back of my mind, but I was hoping for a newfound freedom and being away from the negative vibes. Any dark, hellish plans for my fate would be knocked on its ass, taking with it the dreams of killing Hunter and thoughts of soul-stealing.

Packing didn't take long at all since we didn't have much. All of the room furnishings belonged to the Sanctuary. We'd only arrived with our clothing and a few personal items, not expecting to be there as long as we were. It had only taken about an hour, and with time to kill before Hunter returned, I was getting quite anxious. Would Hadraniel fight him on this and change his mind? Would anyone else? No, I thought, chastising myself, Hunter wasn't one to have his mind changed by anything or anyone, except maybe me, but even I had a difficult time with it.

I thought about telling Hunter everything, coming clean with all I'd done, my evil thoughts, my dreams about killing him. It only seemed right after all he was risking for me. He might even help me try to make sense of them. Maybe he could banish the dreams for good.

By the time Hunter got back to the room, I'd concluded I'd definitely tell him, just not until we were out of the Sanctuary. Now that freedom was so close, I would do nothing to jeopardize it. Once we were settled in back home, I'd spill my guts.

"Good, you packed up everything," he said eyeing the bags near the door. "It's all set. We'll leave early in the morning."

"You told everyone?"

"Yes. Most of them understood, even expected it, and gave us their blessings. Those who didn't... well, I told them to fuck off. Eric and Nora, along with the other demons, have agreed to leave with us."

None of this surprised me. The demons obviously wouldn't feel comfortable staying at the Sanctuary without us, and I knew Nora would go wherever Eric went. I made a mental note to talk to her after dinner tonight, to apologize, and let her know I planned to tell Hunter everything. The last thing I wanted was for her to feel obligated to warn Hunter of my misdeeds before I had the chance to talk with him myself.

"And Hadraniel?" I asked, wondering if we were creating some sort of holy war with our exit.

"He was one of those I told to fuck off..."

I gasped.

"At first. But eventually he saw it my way and we agreed on terms we could both live with. Rest assured, he and his army will still align with us should the need arise."

I exhaled with relief.

"Ready for your last supper with the angels?" he asked with a smirk.

I laughed. The sound seemed foreign. It had been so long, but it was definitely therapeutic. "You mean the angels are actually joining us tonight? They must be really happy we're leaving."

Hunter chuckled. "No, I'm joking, they're not coming. I might be suspicious of an ambush if they were to join us after all this time."

"You're suspicious of everything."

"I'm suspicious of you right now. Are you trying to seduce me?"

"What?"

His eyes seemed to cloud over as they trailed the length of my body and back up again. My skin flushed as I watched his tongue dart over his lips while he slowly sauntered up to me. Hunter kept me locked in his gaze until he refocused and watched his fingertips skimming the edge of my blouse at my chest. Goosebumps formed from the light touch, and I sucked in a breath, causing my chest to rise directly into his fingers. He let them ride the wave as his eyes followed.

"I like this." His voice was deep and sultry. My nipples seemed to be in direct communication with it.

"It's just a blouse." I could barely catch my breath enough to let the words out. And it *was* just a blouse. One of that flimsy material kind. He was probably so used to seeing me in T-shirts and tanks for working out or lounging around the Sanctuary, making this one seem dressier than it was. Or he was simply easily aroused.

"Mmm hmmm." His fingers slid down between my breasts to play with the tiny pearl buttons down the middle of the blouse.

My gaze was hypnotized by his features, lured in by their blatant desire and intensity.

Slowly, he raised his head and looked directly into my eyes. "Then you wouldn't mind if you could never wear it again?"

"Hunter, we can't. We have to g—"

My words were cut off by the sound of material ripping, and my gasp as the chilled air hit my breasts.

"Hunter," I moaned, trying desperately to hold the two pieces of my blouse together. It was impossible, of course, because Hunter had already planted his hands beneath it on my breasts. Not to mention his mouth was suckling my neck in the most divine manner, rendering my motor skills useless. "Dinner," I managed on a breathy whisper.

His lips left my neck, causing me to shiver from the cold air blowing over the wet path that remained. Without a second to recover, his hot breath was in my ear. "I can't think of a tastier meal."

Another moan escaped my lips, and I leaned closer. My breasts pressed into his hands while my core found his thick hardness to rub against, sending a burst of ecstasy throughout my body. The contact, along with his mouth, most definitely making a meal out of me, made me ravenous for more. But I knew we had to get to dinner. I needed to talk with several people before we left early in the morning. *But...*

He spread his legs, caging mine in between while his hands swept behind me and grabbed my ass. His hips rotated, grinding the erection against me, causing the pressure between my legs to become almost unbearable. I latched onto the back of his neck and pulled his head down, smashing my mouth against his, not caring about the bruising it would leave later. I only wanted his tongue in my mouth, a fleshy part of him invading my body, claiming it. It was exactly what I got, and I lashed at his tongue with my own, using the same urgency and greed he used to grind against my core.

As our mouths continued melding together, his hands left my backside and moved to the front of my pants. Hot against my belly, his fingers teased at the waistband, threatening to relieve the pressure not far from their tips.

"Oh, God, Hunter," I said against his lips.

His mouth left mine while his tongue trailed a path along my jaw and up my neck. A sharp pain cut through the pleasure humming throughout my body as he bit into my earlobe.

I cried out, but there was no mistaking it was a cry of pure pleasure.

"You like that?" His breath was hot on my ear, heating my lobe where he'd just sunk his teeth.

"Yes." My answer was automatic as if my body was replying for me, and my mind had nothing to do with it. That's not to say my mind wasn't enjoying every second.

"It seems this is the only way I can control you."

One of his hands skimmed up my body and yanked down the cup of my bra. I heard the elastic strap give way, but I didn't care because his fingers were pinching the nipple, sending sweet, pleasurable jolts throughout my body.

His other hand inched down my pants, teasing as it went.

"Are you wet for me?" His fingers were ever so close to where I wanted them. I almost came from the sheer anticipation.

I sucked in a breath to give them more room.

"Why don't you find out?"

He chuckled, and I opened my eyes to find him staring at me, his bottom lip between his teeth, a gleam in his eye. I wanted to ask him what he was thinking but couldn't stop panting long enough to utter a word.

"Cassandra?"

"Hmmm?"

"You're going to need new pants, too."

Before I could even process the words, the item in question was torn away from me. *Torn. Away.* With one forceful pull of his hand. It happened so fast, I wasn't even sure if my feet came off the floor, but there I was... standing in my panties. By the hungry way his eyes swept over me, they'd be gone soon too.

I smirked as I glanced at myself. "Well, this isn't proper dinner attire."

"It is for our menu."

With that, he swept me up into his arms and stalked over to the sofa, where he set me down gently, adjusting the throw pillow behind my head before straddling my hips and hovering over me.

All thoughts of dinner vanished. My body pulsed with need as Hunter leaned over me. I was desperate for more, his hands, his lips... *hell*... any contact with his body. The mere brush of his thighs against my lower half had me rocking toward him.

His passion-filled eyes met mine as he slipped fingers beneath the straps of my bra. An eyebrow shot up, teasingly, and I shook my head. He grinned while deftly undoing the clasp at the front, releasing my breasts for his enjoyment.

And mine.

Instinctively, my back arched when his lips latched on to one of the tender buds, his thumb simultaneously playing with the other. My hips continued to undulate upward of their own accord as if dancing to a silent tune, seeking the hardness between his legs. Hunter remained hovered over me, barely out of their reach. It was excruciating and frustrating while being powerfully erotic at the same time. I feared one touch of the sensitive spot between my legs would put me over the edge of bliss where I teetered.

"Hunter, *please...*"

A deep growl-like sound came from his throat before he switched his mouth to the other breast and gave it the same affections he'd done with the previous one. While the gesture seemed to even me out, it drove me more insane for release at the same time.

Unable to stand it any longer, I pushed at him with my hands, frantically pulling on his shirt to lift it off and gain access to his pants zipper. Instead, he grabbed my clumsy arms by the wrists and held them together over my head in his powerful grip.

He nibbled on my ear before whispering, "Oh, no, sweetness. I plan on savoring this meal."

I barely processed the chaste kiss placed on my lips before his mouth inched its way down my body. Leaning in to every suckle, every tongue lash was my only option. The idea of where he was headed killed me with delicious anticipation.

When his hands parted my thighs, I realized my wrists were no longer being held. They'd stayed up on their own accord as if paralyzed while he made a meal of my body. That situation changed when his tongue laved the tender folds of my core, and I had no choice but to grab handfuls of his hair and hold on for dear life while he feasted on me.

I rocked my hips into him, lost in the waves of pleasure he was creating.

"Come for me, baby. I want all of it."

They were the only words I needed to send me into complete erotic oblivion. And he took all of it. I could barely handle the sensory overload his continued strokes caused. Finally, he stopped, and I was able to breathe in enough air to bring me down from the high, but his hot breath remained so close, it continued to tease enough to keep me from recovering completely.

When my eyes regained focus, I looked at his self-satisfied smirk only a man with such carnal skills as Hunter should wear.

"That was insanely wonderful," I said, surprised I could even form words.

"Oh, really? It wasn't even the main course."

He crawled up my body, staying between my legs. I wasn't sure I could stand much more. I'd already overdosed with sexual gratification, but when he entered me, I was ready again.

Buried deep inside me, his arms on either side of my head, he lowered himself onto his elbows until our faces were only a breath apart. "Open your eyes, Cassandra."

I did as I was told and couldn't help but fall into the glowing blue orbs staring back at me, making me feel as if he were taking me in metaphysically and melding our souls together.

"Burn this feeling into your memory. Us. Right here. Right now. Use it as your beacon anytime you feel lost. This is your world. With me. Nothing else matters."

His words were like a spotlight on my heart, chasing away the darkness that had taken up residence there, casting shadows on everything that mattered. It all made sense, but he had it all wrong. The memory of a feeling wouldn't lead me back where I was supposed to be. He *was* my beacon. Hunter. His whole being, his very essence, everything that made him who he was. Whenever I was lost, all I needed to do was think of him, my angelic demon. He was, and I knew he always would be, the guardian of my fate.

"I love you, Hunter."

His eyes closed slowly as if he were taking my simple sentiment and letting it bury deep inside his soul. When he opened them back up, they were the brightest I'd ever seen them. He brought his lips to mine in a kiss that lingered, sweet and telling of his love for me too. But then, as if he wasn't satisfied with the kiss's portrayal of his love, his mouth came down hard on mine.

Demanding entrance when I opened my mouth for him, his tongue desperately sought mine as he groaned. Our flesh collided, and I became lost in the sensual dance happening inside my mouth. Hunter shifted between my legs and our bodies took on a rhythm that seemed so natural, so innate, it was as if they were meant to move together in exactly this way.

Waves of pleasure turned into complete bliss with the humming of my body, building in pitch until it seemed to explode throughout every inch of my body. Bursts of orgasmic pleasure thrummed within me, leaving me breathless, while Hunter continued to thrust against me, increasing the speed and intensity, demanding his own release. I knew he had finally found it when he cried out my name.

We lay there for a while, Hunter's spent body covering mine, his face pressed into the side of my neck. Neither of us could speak, but words weren't really needed as our bodies had said everything in our hearts.

The world seemed right again. It was no longer dark inside my soul. Hunter had chased all my inner demons away once again, and I was reluctant to move or say anything to change that. Knowing we had to go downstairs and face everyone wasn't easy. This was simply a temporary respite from reality.

As if he sensed my foreboding, Hunter kissed the side of my neck and whispered in my ear, "We have forever. And this is how forever will be. Always."

I smiled. With that in my heart, I could get through anything.

CHAPTER TWELVE

As reluctant as I was to leave the warmth of Hunter's arms, we couldn't shun dinner plans. It would be our last night at the Sanctuary, hopefully for forever, and I was sure there would be tons of questions everyone desired answered. Plus, I wanted to make sure I had a chance to speak with Nora before leaving. I needed her to know Hunter and I were good, and everything was back to normal. Whatever had happened at the construction site was due to some kind of internal misguidance on my part. I'd been set straight once and for all. Hopefully, she'd understand and things could go back to the way they were with us.

We dressed without further delays, knowing we were already late and everyone was probably already well into the meal. Hunter made me promise we'd have a graphic encore performance when we returned from dinner. As his hungry eyes watched me pull on a brand new pair of pants, his detailed description of what he expected almost made me re-think the direction those pants were going.

While we made our way to the dining hall, I realized how ravenous I was. I hadn't eaten all day and with all the physical activity throughout the day, I was running on empty. No surprise, everyone was already seated at the table and partaking in the feast set before them. Several more faces were present than normally joined us for dinner, and the atmosphere almost seemed celebratory, aside from a few forlorn faces, notably my mom and dad. Voices in the crowd were upbeat, with mini-conversations going on all around the table and smiles given freely.

Hunter's arm seemed planted around my waist, and he led me over the threshold, toward two empty chairs at the head of the table. Nora was the first to notice us. She studied our demeanor, her eyes going back and forth between the two of us as if trying to read where Hunter and I stood on the previous issues. I tried to give her a reassuring look, but her eyes wouldn't meet mine.

By the time we were halfway to the front of the table, the conversations had turned to a slight drone, followed by complete silence. Everyone's gaze was on us.

My mom popped up out of her chair and spoke as if out of breath, "Oh, Cassie. I was starting to think you weren't even going to come."

I leaned over and gave her a kiss on the cheek. "I wouldn't do that, Mom."

"We certainly hoped not, especially since you're leaving tomorrow."

It was a direct statement, designed for my elaboration, but I wasn't ready. I needed to eat something, fill my belly with sustenance before I tackled that elephant, knowing they'd be against our decision to leave. My parents wanted to keep me close, where they could watch over me, know I was safe. It was a tough argument to fight, but my mind was set.

"I promise. We'll talk after I eat. I'll explain everything."

"Hunter did that already," my Dad said, standing. "That doesn't mean we're not going to try and talk you out of it."

Hunter's whole body stiffened next to me as if he had something to say, but I reached my hand back and touched his arm. "I know, but let's wait to talk in private," I said. "After dinner."

My dad's jaw tightened, making an effort to hold back. He focused on Hunter, who stood behind me, and then back down to me and nodded.

"Thank you."

Hunter and I finally reached our chairs. As he pulled one out for me, I noticed every eye in the place was on us.

"Please, continue eating," I told them. "This looks wonderful. I'm starved."

After Hunter had taken his seat beside me, one of the Sanctuary maids came out and asked us for our menu choices. I looked again at all of the food on the table. There was so much—roasted ham, turkey, beef in dark gravy, steaming vegetables, rolls that looked like they'd just come out of the oven. I couldn't decide, so I told her I'd take a sampler of everything.

Hunter's eyebrows rose up at me.

I leaned over and whispered, "It's your fault I'm famished."

The corner of his mouth lifted in a sexy smirk. "I'll make sure to bring leftovers back to the room with us."

I giggled and relaxed back in my chair, catching Nora's eye as I did. Her expression was curious but guarded, uncertain if my behavior with Hunter was authentic. I smiled at her, silently letting her know everything was as it should be. Hunter and I were good. *I* was good.

Her face expression lightened up slightly, her eyes seeming to smile back at me, or maybe that was just what I wanted to see. Either way, she nodded my direction before concentrating back on her own plate.

My heart lifted. It seemed everything was settling back into place. Our plan to leave was dissolving the heavy, dark fog that had been hanging over all of us. Soon, I'd be able to breathe easy again.

Loud voices from the hallway echoed into the dining room, startling me and apparently everyone else at the table. We all turned in the direction of the doorway, but it was empty.

"I said, we'll talk about this later, Braydon. Now go and get some rest. Tomorrow will be a big day." No one could mistake Hadraniel's authoritative voice, and as I'd made the connection, he appeared in the doorway.

He checked around the table, once realizing he'd caught everyone's attention.

"I hadn't meant to make such a grand entrance." His eyes focused on me as he stepped farther into the room. "I only meant to wish you a safe journey after your departure." Hadraniel stopped at the opposite end of the table. His composure was tense. No one would be shocked to know this was the last place he wanted to be.

"I will admit," he continued, "when Hunter told me you were leaving, I was adamantly against it. But to his credit, his arguments were difficult to refute. So, I relented. While I still feel it's the wrong decision, as your safety is one of my top priorities, I give you my blessing. And should you need me... us... you only need to let us know, and we will do everything in our power to help."

I wanted to laugh at his comment about my safety being one of his *top* priorities, but the fact that he put his pride aside and came down to wish us well amazed me enough to squelch an outburst.

"Thank you, Hadraniel," I said. "Your support means a lot to us."

I heard Hunter guffaw under his breath, and I kicked him under the table.

Hadraniel smiled, and while it could have very well been a smile due to my gratitude, I had a feeling he knew exactly the exchange Hunter and I just had.

"Well, I'll say goodbye to you all now then. I have some matters requiring my attention in the morning when you leave."

"It's been a pleasure," Hunter said in a voice dripping with sarcasm.

I kicked him again.

"Goodbye, Hadraniel," I said in a much sweeter, more genuine tone. "And thank you so much for your hospitality the past few months."

He nodded, rapped his knuckles on the table, turned and left the dining hall.

Everyone continued to stare in the direction of the doorway, even after it was obvious he wasn't returning. Not a common sight to see the leader of the angelic army humbled. It made me think of him in a slightly different light. Not so different that I wanted to stay, however. It wasn't as if they'd made us feel at home or anything there, but they had kept us safe.

I peeked at Hunter through half-lowered lashes. He rolled his eyes and shrugged, not impressed given the circumstances. Everyone had gotten over the moment and resumed eating and talking amongst themselves, so I did the same. Hadraniel's appearance made me think of the one angel who did go out of his way to make me feel at home, and I worried about not saying goodbye to him. Even knowing it wouldn't be possible to see Braydon, not with the little time we had left, hurt. Hunter wouldn't leave my side for a minute before we left the Sanctuary. No way could I risk my relationship with Hunter again by asking to go see the man he fought with over me. Maybe I could get a message to Braydon somehow, thanking him for being so kind.

As I ate, Hunter visited with Eric, who was seated next to him. They were talking about security measures to put in place once we were out on our own. In summary, Hunter would be my shadow until we found Caleb, which I pretty much knew would happen. It was a reality I'd have to live with, but at least I'd be free. And it wasn't as if having Hunter around was horrendous punishment. Who wouldn't want the strongest, deadliest, sexiest man at your back?

I made small talk with everyone for a while, asking whether they were as excited as I was and if they were all packed. We discussed where and when we were meeting in the morning. Hunter had been very thorough with his directions to everyone on every aspect of this last minute move. I thought we'd have to discuss things in depth at dinner, but it seemed I was the only one who hadn't been filled in on the particulars. For once, I didn't mind being left out because I knew Hunter was taking care of me.

Eventually, we all finished eating and my mom and dad were ready to talk with me. We agreed to speak in private, but before we left the dining hall, I wanted to make sure Nora would stick around so we could chat before the night was over. She was cold, suspicious even, when I told her I wanted to discuss a few things, and that stung, but she eventually agreed to stay until after the meeting with my parents.

The conversation with them was more difficult than I'd imagined. At first, they argued for me to stay, and when they saw my mind was made up, they tried convincing me they should come along. Of course, I wouldn't hear of that either. They were much safer in the Sanctuary, and I'd be much too worried about them to be helpful in the search for Caleb if they came with us. It took longer than I thought, but they finally conceded to my wishes, with promises to keep in constant touch.

By the time I made it back to the dining hall, most of the people had already gone back to their rooms. Hunter was in a discussion with a few of the demons at the end of the table, including Eric. Nora was nowhere in sight.

"Eric, where's Nora?" I asked.

"She said she had some business with Hadraniel, and then she was headed to bed. Nora told me to tell you she'd meet up with you in the morning."

That hurt. She hadn't waited. I'd taken a while with my mom and dad, but it hadn't been that long. Besides, I'd made it quite clear how important it was for me to talk to her. She hadn't cared.

I was hurt big time, but that wasn't the cause of the panic that unexpectedly paralyzed me. If she told Eric what happened at the construction site before we set out tomorrow morning, I knew they'd never allow me the freedom I was craving.

Eric and Hunter couldn't realize my desperation to talk with Nora, so I sat with them, pretending to be interested in the strategies they discussed. I was barely listening, my thoughts obsessed over what I might say or do if Nora leaked my secret, but nothing came to mind. No logical, or even illogical, explanation could be made for what I'd done. I was a guardian and was supposed to save lives, not take them. If anyone knew, I'd never get to leave the Sanctuary.

On the inside, I was panicking, but I tried to appear calm and attentive to Hunter and the guys at the table. My hands wouldn't stop shaking, however, so I hid them under the table.

"You have something you want to say, Cassandra?"

Leave it to Hunter. He never missed a thing.

I'd been staring at my trembling hands, willing them to stop. Everyone was watching me.

"No, why do you ask?"

Hunter reached over and put a hand on my knee, applying enough pressure to force my leg to stop bouncing, which I hadn't even realized it was doing. He was looking back at me expectantly when my gaze met his again.

"I guess I'm just a little anxious about leaving tomorrow." *Like whether or not I'll be able to.*

"Is everything settled with your mom and dad?"

"Yes, as best it can be anyway. They're not happy about us leaving, but they understand."

"Good," he said and squeezed my knee. "Why don't you go on up to bed? It's late and we want to be out very early. I won't be here much longer."

I nodded and pushed up from the chair. "Wake me if I'm sleeping when you come in?"

"Definitely," he answered with a sly smirk. It was a simple answer packed with an underlying... sexual meaning.

My cheeks warmed, knowing everyone at the table had the sense to draw the same conclusions, but embarrassment couldn't stop the tiny shivers of anticipation from washing over my body.

Attempting to keep some composure in front of the others, I leaned down toward Hunter for a chaste kiss goodbye, but he held my face to his.

"See you soon," he whispered against my lips, flaming the heat all over again.

I smiled at him as I returned to a full standing position and gave him a wink. Then I left Hunter and the guys to finish their boy talk, willing the simple breeze from my movements to cool me down.

Hunter's cryptic promises buzzed through my head while I made my way back to our rooms. I'd gotten pretty far when a tiny hint of the anxiety over not being able to speak to Nora crept into my thoughts and stopped me in my tracks.

I stood there, in the middle of the hallway, arguing with myself over what to do about it. The message she'd sent was pretty clear. She had no further concerns about what I needed. My actions at the construction site had taken away the right to her compassion.

As ashamed as I was about what I'd done, or almost had, I couldn't help being pissed off at her for not considering our friendship strong enough to bother listening to what I had to say about it. She'd lied to me for years before I'd known the truth about her, and still I'd forgiven her. The least she could do was extend me the same courtesy of a chance to explain.

With that anger, I spun on my heel and made my way back through the hallway to the rooms on the opposite side of the floor. Unlike our rooms, Eric and Nora shared a hallway with the other demons of the group. Rooms flanked each side, not all of them filled with occupants because there weren't that many demons in the group. Eric and Nora's quarters were at the very end.

Without wasting any time, I knocked on the door. I wanted to get in and out before Eric returned, and before Hunter realized I hadn't gone straight to our room. While waiting, my senses kicked into overdrive, listening for a rustle in the room to tell me she was coming. When no one answered after a few moments, I knocked again, a little harder, but not much. I didn't want to alert anyone else in the area to my anxious situation.

More moments ticked by and with each one, I knew she wasn't coming.

Was she really not there? Or was she flat out ignoring me? If she hadn't gone to the room as Eric said, then where was she? What was she doing?

All these questions jumbled around in my head without any hint of an answer. I had no choice. Feeling defeated, I turned and walked back to my room.

When I rounded the corner to our wing of the Sanctuary, I came up short at the sight of Braydon leaning against the door of our room.

Was he crazy? If Hunter saw him...

I sped down the hall toward him.

"Braydon, what are you doing here?" I said, trying my best to keep the volume down, lest anyone was in the area.

"We need to talk."

"Here? Now? About what?"

"Us. You can't just leave, Cassie."

"What do you mean, us? Braydon there is no *us*."

"There is an *us* and you know it just as well as I do. Does he know you kissed me?"

Oh. My. God. Was this really happening?

"Braydon, I can't talk about this right now."

"Then when, Cassie? You're leaving tomorrow." His words were an accusation, and his narrowed eyes bearing down on me told me he wasn't going anywhere until this was resolved.

"Okay, okay," I said. "We'll talk, but not here. If Hunter comes back—"

"Where then?"

Where? Where? I scrambled to think of somewhere we could go where Hunter wouldn't find us. No doubt he'd come looking for me if I wasn't in our room when he got back.

"The gardens."

"Fine."

Still leaning against the door, he stared back at me.

Why wasn't he moving?

"After you," he said with a wave of his hand.

Oh, for God's sake. I turned and hurried toward the gardens, praying all the way we wouldn't run into anyone. Luckily, Braydon was right on my heels.

We made it to the gardens without someone spotting us, and I made sure we were off the main paths when I finally came to a stop. Spinning around, I almost face-planted into Braydon's chest.

"Jesus, Braydon," I said, putting my hands there to catch my balance. "A little space, please?"

But he didn't give me any space. Instead, he grabbed my wrists, gluing my hands to his chest. My palms burned as if they'd been placed on a hot stove, before a tingling sensation washed over them, settling in my fingers like tiny icicles prickling from the inside out.

I snapped my head up to meet his gaze fixed on mine, a determined gleam in those sexy eyes. No time to process it before his mouth came down hard on mine. The burning sensation seared the tender flesh of my lips, just as it had my palms, and I welcomed the same tingly feeling that followed, almost making me want to moan from the relief of it. *Or had I actually moaned?*

My breath caught when he pushed back.

"No us, huh?" Braydon said with a self-satisfied smile.

"I don't... that wasn't..."

"Bullshit, Cassie," he said. His fingers dug into my upper arms. "You're throbbing right now, and I'm the only one here. You want me. You need me."

I wanted to deny it. *Dammit, why couldn't I get the words out?*

I stood there like some dumbstruck lover as he raised his hand and lightly brushed his knuckles down my cheek, my neck, farther... and, *oh God*, those damn quivers followed their path and left me taking short, quick breaths.

"Be with me, Cassie. Let me show you how you were meant to feel. Right here. Now."

What the hell was wrong with me? My body had completely taken over and shut down my brain. He was right, I was throbbing. Everything was pulling me toward him. My skin begged to be caressed, my nipples ached to be tugged, and the pressure low in my abdomen was almost unbearable. Those feelings weren't supposed to happen. Not with him.

Somehow I managed to shake my head. Denial followed. "I can't. I belong with Hunter."

His lips curled at the mention of Hunter, and then his finger quickly trapped my lips before I could say more. "See, Cassie, that's exactly why you need me. Being with him, that... *demon*... has caused the darkness within you to spread." His finger left my lips and slowly slid down my neck to my chest while his gaze remained transfixed on its movement. My heart rate increased when he inched his fingertip between my breasts. He splayed his fingers wide below my breasts, nearly covering my stomach, and continued the descent on my body. "It's stretching within you, trying desperately to extinguish your light. It's feeding on your feelings for him, and if you let it go any further, that light will be gone from you forever."

How had his hand gotten so far down, so close to the place between my legs that was screaming to be touched? I couldn't breathe, but I was afraid to release the breath I'd held for fear he'd finish the obvious path he was on. At the same time, I thought I might die if he didn't. He'd watched his own hand all the way down my body, but almost as if the last layer of my composure called to him, he snapped his gaze back up and locked it with mine. The passion in his eyes was so intense, I let out a whimper before I could catch myself.

That was all the invitation he needed. His hand cupped between my legs, and he moved into me as he applied pressure to my core. I cried out, the pleasure had reached a level too much for me to keep inside.

"I can help you stop the darkness, Cassie." The wind of his whispered words blew gently across my ear. His lips barely brushing against it, sending shivers down my body. "With me, your light will always shine. There will never be darkness. Let me show you."

My body said his words were true, that everything was exactly how it was supposed to be. Hunter was darkness. Braydon was light. That if I didn't choose now, right this second, I would lose myself in the darkness and never find my way back. I didn't want to be bad. Every ounce of my soul wanted to be good. And being there with Braydon felt so good at that moment. *Too good.*

What was I doing? Inside, I wobbled like a rag doll, my emotions tossing and turning from one minute to the next, completely out of control. My body was responding on its own to caresses it had no business experiencing. I had to stop it. *Now.*

Somehow my brain connected with my limbs, and I put my hands out, pushing Braydon back. He was surprised by the rejection, and I used the space to catch my breath. Air to my brain cells... that's what I needed.

"This isn't right. I can't do this."

"It *is* right. You know it." His hands moved to rest on my hips. "It's more right than anything I've ever felt. I can tell you feel it too. Just let go."

I almost got lost in his words again, his soulful eyes reaching in, taking hold of my muddled emotions. It wasn't helping any.

"Why are you doing this to me? You barely know me. You're an angel. You shouldn't even want to be with me."

"Does it feel like we barely know each other, Cassie?"

He was right. A definite pull had existed between us from the moment I first saw him. It was almost palpable. And familiar. Familiar because I had the same kind of pull with Hunter. I was very confused. They were such opposite entities. How could I feel the same pull to both? Or was it the same? I didn't know anymore. I couldn't think.

"No, it doesn't," he answered for me when I couldn't. "Look, I don't know what it is either. It just is. Everyone has a guardian. Maybe I'm yours."

No. *No.* I wouldn't believe that. It was etched in my heart. Hunter filled that role. I refused to give up that conviction. This had gone too far.

"You're wrong. *This* is wrong." I pushed his hands off my hips and stepped out of his reach. I half expected him to come at me again, but he remained where he was.

He dropped his head to his chest with a defeated sigh. I should have left. Instead, I stood there like an idiot watching and waiting for what I didn't know. He slowly shook his head before looking back at me. Taking his bottom lip in with his teeth, he studied me.

"You're making a big mistake, Cassie."

"No," was all I could say. I had no reasoning to back it up. Just, no.

"I guess I have no choice but to let you go," he said. "I wish it didn't have to be this way."

"I'm sorry, Braydon."

I turned to leave, so on edge and not trusting myself to stay and hear anything more.

I'd gotten a few feet away when he called my name. My heart dropped. I didn't turn around... couldn't look at him again and froze in place, unable to take another step.

"This isn't over."

I fought the urge to turn and ask him what that meant but had no courage or energy. Or maybe I just didn't want to know. It was hard enough walking away from him, and for the life of me, I couldn't understand why that was. I was making the right decision. Hunter would always be my choice.

***

My thoughts were locked in the gardens with Braydon, although somehow I put one foot in front of the other and returned to my quarters.

What was I thinking? Why did I keep reacting the way I did with Braydon? My heart should be leading me to Hunter. *It was with him, always had been.* So, why was it so difficult to walk away from Braydon?

Fingers grappled my wrist and twisted my body around. I would have fallen if it weren't for the solid body I'd been pulled into.

"Where were you, Cassandra?"

I looked up into Hunter's steely gaze with a gasp.

"Hunter."

"I'll ask again, where were you?" His words were low and controlled, a tone he used to provoke the truth from someone, holding promises of extremely unpleasant things to come from lies.

If I lied, he'd know.

"The gardens. I... it's one of my favorite places here. I wanted to go there one last time. I figured I wouldn't have the chance tomorrow and you were busy and..."

"Alone?"

Oh. God, did he know? I searched his face for signs I'd been caught, but in typical Hunter fashion, he was a stone.

"Yes. It helps clear my head being there alone."

"Apparently, it didn't help you tonight."

"Excuse me?"

"You walked right past me, Cassandra."

I let the breath I'd been holding in ease through my lips. It didn't appear he knew I'd been with Braydon, but I needed to tread carefully as Hunter liked to play with his prey before he pounced in for the kill.

"I'm sorry, Hunter. You're right, it didn't help too much tonight. As much as I want to go, I'm still worried about what we're leaving behind."

"Such as?"

"My mom and dad, the Sword. What if Caleb has figured it all out and is just waiting for us to leave so he can come for the Sword? My mom and dad are still here. They could be in danger. We won't be here to protect them."

Hunters gaze softened on mine as his hands reached up to cup my face.

"They'll be fine, baby. They have an army of angels here to protect them. Hadraniel won't let anything happen to them."

"How do you know that?"

"Because Anael will make sure of it. And as much as he doesn't like anyone to think it, she has him by the balls again. Just like you have mine."

His sexy smile filled me with relief, and I laughed.

"I hardly have your balls."

"You have my everything, Cassandra." He leaned in and gently placed his lips on mine for a sweet kiss. "Now let's go back to our room so we can practice on how you hold them."

"Yes, let's." I shot back my own mischievous smile. "I've wanted to perfect my grip."

A growl rumbled deep in his throat, and I was caught off guard as he lifted me off my feet and tossed me over his shoulder, caveman style.

I couldn't stop the little shriek that escaped my mouth, along with the laughter that followed. "Hunter, what are you doing?"

"You walk too slow. And my pants are way too tight to wait for you."

I slapped him on the ass.

"I'm going to love paying you back for that," he said, rubbing my own.

I laughed again, but a shiver of pleasure went through me from his promise. I had no doubt he'd own up to it.

And he did. Several times throughout the night. We had wild, ribald sex, and made sweet love for several hours, despite knowing we had to rise early. He made me forget all my worries, as he always did. I knew as I closed my eyes to sleep, exactly why I was making this choice—I loved Hunter—with everything I was, good and bad.

Unfortunately, my subconscious didn't take the hint.

CHAPTER THIRTEEN

Something was wrong. I knew it the second I woke. My body was covered in a film of sweat, and I couldn't stop shaking. It had only been a few hours since Hunter and I went to sleep, but it was enough for a nightmare to sweep in and leave me emotionally scarred.

This was the first time my nightmares hadn't been about sticking the Sword through Hunter's heart, but the relief in that was outweighed by the horrific feeling of being torn in two. And it was quite literal. Fragmented images hit me like strobe lights, disjointed, fleeting images, revealing snippets of the scene I was thrown in. While my vision was hampered, the violent, physical torture was not. It was constant. Like a rope in a strongman's tug-of-war, I was pulled at the wrists by Hunter and Braydon, stretched until my muscles were slowly tearing apart. Back and forth they pulled, their matched strength evident as my body ripped more every second.

It hurt like a son of a bitch, but that torment paled compared to the white-hot pain radiating from the blade of the Sword that lay within my belly. As my gaze followed the long length of glistening steel, an evil laugh echoed from its holder. I flinched at the familiar sound and slowly peered up into Nergal's lecherous smile. He tugged at the hilt, and my body flung forward as much as Hunter and Braydon's hold would allow. I could swear I heard something crack inside of me, but the pain by now was so extensive, anything new probably wouldn't register.

Just when I thought I couldn't take any more, I was yanked backward and a piercing heat flamed from a point on my back as if the Sword had been yanked from it. I looked down and the hilt was still in Nergal's hand, but he'd come within a few feet of me. Another laugh came from behind, and I stiffened. It was as familiar as Nergal's but so unexpected, I had to crane my neck to confirm my suspicions.

I wanted to scream at the sight. Hadraniel stood behind me, the hilt of the Sword in his grasp, a similar cynical smile on his face as Nergal's. The Sword had morphed into something similar to a two-handed saw, hilt at each end, its blade extended through my body. Hadraniel tugged at it one more time, and I felt the cut deep inside, both physically and emotionally.

"Why?" I managed with a guttural breath.

My answer was deafening laughter from all of them... as they ripped me apart.

Disoriented and scared, I checked around the room, half expecting to see Nergal standing at the foot of the bed dangling the Sword at me, but I was alone.

Where was Hunter?

The clock on my nightstand indicated eight o'clock. Then, it finally dawned on me, this was the morning we were supposed to leave. I scrambled out of bed, grabbing scraps of clothing off the floor to wear, all the while thinking something had happened, an incident of some sort that would prevent us from finally getting out of there. Why else would Hunter leave me to sleep so late?

"Hunter," I called out, my voice full of desperation.

When I heard nothing, I started for the door, determined to find him, wherever he was.

Just as I reached for the doorknob, the bathroom door opened and Hunter walked out, wearing nothing but a towel wrapped around his waist. On any other given day, the sight of him recently showered, jet black hair, dripping rivulets of water down his muscled chest and arms, would have caused my heart to race from a dead stop. Today, the sight of him there, in the room, made me groan with relief.

"Where are you going, Cassandra?" Hunter asked, studying me.

"I... I woke up... I didn't know where you were. I thought something might be wrong, so I was going to look for you."

"Like that?" He scoped out the length of my body and back up. One eyebrow arched as he looked back at me... expecting something... maybe a different answer.

I looked down at myself, totally oblivious until then that I was about to race out of the room in a T-shirt and panties.

"Oh, crap. I didn't even think."

"You must remember to do that, Cassandra. It's a good idea, and I would not have been happy."

"But you're happy now, right?" I said with a mischievous smirk after my gaze eased down at the bulge tenting his towel.

Hunter stalked toward me. "You make it difficult not to be." He tugged me against him with one arm wrapped around my waist, the other snaking up my shirt, as he nestled his erection into the V between my legs. My body instantly tingled.

His mouth came down on mine, and I opened up to his demanding tongue. He possessed me with it, claimed me. The arm around my waist slid to my hip. One finger hooked under the side of my panties.

"Don't we have to go?" I breathed against his lips, barely able to stop myself from getting lost in his lusty passion.

"They can wait. I can't."

He wouldn't get an argument from me and was making damn sure of that with the way he was playing with my nipple.

I moaned and leaned back into him, plunging my tongue deep into his mouth.

Pounding at the door gave us pause. We both froze, and I mentally groaned at whoever was behind it.

"Must they always pick the worst times to knock on that damn door?" Hunter growled, more to himself than to me. After a minute, he said, "Fuck it. Ignore them."

He picked me up and started toward the bed, but another round of pounding ensued. "Hunter, Cassandra, there's a matter I need to bring to your attention. Open the door."

Hunter frowned at me as he cradled me in his arms. "I might kill him this time."

"It sounds important. We should probably let him in."

"This is important, or haven't you noticed." He wiggled my backside against his very hard, very ready erection.

I laughed. "Yes it is, and we'll have plenty of time after we get out of here to be alone, with no one who would dare knock on our doors."

His jaw clenched in his typical *I'm not happy about this* way, but he swung me around and set me down on my feet anyway. "Get dressed. I'll let him in. It better be important," he said with conviction.

I found a pair of sweatpants and put them on as Hunter went to the door.

"This better be good," Hunter said to Hadraniel as he opened the door.

Hadraniel glanced down at Hunter's towel before rolling his eyes and looking back at him. "It's not good. In fact, it's very bad. I thought you'd want to know before you left. The demon we were holding captive has escaped."

My first thought was Hunter had killed him after I'd left them alone the night before but rethought that possibility when I saw Hunter's angered features. "When and how?"

"Sometime during the night," Hadraniel answered. "And I don't know how. We're still investigating." He was looking at me as if gauging the authenticity of my reaction, and it pissed me off.

"Why are you looking at me? You think I had something to do with it?"

"Now, why would I think that?" he asked with enough sarcasm for me to know it wasn't a question but an accusation.

I straightened, slamming my hands on my hips, fixing him with a pair of narrowed, glowing eyes.

"Look, assho—"

Hunter stepped in front of me to face Hadraniel before I could finish. "I can assure you, Cassandra was too busy last night to free any demons. You'd be wise not to accuse her again. If the demon escaped, it was from your proven lack of security. Or maybe this is just your attempt to get us to stay."

I stepped to the side so I could see Hadraniel's reaction to Hunter's accusation. He didn't seem fazed, but not much bothered Hadraniel. I didn't think he'd have anything to do with letting a demon go, but that didn't mean he hadn't done something else, like kill him.

"If I wanted you to stay, I would have simply asked you to. I didn't. As I told you before, I agreed with your conclusion. Caleb didn't seem to want the bait we'd set." His gaze fell on me. "No longer a need for you to remain."

"Who was on duty?" Hunter asked.

"Jeremy, a very trusted and capable Sanctuary angel."

"What did he say happened?"

"Nothing. We're still looking for him, as well."

"Was there damage to the cell door?"

"No. It was unlocked."

"So, Jeremy could be a mole," Hunter pressed.

Hadraniel's jaw ticked a couple times. "Maybe you didn't hear the part when I said he was very trusted and capable."

Hunter chuckled and rubbed the back of his neck. "Forgive me if I don't trust your judgment of those qualities. Your track record hasn't been too good in that regard. I could loan you a couple demons to show you what to look for if you'd like."

"Do you think this might have been Caleb's doing?" I asked. They were wasting time. Pissing on each other's boots wasn't going to get us anywhere.

"It's possible," Hunter said.

"So, he could be here?" I almost hoped this was the case. If it was, we had a chance of capturing him and being done with this whole mess.

"Highly unlikely," Hadraniel answered. "There's no way he could have gotten down to the holding areas without us knowing."

"I don't know if you're just getting old or you've always been this naive," Hunter said. "Caleb always has a plan. He plotted to kill the most powerful force of the Underworld, something you couldn't do for centuries. He's not some special ops demon who hangs out in the shadows and waits for the guards to piss or sneak a smoke break. He's a smart, cunning, black-souled fiend. He looks for weak links and smashes his way through. It's obvious your army is riddled with those. You need to round up every angel who had knowledge of the demon in that cell and find out what they might know. If it wasn't your trusted, capable Jeremy that freed the demon, then someone else did."

Hadraniel's lips pressed together as he narrowed his eyes at Hunter. "It's already being done. We're assembling them all in the dining room."

"Good. I'll be there in ten minutes to question them myself."

Hadraniel was being dismissed and from the death stare he was giving Hunter, he knew it. Surprisingly, without a word, he turned and left.

Hunter and I stared at the closed door after Hadraniel left, both wrapped up in our own thoughts over what this turn of events might mean.

Finally, I broke the silence and voiced the inevitable. "So, I guess this means we're not leaving today."

I looked over at Hunter and watched his jaw tighten as if he wanted to say something, but didn't trust himself to open his mouth yet.

He turned to face me and put his hands on my arms. "We will, baby. I promise." He slid his palms up and down my arms. "I'm going to take you far away from this place. The only difference is it won't be today. I've got to question the angels because I don't trust Hadraniel to be unbiased enough to see if one of them is lying."

"You're going to try and make me stay here while you do that, aren't you?"

He smiled as if he were amused at my question. "Something tells me that wouldn't be an option anyway, but no, I was not. In fact, until we figure out what is going on, I'm not letting you out of my sight." He leaned down and sealed his promise with a gentle brush of his lips on mine. "Now go shower, so we can get this over with. I still want to get the hell out of here as soon as possible."

"Yes, sir," I said, smiling at him and raising a hand in a mock salute. Shocked, but relieved I was actually being included on something useful to our mission, I went straight into the bathroom, stripping my clothes off along the way. "I won't be long."

Hunter groaned. "You better lock that door, Cassandra, or neither of us will be leaving this room anytime soon."

With a laugh, I closed the door behind me and clicked the lock into place. It was just for show. A lock would never keep Hunter from anything he wanted. That's how I knew we'd get to the bottom of the demon's disappearance, one way or another.

***

The dining room wasn't nearly as crowded as I thought it would be. Hadraniel obviously felt the need to keep the imprisonment of a demon as discreet as possible, whether out of fear for his angels or of what they'd do about it. Whatever his motives, it would definitely benefit us now with so few to question.

With only fifteen or so angels and about half that many demons in the room, I doubted any of them had anything to do with the disappearance of their kind. Hadraniel and the angels weren't so assured. It was only fair everyone with knowledge of the demon should be questioned equally. I wondered if we weren't wasting our time outright with all of them.

"We'll start with your demons," Hadraniel stated when he met us at the door.

"It's a waste of time," Hunter said, sounding bored, "but if it'll make you feel better to throw your weight around before you find out another of your noble angels has turned traitor, then by all means."

"You know, demon, I find it amusing that someone who used to send the souls of innocents to eternal slavery in Hell should speak of his own kind as if the blood of angels ran through them."

Without another word, Hadraniel turned and approached a couple of demons, who were leaning against the far wall, deep in conversation.

"We better get over there," Hunter said, his gaze on Hadraniel's back. "I have a feeling if we're not there to supervise, King Halo will find some reason to lock every one of my men up."

I nodded and with Hunter's hand at my back, we approached the small group.

We'd almost reached Hadraniel when I caught a glimpse of Nora standing amongst some angels. I hadn't been seen her from our vantage point before, especially with the way the angels towered over her, but I did now. And as our gazes locked, I knew she saw me too.

I stopped and caught Hunter's attention. "Why don't you go ahead? I trust the demons. I don't need to see their reactions when you question them. Nora's here. I'd like to talk to her since I didn't get the chance last night."

"Of course. This shouldn't take long anyway. Join me when you're done."

After a chaste kiss on my cheek, he left me to join Hadraniel by the demons.

I had to walk the length of the table to round it and get to Nora on the other side, and as I did, I saw her glance over at me before she excused herself from the group of angels. At first, I thought she was coming to meet me, but then she started walking fast in the opposite direction, toward the door.

Her action froze me in place, open-mouthed. Without so much as another nod my direction, she left the room.

I wanted to yell to her. I wanted to yell *at* her. Did she hate me that much now she'd blatantly turn her back on me? If she hadn't seen me coming, her leaving would have been innocent enough, but she looked me dead in the eyes before she'd gone. There was no question, she'd pretty much just given me a big *fuck off.*

"What's up with you and Nora?"

I closed my eyes after hearing Braydon's voice behind me. Could this day get any better? Maybe, if I were lucky, I'd get to see another testosterone-filled brawl.

I turned to face him. "Nothing."

"Is that nothing, as in... it's just a tiff that will blow over too soon to talk about... or it's none of your business, Braydon."

"It's none of your business, Braydon."

He wanted to say something more about it but studied me with curiosity instead.

"I didn't think I'd see you again after last night."

Jesus, he had no sense of discretion. I glanced behind me to make sure Hunter hadn't caught our conversation, or the attempt at a conversation I was about to kill. Anyone in the room had the ability to listen in if they wanted. That was part of the problem of hanging with a bunch of super-sensory angels and demons. Good thing was, most of them tuned out everything but what was pertinent to them in order to keep their sanity. Lucky for me, and even more so, Braydon, Hunter didn't deem my conversations pertinent at the moment.

"Yeah, well, we didn't expect to be here either."

"I won't say I'm sorry."

"I didn't ask you to."

An awkward silence ensued until I could no longer take Braydon's intense gaze.

"So, did you know this Jeremy guy?" I asked, trying to veer the situation somewhere that felt less... personal. I figured I might as well try to get some information out of him.

"We worked together a few times."

"Did he seem like the type to turn traitor?"

"No."

I waited for him to elaborate, but after a few moments of silence, it was clear he wasn't going to.

"Okay. What about him makes you say that?"

"Because he was just like the rest of us—the angels, the demons, you, me, even your precious Hunter. Watch any one of us and you see someone fighting for something. But that isn't always representative of what's inside, what they truly believe in. You, of all people, know this, Cassie. The truth of a person's essence lies deep within and can only be seen if they want it to be."

While his words may have applied to Jeremy, he was talking about me. The aimed look he gave me as he said it, put weight into every word as they fell on me.

"So, what you're saying is any one of us could be a traitor."

He didn't miss a beat. "For the right reasons."

Oh, no. Could it have been Braydon who set the demon free? Would keeping me here be reason enough for him? I hadn't even considered it.

"I can tell what you're thinking, Cassie. It wasn't me."

"Why should I believe you?"

"Because I wouldn't want you to stay for any other reason than to be with me. I wouldn't trick you into it. I want you, not your obligations."

"Dammit, Braydon," I whispered, as I glanced over at Hunter again. He was talking with some of the other demons and still didn't seem to catch our conversation, thank God. My luck wasn't going to last much longer, however. "You've got to stop saying things like that," I said through clenched teeth.

He glimpsed over my shoulder at Hunter and then rolled his eyes before smirking back at me. "I'm just being honest."

"Well, sto—"

Angered shouts near the door cut me off. An angel and demon were exchanging accusations and insults that were quickly escalating. The tension was thick all the way across the room. When the angel managed to sucker punch the demon, Hadraniel and Hunter descended on them to break it up.

"Seems the natives are getting restless," Braydon said.

I shook my head as I watched Hadraniel and Hunter reprimanding the two brawlers. "They can't even be in the same room for more than fifteen minutes without wanting to tear each other apart."

"It's a natural instinct."

I turned to look at him. His gaze was set on Hunter.

"Is it?" I asked.

His eyes met mine, and I could tell the moment he knew why I was asking, but I made my point anyway. "Maybe I shouldn't let my guard down around you."

As soon as his mouth opened in response, I walked away before he had the chance to get it out.

Hunter was headed my way. I rounded the table to meet him, thankful I'd gotten away from Braydon before he'd decided to join me.

"What's going on?" I asked.

"They're all getting restless. Hadraniel is having some food and drinks brought in to give them something to occupy their time while they wait. I'm all finished up with the demons so things should settle down in here anyway."

"Did you get anything from them?"

"No. Ceril was the last to see the demon. He went down on a round right after dinner and said he looked in on the demon while Jeremy was on duty. Nothing seemed out of place."

"Did he actually see the demon in the cell?"

"Yes, said he even razzed him a bit through the door. The demon was smug but not more than usual."

"Okay, so that leaves Jeremy the last to be around him then."

"So far."

"Who's next?"

"I think we'll start with Chris once the food comes," Hunter said, motioning with a nod toward the angel they had restrained moments ago. "He seems the most tense, which may mean he has something to hide."

No sooner had he mentioned food, than a few servants appeared with platters, setting them out on the table. The aroma of steaming meats and ripe fruit filled the room. It looked and smelled wonderful as if it had come from the roaster or was freshly picked from the vine. How did they manage to have so much ready on such short notice?

The angels migrated to the table and began to fill their plates. Most remained seated there to dine, but a few took their plates and lounged against the walls together to eat as they chatted. Hadraniel's plan to ease the angels' anxiety with food seemed to be working. The air around us was definitely more breathable now.

Apparently, my stomach also wanted in on the scheme because it released a loud enough rumble to gain Hunter's attention.

"Sit. Eat," he said, pulling out the chair in front of us.

"Shall I roll over and beg too?"

I didn't catch the duplicity of my words until a roguish smirk appeared on Hunter's face. "Ask me later."

Unable to help thinking I just might do as he asked, in private, I laughed. Reaching across the table, I picked pieces from several platters to fill my plate. Hunter added to it from those I couldn't reach before he sat down next to me.

"You're not going to have anything?" I asked, noting the empty table in front of him.

"You know I'm never hungry for food," he said, stealing a slice of ham from my plate and plopping it into his own mouth.

"Hey."

I made a fist to give him a playful punch while he laughed at me, but I ended up bumping Hadraniel's arms as he reached between us to set two glasses on the table. Liquid sloshed over the rims, splashing both Hunter's lap and mine.

"I guess I should have announced myself," Hadraniel said, handing us each a small cloth to clean ourselves up while he did the same. "And here I was trying to be a gracious host for once by bringing you a drink."

I couldn't discern whether it was a grunt or growl that came from Hunter, but it was something low and gritty, definitely not complimentary.

"Well, it wasn't a total loss," I said, picking up the glass nearest me. It contained more than half the original liquid in it. I took a sniff. "White wine?"

"Yes. I'd heard that's what you preferred."

I nodded as I took a sip. A perfect blend of fruit, but not too sweet.

"Why *are* you so hospitable now?" Hunter asked eyes narrowed up at Hadraniel.

"Oh, I have my reasons."

The words had barely left his lips when the room started to spin and my lids felt like lead sheets over my eyes. They closed of their own accord, and the muscles in my arms and legs seemed to disappear.

"Rest, Cassandra," I heard Hadraniel say. A hand was at my back, urging me forward until my head rested on the table.

"You son of a bitch," Hunter shouted.

Grunts and scraping furniture sounded all around me, but I couldn't process what it meant. What was happening? What was wrong with me?

"Hunter?" I called out, my tongue so thick it garbled his name.

Somehow I managed to lift one of those heavy lids enough to see Hunter surrounded by angels. He was gagged and being restrained.

I opened my mouth, willing a scream to come out, but everything went black before I could catch my breath.

CHAPTER FOURTEEN

My skin trembled, but I was burning on the inside. A draft flowed over me, a cold and wet one, like a thick fog leaving a chilling mist behind. But I couldn't raise my hands to wipe it off. I was powerless to lift anything, not even my eyelids. They were too heavy.

Sounds surrounded me. Echoing sounds, like voices in a distant tunnel. I couldn't make out what they were saying because the fog seemed to have entered my brain, and when I willed myself to shake my head to clear it. Nothing.

What had happened to me?

Even my thoughts seemed lost. Fleeting impressions inundated me, but I couldn't grasp them. I was at home with Nora. I was in the park with Hunter. No, I was in Hell. Had the darkness overtaken me for good? Oh no, I was with the angels. I was safe with them. Hunter was here. Or was it Braydon. Was I dreaming?

The voices grew louder. I tried to call out to them, but my lips failed me.

My body seemed anchored or tethered, but to what I didn't know. I just wanted to move to know I... existed, to know I was *somewhere*... any place real.

A deep, muted voice was suddenly so near me I might have jumped if I'd had any control over my body. Then something whispered over my cheek, like a feather brushing against it.

I flinched from the contact, and it was the most welcomed awareness. In fact, I *did* exist.

My body started to wake. Blood flowed within, leaving needle like sensations along its path.

Then, without assistance from me, my head began to clear, and along with it, the voices.

No, it was only one voice, and that familiar voice froze my blood once again.

"Wake up, sleepyhead," he said in a lover's croon. "I've missed you."

I wasn't in Hell. I was somewhere much worse.

Caleb.

I wanted to slip back into that nothingness. Feel nothing, *be* nothing. The unknown was better than hearing that voice in my ear again.

"Come, my queen. I have so much to show you."

Once again, fate had come down like a lightning bolt splitting the earth in front of me, jarring me from my path, forcing me to step into the darkness I was so carefully trying to avoid. It seemed no matter how much I tried to shape my destiny, it kept molding it in such a way as to make it unwieldy.

"Hmmm... maybe a kiss to wake my Sleeping Beauty."

I fluttered my eyes open.

"Ahhh... there she is." He loomed above me, his face mere inches from mine, a smirk covering it from ear to ear. "Welcome home. Well, technically this isn't home, but close enough."

"How?" I managed to ask, my tongue so thick it was difficult to form words. "Where?"

"So many questions," he said, staying next to me as he stood back up. "We'll get to them soon enough. First we must say our goodbyes to your escort. I'm sure he's eager to get back."

He turned his head toward someone or something in the distance, but I couldn't see from my angle. I was lying on a cot or bed of some sort and tried to sit up. That was when I realized I was bound to it at the wrists and ankles by metal shackles.

Caleb stared down at me with a spark in his eyes. His features were harder, more prominent, stronger than I remembered. His entire body appeared more powerful than the last I'd seen him. And if he had seemed confident back then, he appeared to hold the world with his bare hands now.

"For your own safety, of course," he said, referencing my binds.

Don't you mean yours? I wanted to spit out, but I knew the best way to deal with Caleb was not with idle threats, especially ones my body wasn't ready to give substance to. My brain was still too fuzzy to process everything, so I lay back down and closed my eyes to try and let it clear.

"If you think I'm leaving here without the body, you're not as smart as I gave you credit for."

I shot up again, eyes wide with surprise at Hadraniel's voice. There he was, standing near the bed now, looking at Caleb as if expecting something. Payment maybe? If I hadn't seen him with my own eyes, I would've thought it was my muddled mind playing tricks on me. But then, the memory of the dining hall, feeling lightheaded, Hadraniel telling me to rest. It all came flooding back.

"You," I said, with awe and disgust. "How could you?"

His gaze met mine, and I don't know what I expected to see in his eyes... disgust maybe, but there was nothing.

"Don't be so surprised, Cassandra," he said. "I have a universe to protect. Some sacrifices are expected."

I clenched my teeth so hard, I was sure they'd break from the pressure. The hatred I had for him at that moment emanated from me. I only wished it was palpable and able to knock him on his sorry, sacrificing ass.

"You see, sweetheart," Caleb said, his enjoyment of this whole scene giving an extra lift to his voice, "your great, great, great granddaddy here and I made a deal. He'd bring you home to me, and I'd give him the other piece to his almighty collection—Nergal's body." Caleb looked back at Hadraniel. "It's too bad he didn't pay attention to the fine print. The part that reads, 'Never make a deal with the devil.' Nergal taught me that one."

I pierced Hadraniel with a look of complete loathing. "You're a fucking idiot."

Caleb laughed.

Hadraniel kept his gaze on Caleb, ignoring my outburst. "Without the Sword, you're still no closer than before I brought the girl. You've gained nothing."

So, I was just a girl now. Before I was the girl, I'd been the angels' only hope of luring the big bad wolf in. Caleb wasn't the only manipulative prick in the universe. Apparently, the most powerful and highest angels hid their horns well.

"I've gained a queen," Caleb said, smiling down at me, making my skin crawl.

"A queen can only satisfy your desire in bed, not your desire for power. You'll never get the Sword," Hadraniel argued.

"You do underestimate me, Hadraniel. I'm much smarter than you give me credit for. In fact, the Sword is already on its way to me. You're not the only angel on my shoulder, you know."

"You're lying."

"I'll bid you goodbye so you can go see for yourself."

"And I'll come back with a thousand angels more than your pitiful group of demons could ever handle."

Caleb fixed Hadraniel with a smug look. "It seems you're in a bit of a catch twenty-two situation then. You see, if you leave, we'll be gone by the time you return, and you'll be back to square one, with one less beautiful woman to sacrifice. But if you stay, how will you stop the Sword from making the way to its rightful owner?"

Hadraniel's forehead creased as he narrowed his eyes at Caleb. After a time of silence, when he seemed to be contemplating the scenario that had just been painted, he said, "I'll find you."

He was leaving? No. No, he wouldn't leave me this way. While listening to him, I'd hated him, but a tiny glimmer of faith had me clinging to the hope he had some ulterior plan, that I really wasn't being sacrificed and left here with Caleb, to be his plaything. He was an angel, for chrissakes.

"You're leaving me here?"

My last words dissipated into the air where Hadraniel no longer stood. He was gone.

"I thought he'd never leave," Caleb said, smiling down at me. "Talk about overstaying your welcome."

"This will never work. They'll find you. You know they will and when they do, they'll shove that Sword down your lying throat."

"Now how would they do that when they don't even have the blessed Sword? That, my dear queen, was not a lie. It will be in our possession soon enough."

Our possession. As if I'd have anything to do with his psychotic plan. He was more demented than he'd ever been.

"You can't keep me here, Caleb. I'm stronger than you. You know that."

"You don't look too strong right now."

"These drugs won't last forever. And when they wear off—"

"We'll be far enough away, and you'll see where you belong. You'll *feel* where you belong."

"I know where I belong. No drug in the world can take that away from me."

"You'll change your mind. I have no doubt about that. Now let's stop arguing and get this party started." He started climbing up onto the bed.

"What the hell are you doing?"

He straddled my hips and leaned over me, his face practically nuzzling my neck. I heard him breathe in deep through his nose, smelling me. After a moment of nothing, as if he were holding my scent in, he slowly let his hot breath out while he made his way to my ear. Lips brushing my lobe, he said, "You're going to thank me for this, I promise."

With all my strength, I raised my fists, wanting nothing more than to beat them over his head, or grab him by the neck and twist it until it no longer supported his head. But the manacles held my hands fast and too far away to reach him. All I could do was twist my head in his direction, hard enough to force him back.

"I'm going to kill you, Caleb. That's *my* promise."

He smiled at me with that evil smirk I despised and hoped I'd never see again.

"I love it when you're spunky," he said, right before he put all of his weight on me and hugged me to him.

I braced myself for what I thought was next, but all that came was darkness. A sweet, welcomed darkness.

***

Cassandra.

The breathy, melodic sound of my name echoed in my head, waking me from what seemed like the deepest sleep I'd ever been under.

Cassandra.

Cassie.

A different voice. That one didn't sing. One that grated on my nerves like steel against stone.

I opened my eyes to what I'd hoped was a nightmare.

"We're home," Caleb said, still straddled over me. "Well, close."

I closed my eyes. Definitely a nightmare, a living, breathing one.

"Come now, sweetheart. Don't be like that."

"Don't call me that."

He laughed as he shifted off the bed... and me.

I opened my eyes again. Torch sconces dimly lit the room, dancing light over the stone walls that surrounded us, as far as I could see. An old, dank smell permeated the air, like that of an ancient castle.

The scenery was much the same as the last place we'd just left, but the vibes here smothered me like a dark, weighted blanket. I wanted to be repelled by it, but much to my disgust, it gave me a strange, comforting feeling. *Must still be drugged because it seems I'm exactly where I was supposed to be, but I know better.* It made me think of the melodious voice I had heard or *thought* I heard when we first got there—inviting, welcoming me.

I shook my head to rid myself of the traitorous thoughts.

"You feel it, don't you?" Caleb asked. He was studying my face as if he could read my thoughts.

"I have a lot of emotions right now, Caleb—hatred, repulsion, rage. But you know what I feel the most? Bloodthirsty." I sneered.

One of his eyebrows lifted when a smug expression came over his face. "Good. I knew you'd be the perfect queen."

"You're delusional. I am not your queen and never will be. Do whatever you want to me. I've already been through worse than you could ever dream up. You're nothing but a flunky wannabe."

"Be careful, Cassie."

"Oh, please. I was tortured for months by Nergal, someone more powerful than you."

A searing pain shot through my head, like a knife slicing through my brain. I squeezed my eyes shut and cried out. Shit. Where'd he learn to do that?

"Are you sure? I've got more tricks I wouldn't mind showing you. You could take notes, then we could compare."

"Fuck you."

Another blast of pain erupted under my skull, and I swear my eyeballs bulged out of their sockets from it.

"Are you ready to be a good girl?"

The pain eased up, but tiny aftershocks echoed. Once they were finally gone, or at least bearable, I opened my eyes and glared at him, but said nothing.

"You really need to lighten up, Cassie. Once you do, you'll see this will be a very pleasant and uplifting experience for you. You're finally on the right path. Fate has beckoned you here for a reason."

Yeah, to kill you.

"No, sweetheart, not to kill me."

Wonderful. He'd added mind reading to his big bag of tricks. That wouldn't be helpful.

He smiled. "To rule with me. With me, you are an integral part of the world order, fate's plan. Without me, you're only a lost little hybrid."

"I'm not lost," I said through pursed lips, unable to hold my tongue through all his bullshit.

"Oh, really? Was Hadraniel showing you the way? Did he take you in with open arms, horns and all?"

I narrowed my eyes at him.

"Ahhh, that's right. Grandpappy sold you to the highest bidder. Oh, but then there's Hunter," he said, looking thoughtful. "Tell me, how long do you think it would have taken before you acted out those deliciously murderous dreams you were having of him?"

He couldn't know my dreams. But he did. That sparkle in his eyes as he gazed down at me told me so.

Caleb leaned down to me and put his lips to my ear. "Still think I'm a flunky wannabe?"

After placing a soft kiss on my cheek, he stood back up. "Unlike them, I want to help you reach your full potential, Cassie. That's all I've ever wanted. Well, maybe a wee bit more than that," he added with a devious smirk, "but my desire for you only makes me want you to realize your true calling even more. And now, after all this time, I have the knowledge and the power to make it happen. But I need you to work with me on this. The more you fight, the more difficult, and painful, it will be."

His proclamations of grandeur sounded like the same old Caleb, but the powers he was displaying warned me they might not be as delusional as they were before. He'd obviously become more powerful, but how?

Defiance was not working, so I wasn't going to waste more energy on it. One thing I was sure hadn't changed about him was his ego, and how he loved to have it stroked.

"You've obviously been working out. Where'd you learn all those cool new tricks?"

He smiled. "Be my queen, and I'll show you."

"Always the fine print. What happened to Alison? She was the one who helped you escape, so obviously she had a thing for you. Why didn't you just pick her to be your queen?"

"She helped pass the time, but she was never queen material. There's only ever been one queen in my eyes, Cassie. Alison found that out the hard way."

The hard way meant he killed her, of that I had no doubt. Although I might not have been in this situation had Alison been his queen *material girl*, I couldn't say I was saddened to hear she met a fitting fate.

"Am I to be your queen bound to this bed?" I asked, changing tactics.

He closed his eyes and smiled languidly as if savoring something delicious. "Oh, the fantasies you arouse."

"Free me, Caleb."

He contemplated the possibility. "Not yet," he said, shaking his head. "I can see you're still not fully succumbing to your fate. I'll give you some time."

Caleb started to walk away.

"You can't leave me like this."

Who was I kidding? He could leave me any way he wanted.

"Don't worry, Cassie. It won't take long for you to realize there's no other way."

***

After a while of seething over Caleb leaving me tied to a bed in the middle of some dank, archaic room of what was probably a primeval castle in the middle of no man's land, I finally told myself to calm down and let my energy regenerate. I was too wired up to even think about sleeping, so I lay there, staring up at the cracked stone ceiling, listening.

Somewhere beyond the walls, the clanking of metal echoed. I could barely hear it. No voices to be heard so I couldn't discern how many were here with Caleb. I knew there were others because Hadraniel had been flanked by two other men. Caleb's minions, I assumed. I wondered how many more existed. He'd already assembled a small army when we'd been in Hell. In the time he'd been gone, it could have grown to any number. Power was a magnet to demons, and he seemed to have plenty of it.

My smart move was to tread carefully. He wasn't stupid, by any means. He'd be wary if I showed too much interest in being his queen. I'd have to take things slow, get him to trust me, and then I could...

Could what? The truth was I had no idea what to do, with or without Caleb's trust in me. I didn't even know where the hell I was. And it wasn't as if I could transport back to the Sanctuary. As far as I knew, I didn't have that power. The only times I'd transported anywhere was when someone else was in control.

The situation here was feeling more hopeless than when I was chained to pillars in Hell at the tortuous mercy of the devil. At least then Hunter knew where I was. I doubted anyone knew where Caleb had taken me. Since he had eluded us for months, this was quite possibly where he'd been hiding out.

My head throbbed from hitting mental brick walls.

Cassandra.

It was the same voice I heard before. The silvery quality of it was just as pacifying, but now with the knowledge of my whereabouts and company, there was no way it could charm me.

"Who's there?" I called out.

I've been waiting for you. Come to me.

I searched the room from my supine position as much as possible but saw no one. The room wasn't that big, so whoever it was would have to be crouched down somewhere behind me, but it didn't sound like it was coming from there. The voice echoed in the air around me, near but distant at the same time, as if it had been caught somewhere else on the wind and brought to me.

"Where are you?" I whispered.

Close.

Without thinking, I lurched up, intent on whipping around to see the full extent of the room, but my binds jerked me in place. I let out a loud, frustrated growl.

"Where *are* you? *Who* are you?"

"Miss me already?" Caleb sauntered through the door. "I haven't been gone long. And I'll never be too far away, I assure you. As far as who I am, well, I guess you could say I'm the new and improved Caleb. I still have all the same parts. Would you like to see?"

"I'll take your word for it."

"Ah, so you're starting to trust me. We're on the right track."

"I won't lie. I still don't trust you. Your track record has me stepping very carefully, Caleb."

"At least you're honest. I'll give you that. I wasn't a very trustworthy person then, was I? I was desperate for power, but now I have it."

"Not the ultimate power. You still don't have the Sword."

"True, but I will."

"So, why do you need me then?"

"I told you, you're my queen. We're connected, Cassie, in so many ways. You may not appreciate that fact right now, but you will. It's fate's plan, and the quicker you realize it, the sooner you will be free."

"So, what? I'm stuck here in this bed until I reach some kind of epiphany? I'm just supposed to find it in my heart to believe you? You know it doesn't work that way with me anymore, Caleb. I've been burned too many times... quite literally, as you well know."

He stood next to the bed and took my hand in his.

"What are you doing?" I asked.

"A peace offering."

With less than a blink of his eyes, my bindings disappeared. Instinctually, I went to draw my hands together, but Caleb kept his grip on the one he held.

"They go back on as easily as they came off, Cassie. Don't forget."

His powers scared the hell out of me. They reminded me of Nergal. Was it possible he'd gained them just from having Nergal's body in his possession? Had he found some way without the Sword to extract powers? Maybe the angels weren't as all-knowing as they claimed. But then, he still wanted the Sword. It was all quite confusing. Too many questions swirled in my head that only he seemed able to answer, but I was horrified to put any trust in Caleb to get that clarity.

Then again, what choice did I have?

"Thank you." It was all the peace I could stomach.

His friendly smile was enough to show me he appreciated it.

"How'd you like to get out of this room?"

"You even have to ask?"

He laughed and pulled at my hand to help me off the bed. "A tour?"

I nodded as my feet touched the floor. Standing, I realized my limbs hadn't fully recovered from whatever Hadraniel had given me, so I was forced to lean on Caleb in order to walk with him. By the smug expression, I knew he was more than happy with the circumstance.

As we got closer to the door, locks clicked. The door eased opened of its own accord.

"You already know that trick," Caleb said, squeezing my arm.

Great, more mind locks. Loved those.

The room we'd been in was at the end of a long, dark corridor with walls and a ceiling made up of the same cold stone as the room. Torches lined the walls at intervals, lighting up the seemingly endless length of the hall but creating pockets of shadows where the glare didn't reach. It reminded me of the shadows I used to hunt down when I was merely a guardian. That seemed so long ago, a much simpler time. There had been only one goal... to save lives from the shadows of death. Now it seemed the fate of the world was on my shoulders. The darkness was nothing compared to the monsters I faced now, the worst being the one who seemed to lie in wait within me.

"So, where are we?" I asked as we continued to walk down the corridor. I could faintly make out a solid steel door at the end of it.

"In the middle of nowhere."

"Well, that's enlightening. Guess I'll just throw that in my GPS next time I want to visit."

He laughed and squeezed my arm again.

"No, I mean that quite literally. We are nowhere that exists in the world as you or any mortal knows it. We are in a different realm entirely."

"You mean, like an alternate universe or something?"

"Yes. That's exactly what I mean."

"If no one knows it exists, how did you find out about it?"

"I said, no *mortal* knows about it. The higher beings know it's here."

"The angels know about it?"

"Yes, they do. They just never think about it."

"I don't understand."

We'd come to the steel door. Caleb stopped in front of it and turned to face me, grasping my upper arms to hold me steady, although I'd already regained some strength since we'd left the room.

"When we transport from place to place in the mortal world, we go through a parallel realm to get there. This realm. Most don't think to stop in it, they just ride right through to their destination."

"And you decided to stop and build a castle?" My mind was spinning with this new information. The situation was looking more and more hopeless. If we were in some universe no one even stopped to blink in, I had no chance of anyone ever finding me.

"This castle was built thousands of years before my time. I was merely informed of its location and took up my rightful residence."

"By whom?"

"You'll see," he said with a mischievous smile.

As if on cue, the locks clicked on the door in front of us and slowly opened outward.

I looked through the entrance into a huge, glorious room that didn't seem to belong to the corridor we were in. My jaw hung open as I peered in.

"I've made a few renovations," Caleb said with a chuckle. "Go ahead in, Cassie."

Coaxing wasn't necessary. I was in awe of the room in front of me. It was like stepping into a movie, set to the theme of extravagant kings and queens of ancient times when luxurious surroundings reflected your status in life. The floor was made of a polished stone, which appeared to reach up at evenly spaced intervals along the wall, creating arched doorways opening to deep alcoves. Within each alcove, cushioned divans were placed against stained glass backdrops. Floor-to-ceiling columns lined the alcoves and seemed to find life toward the top like trees with stone branches reaching out to the ceiling in symmetrical patterns, giving the whole room an odd earthy feel. Pedestals stood uniform along the walls, each wielding a medium-sized ball of dancing flames that never seemed to lose strength.

Maroon rugs and tapestries were laid and hung throughout the room, the gold swirl patterns bringing out the sand-colored stone of the floors. A huge wooden table sat central, with chairs surrounding it, but one chair stood out at the head of it. Throne-like in nature, its maroon, cushioned fabric matched the rugs and tapestries, including the gold edging, which seemed to swirl in a perfect pattern. I had no doubt it was where Caleb reigned over his minions.

"War room?" I asked.

"Sometimes," he answered. He led me over to one of the alcoves and encouraged me to sit on the cushioned divan. "It can also double as a sitting room with all the comforts of home, don't you think?"

As I sat, I peered up at the stained glass backdrop. The design included a blue winged devil, complete with horns and staff, crouched on a rock, appearing as if it were looking down upon anyone sitting on the divan.

"Yeah, sure," I said. "I love kicking back with a good romance novel while some hellish fiend hovers overhead looking to devour me."

Caleb placed both hands on the seat at each side of me, caging my body from escape. He bent near, causing me to lean back as far as I could without falling off completely. "Cassie, you must stop painting these delicious pictures in my mind, or I'll lose all self-control before we even make it to the altar."

I felt his breath on my face and panicked. Trying to catch him in the goods, I threw my knee up between his legs, but before I could hit pay dirt, he grabbed me by the neck, picked me up, and threw me across the room like a banished rag doll. I hit high up on the wall opposite, feeling things crack under my skin on impact before I dropped to the floor in a heap. While trying to feel what part of my body was workable without actually moving, a force lifted my heavy, lifeless body up the wall I'd just slammed into, straightening it out as it went, until my feet dangled inches from the floor.

Caleb was still across the room, but his narrowed eyes were intent on me, and I knew they were the force holding me up against the wall. He took measured steps toward me. My lungs were obviously still intact because they were working harder with every step he neared, until I'd forced them to stop when he was standing right in front of me. I cast my gaze down at him. My eyes were all I could move because my head was pinned securely against the wall. It was a horrible feeling, made worse when I noticed Caleb's face in a direct line with my chest, and his lecherous eyes made sure they let me know it.

"That was not nice, Cassie," he said, finally lifting his glower to mine. "I think you owe me an apology."

"Screw you. I'm not going to let you paw at me whenever the hell you want to."

"Really?" He stepped closer, put his hands on my hips and started inching his palms up under my shirt. "And what makes you think you have that choice?"

I closed my eyes and sucked in a breath, which was the worst thing I could do since it pushed out my chest even more, feeding his evil desire. Unable to help myself, it was all I could do to withstand his scorching hands on my skin, and I pulled my lips into my teeth and bit down as his fingertips neared my breasts.

"Obviously, you don't fully comprehend the extent of my power over you just yet," he said. "Maybe I just need to give you a hard, fast lesson and be done with it."

My arms flung up over my head of their own accord, or I should say of his, and then my legs spread out against the wall. One set of hard clunks on the wall and tight, cold steel restrained my wrists and ankles. He'd shackled me again. This time, hanging on the frigging wall.

"You've had your warning, Cassie. I won't offer it again."

The brush of his thumbs on the underside of my breasts made me ill, but I didn't dare gasp. Hell, I couldn't even breathe.

"Look at me," he ordered, his voice low and commanding. I lowered my gaze to his. "While the thought of fucking you against this wall makes my cock harder than it's ever been, I won't do it until you've come to terms with our relationship. But know this, Cassie, you've given me a taste of what is one of my most sinful fantasies of us, and it *will* happen."

Thankfully, he took his hands away.

"I'd rather die than let you touch me," I said through clenched teeth.

He eyed me and sighed as if I were a child who had disappointed him. He stood in that spot for a long time before saying, "Well, I guess I'll just have to let you hang out for a while by yourself then and contemplate your situation. You make me very sad. I was hoping we could catch up today on all the time we've missed. Maybe tomorrow. Goodnight, Cassie." He blew me a kiss and turned to walk away.

"Caleb, what the hell? You can't leave me up here like this." It came out as more of a plea than an order because the farther away he got, the more I knew he very well could, and would.

He turned around when he reached a door at the opposite side of the room. "Sweet dreams, Cassie. Oh, and don't worry about the crew coming in the morning. They've been ordered not to touch you. They know you're mine."

With that, he walked out.

And I was stuck, slapped up against a fucking wall like a smashed, swatted fly. Oh, I'd be contemplating my situation all right. I was already considering about fifty different ways to make Caleb endure an excruciating amount of pain before I killed him.

CHAPTER FIFTEEN

I hung shackled against the wall for what seemed like hours with no concept of time. The room was pitch dark without a glimmer of light from anywhere even touching the stained glass windows. No clocks either. For all I knew, day or night might not exist in this realm, time being only an earthly value. It was difficult to wrap my head around our location in comparison to the world I'd always known. Was this purgatory, that realm between Heaven and Hell? Hanging up on the wall as I was like a prized painting, it certainly felt that way. But if this were Purgatory, where have I come from? Heaven or Hell? And more importantly, where did I belong?

You belong to me.

The voice permeated my senses, the same one that seemed to haunt me only when I was alone in this undiscoverable place.

Scanning the room, as much as possible given my position, I was surprised at how much I could move my head. Caleb probably only allowed it to torture me so I could see where I was unable to go. I couldn't dwell on his maniacal ways at the moment. I had other head-trips to deal with. My own, for starters.

The room looked empty. Between the fires burning on the pedestals and the three mammoth-sized chandeliers hanging strategically from the ceiling, I had a pretty good view of the whole room. Granted, there were many places one could hide, behind tapestries or within an alcove out of my range, but like before, the voice didn't seem to come from a distance. I was certain, it was right there, all around me, within me.

You're not real.

Are you sure? Am I not? the voice in my head asked.

The air shifted by my ankles, and my legs closed to a normal position, now dangling against the wall. The shackles around them had disappeared.

Okay, obviously someone was there with me but not in any physical form, and that situation was even scarier than thinking I was going bat shit crazy. Was it Caleb? Was this one of his new tricks? Was he trying to get me to lose it for good?

"Cool trick, Caleb. Now come out and let me off this wall."

Not Caleb. I own Caleb.

I had nothing to base it on, but from the power that seemed to surround me, I had no doubt it was the truth.

"Then who are you? What do you want from me?"

I want you to let go.

"Let go? What the hell does that mean? Look," I said, flailing my hands lamely over the tops of the shackles, "this is me letting go. Helloo... I'm stuck here."

When that was met with only silence, I demanded, "Show yourself, so I know who I'm dealing with." More silence. "At least get me off this goddamn wall."

You have the power to do that yourself.

"Really? Wow. Joke's on me then, I guess. Here, I've been hanging around on a fucking wall for who knows how long, and I could have been sitting back and having a beer with the guys. Ha ha, very funny..."

Enough.

If I could have jerked from the force of the voice I would have because it was that overbearing, powerful. I swore the wall behind me shook along with the chandeliers above. Who the hell was I dealing with?

You only need to believe and understand the power within you. Let go. Imagine what you need.

"Look, thank you for the imaginary pep talk and all, but I don't have that kind of power. Believe me, I've tried. Please throw me a bone here and free my hands."

After another moment of silence, the words flooded my mind. *I'm disappointed, but if you continue to think yourself as that fly on the wall, then you shall remain that way. Remember, while flies may hear and see everything around them, they are easy targets. Caleb will tear off your wings and eat you alive. Then where will you be?*

The presence was gone. I could feel it... or rather, *not* feel it. And I was *still* stuck on the damn wall. I didn't know what to make of the voice... presence... whatever the hell it was. It seemed to be trying to help me, but why? Whoever it was, obviously believed I had powers and wanted me to tap into them. But for what end? To save myself? To overpower Caleb? It seemed that way, and in that sense, it made me smile inside. But at the same time, heavy darkness lingered like an electrified cloud hanging low over a metal rod, waiting for just the right energy to shoot out a bolt of lightning and destroy everything around it.

I could contemplate what the presence wanted from me until I was blue in the face. The fact remained... I was still shackled to the wall and had only been given one piece of advice in all the hours I'd been there about how to alleviate my situation.

So, what could it hurt?

I closed my eyes and repeated to myself that I could do this. I was strong enough and had the power within to free myself. The chant must have lasted ten minutes, but nothing happened. Either I was doing something wrong or the voice was full of shit.

Okay, okay. I mentally shook myself. The voice had said to believe, let go, and imagine. I tried again, but this time, my mental cheerleader quieted, and I envisioned myself up on the wall, arms shackled. I concentrated on them specifically, made them disintegrate in my mind and imagined a pressure being relieved from my body before I fell to the floor. Watching the whole scenario, relief washed over me and it seemed real from deep within as if it had actually happened.

Two unexpected thumps sounded over my head, and I slid down the wall, landing hard on my ass on the floor.

It worked. Holy Shit. It really worked.

I rubbed at my wrists and slowly began to rise from the floor as I contemplated what I'd just done. When had I acquired that kind of power? Since I'd found out I was a guardian-slash-demon, I'd discovered many skills, but it had been months since I'd gained any new powers. Maybe it was the Sanctuary or the angels holding those powers back. Maybe it was me. The voice had said as much. Either way, it didn't matter. This was big. *Christ*, this was *huge*.

While my head spun with the possibilities of what I could do, the dilemma remained about how it could help me get out of this situation. No longer believing I was helpless and trapped, I had to remember this skill was new. The complexity of how it worked exactly, or how far I could go with it, stayed a mystery... for the time being. Could I simply imagine a door leading me out of this castle and back to my realm and one would appear? Would it work to picture me choking the life out of Caleb and he'd suddenly fall dead at my feet?

With every power came limits. I needed to be careful when I chose to explore those limits, especially with Caleb. He was smart and powerful. Those traits were two extremely attractive qualities in a person, except when it pertained to someone as ruthless and evil as Caleb. In that case, it could be detrimental to my health. Yes, I may have realized a new power within myself but also knew Caleb had an arsenal of ones I hadn't seen yet.

Glancing around, I wondered what to do next. Running wasn't an option since we'd transported to this godforsaken place. I'd only end up going from room to room, and sure as shit, Caleb would find me anyway.

At the moment, my options were limited to roaming around the castle, checking for something that might help me. In my mind, that scenario seemed lame after I'd just found out I had this awesome gift, but I could at least get a lay of the land. *Smart planning, right?*

The door we'd entered wouldn't lead me anywhere. I knew that and was definitely steering clear of the door where Caleb exited. One choice left on the right side of the head of the table.

When I reached the throne-like chair, I stopped, an idea hitting me with so much force, I couldn't ignore it. I closed my eyes and calmed my breath, bringing up a vision in my head and letting the feeling from it rest within me. Finally, I heard multiple clunks echoing throughout the room. When they stopped, I opened my eyes.

Smiling at my accomplishment, I looked around at the masterpiece I'd created with my mind. It was poetic and perfect. Attached to each bare wall between the alcoves were a set of shackles placed exactly the way they were when they held me— two at the top, and two at the bottom. I pictured several demons stuck in them around the room and giggled at the thought. Not believing I'd have the ability to shackle a bunch of demons to the walls, it was more for my own revengeful enjoyment, but I relished the sight in my head just the same. The most important factor related to my self-confidence. I'd again proven the accomplishment of such a power.

There I stood, basking in my selfish glory, when *surprise, surprise,* several demons filed into the room from another door. They stood, beautiful, but deadly, staring at me as I watched them with a deer in headlights shock on my face. Some of them checked around the room as confusion appeared on their faces when they spotted the shackles along the walls. By the time their gazes returned to me, it was with narrowed, glowing eyes.

"Hey, boys. How's it hangin'?"

Absolutely certain the demons would charge at me any second, I was about to make a run for the door when a crowd of them parted and Caleb walked in ahead of them. His demeanor was calm and cool. While he stood gawking back at me with a warm, almost welcoming smile, I hadn't missed the surprise that had flushed over his features at first.

I'd caught him off guard. *Good.* It meant his predictions of me might not be so set in stone. Knowing that was worth any punishment he could dish out.

"Cassie," he said, still smiling, "how very nice to see you back on your feet. You're a breath of fresh air, as usual."

He turned around, motioned to the demons behind him, and said, "Leave us."

I tensed under the steady examination of Caleb's gaze as each of them backed out of the room. Finally, once they were all gone, he broke his stare and analyzed the room. "I see you decided to redecorate," he said. "While I rather enjoy the very macabre nature of it all, it just won't do in here."

As if on cue, the shackles on the walls all disappeared at once. He'd gotten rid of them without blinking an eye, making me envious of the ease with which he accomplished it.

"It'll scare away any guests," he continued, "and we can't have that. However, we do have several rooms here we could experiment with if that is your desire."

He stepped toward me, and I watched him in earnest, trying to determine his intent, but he was as difficult to read as Hunter. My flight instinct was in overdrive, but I knew it was pointless to try and would probably only make the situation worse. I decided my best course of action with Caleb was to engage in his game, only play it better.

"Please, have a seat," he said when he reached my location. "Just, not there."

I'd been clutching the arm of the throne-like chair next to me. I let go as if it burned my hand, and he pulled out the first chair on the right side of the table and waited.

It took me a moment, but eventually I relented and shifted position to sit in it.

"Are you hungry? I could order anything you want."

"I'm good."

He'd taken a seat on the throne and set his forearms on the table, clasping his hands together as he studied me.

"Yes, you are, Cassie. Even better than I thought you were. You continue to surprise me, but I'm very pleased with your progress."

I snapped my head up, shocked by his appraisal. He was pleased? If anything, I would have thought he'd be threatened or mad.

"Why aren't you scared?" The words were out of my mouth before I could think to bite my tongue.

He chuckled. The sound bristled the nerves under my skin.

"I'm not scared, Cassie, because the quicker you gain your powers, your true potential, the faster we can go forward with my plan."

"We?"

"Yes, we."

"You're not afraid I'll use my powers against you?"

He smiled back at me. It was similar to one used to placate a young person who was confused and afraid. I was no child but had to admit the gleam in his eye over me gaining my powers definitely left me confused and afraid.

"Not at all," he said. He reached over and grasped my upper arm before sliding his hand down, causing my skin to shiver from the path of his touch. He reached my fingers, entangled them with his, and rested it on the table between us. "Tell me, Cassie, how did you figure out how to get out of the shackles?"

I'd been staring at our hands held together and slowly turned my eyes up to meet his.

"I just did it."

"No," he said, squeezing my hand, "you didn't. Come now, let's not spoil this momentous time with lies. How, Cassie?"

His eyes bored into mine, and I knew I could do nothing more than tell the truth.

"I heard a voice." *Christ,* just hearing myself say it made me think I should be strapped with a white jacket and led to a padded room.

Caleb nodded. He knew about the voice, which meant he knew who or where it came from. It also indicated the voice was not my friend.

"Who is it, Caleb?"

He studied me a moment. I thought he might actually start talking, but then he shook his head, he said, "Not yet. Too soon."

"For what? Dammit. Tell me what the hell is going on. I'm stuck in the middle of nowhere here. You've got me, okay. I've got no way out, so, just fucking tell me."

"No," he said, his blunt tone left no room for a change of heart. "I may have you physically, but your soul is still not where I want it to be, where I need it to be. When it is, I'll tell you everything you want to know."

I was so frustrated, I wanted to spit. No, I wanted to kill. Being sick to death of the mysteries and secrets ruling my life had me at the end of my rope. Just once, I'd like to know what everyone else knew. Instead, I was always in the dark, having to go through tests and trials to find out what was behind the next curtain. Someday soon, maybe the fates would lay it all out for me so I knew what the hell I was doing or what was expected of me. Maybe then I could make my own damn choices.

"Ahhh," Caleb crooned, breaking me from my thoughts, "but life would be so boring then wouldn't it?"

"Get out of my head. At least let me have that."

"No can do, sweetheart. You're as addicting on the inside as you are on the outside. I can't wait until you start fantasizing about us."

"Dream on."

"Oh, I do, but my dreams are already coming true, and I don't see that changing anytime soon. Yours will too, you'll see. For now, let's get you fed. You still have those annoying human qualities that require you to nourish your body. I can't have you passing out on our tour."

Great. He still wanted to give me the grand tour of my new prison. I wanted to argue I couldn't care less about seeing his new pad, to be belligerent, but I'd planned on checking the place out anyway so I went along with his hospitality and saved myself from a fight which would probably only amount in draining my own energy.

Without Caleb even beckoning them, several women entered with platters of breakfast foods. None of them spoke, and they all kept their heads down throughout the entire process. How typical of him to have women slaving over him. Granted, they were demons, but they were still slaves. It touched a nerve with me.

I thanked each one of them as they set the food in front of me. The feast included every breakfast food a mortal could conjure up, and while I didn't want to grant Caleb the pleasure of knowing he was right, I was famished, so I dug in. The food was delicious and seemed to even out my adrenaline to a nice, calm flow. I was no longer anxious and on edge, and as stupid and petty as it was, I was almost thankful to have that quality of nourishment to fulfill the soul. It kept me human in the far-from-human world I occupied now.

Caleb sat back in his throne, hands clasped together over his stomach, a content smile on his face. He came across as proud, not proud in an *I told you so* sense, more like he felt he was doing a good job and seeing me eat was his reward. I didn't get it. Maybe in his twisted mind, this was the portrait of a happy couple.

When I finished, I sat back in my chair and turned to Caleb with a *what's next?* expression plastered on my face.

"Did you get enough?" he asked.

"Yes." He wouldn't get a thank you out of me. Prisoners didn't thank their jailers for the essentials of life.

"Good," he said, standing and holding out his hand. "Then let's go. There's much for you to see. I really think you're going to love it."

"It sounds like you're trying to sell this place to me. If I don't like it, will you let me go?"

"You've become such a witty one, Cassie. I like it."

He led me to the door where I'd been headed before the demons showed up. His hand settled low on my back, urging me forward. I wanted to shake it off, skin burning beneath my shirt from the gesture, but I let go. Figuring it was better than being led by chains, or worse, I told myself I wasn't growing soft, only biding my time.

"So, that's a no?" I asked.

When we reached another door, he stepped in front of it, facing me.

"I'm hoping you won't want to, Cassie, and I have faith that soon you'll see things in a different light."

His gaze was so focused on mine, it made me extremely uncomfortable. He wasn't flaunting the cocky air he usually exhibited. It was as if he really *wanted* me to want to be there. Normally, he wouldn't give a damn about anything anyone else wanted. This new Caleb was throwing me off. Surely, that was his plan.

I started to argue, but he quickly put a finger to my lips.

"No, let me talk," he said, his voice low and level. He bit his bottom lip for a moment or two, as if pondering what to say next, or maybe how to say it, which was so unlike the old Caleb.

That Caleb never faltered with words. "You and I came from two different worlds, served two different masters, and because of that you still see us as enemies, but things are different now. *We* are different now. Don't you feel it?"

I did feel different, and somehow he knew that. What I really needed was answers and for him to tell me why and how he'd changed.

"Yes. I feel... a connection here."

A smile spread across his lips and he nodded.

"Thank you for telling me," he said.

"I've told you something. Now you tell me something, Caleb."

He narrowed his eyes, and at first I thought he was going to revert back to the cocky old Caleb and refuse, but then he nodded again and said, "Okay. I'll tell you everything after the tour."

"Why not now?"

"Because I need to show you things here that will help you understand. I'll tell you, Cassie. Trust me."

"Yeah, right. I don't feel *that* different. No way do I trust you." Whatever it was he thought would change me obviously hadn't taken root because trusting him was never going to happen. I knew that from the depths of my soul.

His jaw tightened as he glared back at me. After a moment or two of silence, he turned, opened the door, and with his hand at my lower back again, urged me, with some force, through it.

"I told you I'd tell you and I will," he said, his voice strained. "End of discussion. Let's get on with it."

I didn't argue anymore while walking with him through the hallway. Knowing the more I pushed, the more my chances of getting anything out of him dwindled, I backed off... for the moment.

We walked in silence, and I took in my surroundings. The hallway was spacious and bright, the light-colored stone walls and floor gave the area a pleasant ambiance. Compared to the dark, foreboding room from which I'd awakened here in the castle, the sight was spectacular. Ornate light fixtures on the ceiling and walls lit our way, the modernization contrasted with seemingly ancient architecture. Our footsteps on the stone beneath our feet echoed against the walls, creating the only sound around us. It reminded me that Caleb was being unusually quiet, which unnerved me.

"The lighting is a nice touch," I said, to break the silence.

"I'm a slave to modern conveniences," he said.

We came upon a wide stairwell to our left, but we didn't slow as he motioned that direction and said, "Those lead to the servants' quarters."

"Aren't they all your servants here?"

His only answer was a smile for a long moment. Then, he obliged my curiosity. "Yes, I guess they are, but these quarters are for the ones who maintain the castle. There are maids, gardeners, cooks, which by the way, I've hired for your convenience."

"Just for me?"

"You're the only one here in need of human inconveniences, Cassie."

I was really starting to hate that phrase. *Human inconveniences*. Every time he said it, I knew it was his way of feeling superior to me. It made me all the more determined to come into more of my powers if there were more. And if that proved correct, I'd show him just how *inconvenient* I could be.

"Once you're settled," he continued, "they will be at your beck and call. They've already been instructed to service their queen with the same courtesy they serve their king."

"Well, not exactly the same, right?" I asked, my eyebrows raised so he'd catch what I was hinting at. His smirk told me he hadn't missed it.

"If you're insinuating they provide me with sexual services, I assure you they do not. I'm saving myself for a particular redheaded hybrid," he said with a wink. "I have to admit, Cassie, seeing the green-eyed monster in you is a big turn-on. I'm not sure how much longer I'm going to be able to wait."

A sharp retort was on the tip of my tongue, but we'd just passed through the double-wide entrance and into a colossal foyer. My breath caught at the sight. The room was even more majestic than the one we'd come from. The color scheme was the same, all maroons, golds, and tans, but this area had a modern, more structurally savvy appearance, almost making it seem that we'd left a castle and entered a mansion.

Two huge staircases flanked us on the right and left, spiraling up and meeting in the middle at a landing on the second floor. Black filigreed iron railings lined the stairs and floor that circled up above us. A huge chandelier, similar to the one in the war room hung centered from a large, domed ceiling, displaying murals or images I couldn't quite make out. It reminded me of pictures I'd seen in college of the domed cathedrals in some historic churches in Italy, but I was sure these images were far from the saintly ones depicted in those.

Off to the far left was an open sitting room. Heavily cushioned sofas and chairs were scattered throughout the room, tables positioned conveniently amongst them to hold mood-lit lamps. A large, stone fireplace blazed on the far back wall of the room, and its heat seemed to radiate where I was standing at least fifty feet away. Not that I was surprised. The fires of hell burned way hotter than any mortal fire.

Behind the staircases on the north end of the foyer where we stood, the wall was floor-to-ceiling glass, with double doors at its center barely outlined to be noticeable from the rest of the wall. Beyond the glass, I saw an abundance of foliage, flowers, plants, and trees. Natural sunlight emitted throughout the room as far as I could see. It reminded me of the gardens at the Sanctuary.

"Is that a..."

"Greenhouse, horticultural conservatory, take your pick," Caleb answered the question I could barely get out.

"But those are... and you're..." I was still too much in shock to piece together a sentence.

"What?" Caleb chuckled. "Simply because I'm a demon, you think I can't appreciate natural beauty?"

"Well, yeah, I guess that's exactly what I thought."

"You underestimate me. I assure you, I have a soft side for many beautiful things."

Now I was downright uncomfortable. Dealing with a cocky, self-centered Caleb was much easier than a flowery, born-again, romantic Caleb.

"Let me guess, your favorite flower is the snapdragon," I said with full-on sarcasm. It was the only way I could think to right my world again.

"Clever. I'll show you sometime, but not today. There's much more to see. Come along." He grabbed my hand and led me to a staircase on our left.

As we began to ascend, I asked, "What's up here?"

"Our quarters."

My step faltered, causing him to pull back since he still had hold of my hand.

He looked at me, grinning. "Relax, Cassie, it's bigger than you think."

I gaped at his remark, its sexual overtone very clear.

Caleb chuckled. "There are other rooms besides the bedroom up there, but I like where your mind has gone."

I pulled at my hand, but he wasn't releasing.

He sighed and rolled his eyes. "I won't be ravishing you on this tour, Cassie, unless you want me to, so come along."

I studied him for a moment. He still sported a stupid grin, but I somehow knew he meant his words. Besides, Caleb wasn't the type to need a bed if he wanted to take me against my will.

Although, his ego might think getting me in a room with a bed would be seduction enough.

My slight nod must have signaled I was ready to resume and we started back up the staircase, my inner guard kicking up a notch with every step we took. Caleb allowed me ahead of him, probably to ensure I didn't turn tail and run.

Once we reached the landing, I stopped. The air was different. My body had become charged, energized, as though some magnetic surge was pulling at it from somewhere beyond the walls. The sensation was so powerful, it made me breathless, but at the same time, it seemed to renew me, fill me with life.

A circular hallway surrounded us, its color scheme much the same as the floor below, but with plush maroon carpeting softening each step. Three sets of mahogany double doors, evenly spaced, with dimly lit wall sconces in between them, seemed to give them an even richer appearance.

After taking in the surroundings, I finally noticed Caleb standing next to me, his eyes watching mine, studying me intently.

"Which way?" I asked, unable to stand the pressure of his gaze any longer.

"We'll start on this end," he said, motioning to the set of doors closest to us.

He took the lead, and I followed.

When we reached the entrance, Caleb stopped and opened them into the room. It was a massive, but comfortable looking study, its walls reaching far back and to my left, filled with floor-to-ceiling books. Plush furniture was set throughout the room, side tables interspersed between them, along with lamps atop. Another fireplace roared with life at the far end of the room in front of a set of sofa and chairs. The atmosphere was cozy and warm, inviting guests to sit and lose themselves in its peace and tranquility.

"I know how much you like to read," Caleb said as we continued farther into the room. How he knew that was beyond me, but I didn't bother to ask. "We have tons of books, as you can see, but if there's something in particular you want, let me know and I'll have it brought in."

Sitting back and enjoying a book was not on my agenda. Any delay in getting out of here wasn't on my radar.

Caleb cleared his throat, and I looked up. His lips were pursed, and the glare on his face indicated he'd read my thoughts.

I'd warned him to stay out of my head. If he didn't like what he saw there, that was on him.

"Nice room," I said with a smirk.

"Yes, it is, and eventually, you'll really believe that."

"Mmm hmm," I said to appease him.

"Okay, moving on then," he said and motioned me out of the room.

I stepped back into the hallway, and he joined me, closing the doors behind us. I hadn't noticed until then the energy I'd experienced earlier had dissipated when we had entered the study, but it hit me again as I returned to the hallway. With each step, it seemed to gain power over me, and I automatically quickened my footsteps toward the source of it.

"Cassie," Caleb's call penetrated my trance, and I realized he'd stopped back at the middle set of doors I'd inadvertently passed. I was already midway to the farthest set on the right side of the hallway. "Are you that eager to see our quarters?" he asked with a smug grin.

"No." I blurted, glancing back at the door I'd been heading toward. "That's our... your quarters?"

He sauntered over, cocky grin and all, and positioned himself directly in front of me. "Our quarters, yes." His voice was low, intimate. "Did you want to see it, Cassie?"

I wanted to slap his face, scream in it that his bedroom was the last place I'd be caught dead in, but *oh, my, god.* The pull toward that room resembled a delicious aroma of a meal coming from the oven drawing in a starving person. I couldn't shake the sensation. The closer I got to the room, the harder it became to fight. Whatever the force, it desperately wanted me to connect with it, as much as I urgently needed to find it.

"Ye—" I started, but frantic footsteps on the stairwell caught my attention and stopped me... cold.

Caleb and I both waited at the staircase landing when one of the demons rushed to the top.

"Master, I'm sorry to interrupt you, but he's here," he said without coming any closer.

"Is he alone?" Caleb asked him.

My heart rate picked up. Was it possible someone had found us? Could it be Hunter coming to save me? Hope flooded my mind at the thought.

"Excuse me for a moment, Cassie," Caleb said and approached close to the demon. "Did he bring it?" he asked the demon in a low whisper, obviously not wanting me to overhear their conversation.

That was when it hit me. They were talking about the Sword. Caleb hadn't been lying. Someone from the Sanctuary had betrayed the angels and brought him the Sword. Who was it?

The Sword. The last piece of ultimate power.

The words echoed around in my head, much the same as they had in the Sanctuary from the mere mention of it. My body heated as if a flame had ignited a furnace from within. Chills ran over my skin, and energy pulsed within me.

Caleb was standing in front of the demon so I couldn't see his face. I shifted to my left, wanting to see his answer, rather than chance not hearing it, but as I did, a familiar voice penetrated my thoughts.

Cassandra.

It was the same voice from the war room.

I snapped my head back, unsure if it had come from Caleb's quarters, but the door was still closed. I stared at it, unable to draw my gaze away as if I could see through the wooden doors and find the source of the voice within the room. Trance-like, I walked near it and put my hand on the knob.

The Sword, Cassandra. Find the Sword.

Find the Sword?

"Ahhh, see, Caleb said, causing me to jump. I hadn't realized he'd walked up behind me. "It's like we have the same brain."

Had I said the words aloud?

I turned my head toward him, my fingers still clutching the handle of the door. He was smiling back at me.

"Our guest has arrived, Cassie. Come." He gently took my hand from the door and held it in his. "Let's go see what they've done with our Sword."

I allowed him to lead me back down the stairs, oblivious to my surroundings now. My concentration was on one thing: the voice in my head repeating itself over and over again.

My Sword.

But it wasn't the voice from the room. This was my voice because it was my Sword.

CHAPTER SIXTEEN

I interrogated Caleb as we made our way back down to the war room, but he wasn't talking. All he kept saying was it was a surprise as if this whole scenario he had going was some special bestowal to me. I think the words *homecoming gift* may have even come out of his mouth.

Unsure how to feel about it, half of me was hopeful, knowing there was an angel here, someone from the good side who should want to help me escape from the hands of evil that bound me here. But the rational side of me bashed that theory to pieces when I thought of how they'd allegedly come to be here. Someone had stolen the Sword for a chance at greater power. The chance to rule with Caleb. I had to remind myself that angels weren't always good. Hadraniel was living, slimy proof of that.

All demons weren't evil, either.

Thinking about that made me want to take back all the nasty things I'd said to Hunter in the past few months. Everything he'd done was for me, to keep me safe, to protect me from all of this evil. He might be a demon, but he was more righteous and good than any angel I'd met.

A blast of pain shot through my head and caused me to double over on the spot.

"Cassie?" I heard Caleb say over me.

His hand stroked my back, and I twisted as much as I could to try and fling it off.

"Don't touch me." I slowly stood and stepped back. Glaring at him, I said, "I told you to stay the hell out of my head."

His brows furrowed as he narrowed his eyes at me. "I wasn't in your head, Cassie."

"Bullshit. You just sliced my brain in half, you asshole. Don't lie about it now. If you want me as your queen, that is *so* not the way to go about it."

"What did you think before it happened?" he asked.

"Like you don't know."

"I don't. I swear to you, whatever just happened, I had nothing to do with it."

"I'm not an idiot, Caleb. It was the same thing you did to me when you had me shackled to the bed."

He studied me for a moment before the corner of his mouth lifted.

Smug asshole.

"I'm not the only one with those powers here," he said in a low voice, "but you already know that."

My face contorted with confusion, but deep down I knew who he meant, or at least what he meant. He was referring to the voice. I was starting to get a really bad feeling about who, or what that voice belonged to.

"Come," he said. "Let's go get the Sword, and I'll explain everything. I think you'll be ready to hear it then."

Oh, I was ready to hear it the second I woke up in that room, heard that voice, and thought my last reality check had checked out, but the mention of the Sword changed my gears again. Finding it was everything right now. I didn't know why, but it was a fact.

I didn't bother agreeing with him, but we walked in the direction we'd been going before my brain was zapped. Caleb caught up to me as I stood in front of the war room door.

"You're going to make a fine queen, Cassie," he said with a smile on his face as he opened the door.

I rolled my eyes at the comment, but he didn't see it since he'd already entered the room.

A small group of demons was milling around inside, some standing near the long table. Whatever discussion they'd been having stopped short when they noticed Caleb and I coming toward them. Each of them bowed their heads once and watched us until we made our way over there. Christ, they really did treat Caleb like a king. I wondered how many he'd managed to convince of that. With enough of them serving him, he just might have the power to overtake the angels, with or without the Sword. It was a scary thought.

"Did you put him where I told you to?" Caleb asked them.

"Yes, Sir," one of them answered.

"Has he told you where he has the Sword yet?"

"No, Sir," the same one answered. "He says he has it but won't tell anyone except you where it is and only after you give him what you promised."

Caleb made a *tsk tsk* sound as he shook his head. "Very well," he sighed. "I guess we have to do this the hard way. You three, guard the second floor while we're gone. No one goes up those stairs. Have the others ready in case he's managed to pull one over on us, although, I don't think he's bright enough for that. You may go."

"Yes, Sir." all three of them said in unison, before bowing again and turning to leave.

One of them looked my way as he passed, his glowing blue gaze meeting mine.

They'd almost reached the door we'd come from when Caleb called out, "Seran, a word before you go."

The one who'd caught my eye turned back to face us, and I caught a flash of fear streak through those blue orbs.

"Yes, Sir," he said as he made his way back to us. His trepidation was obvious even though he walked with a steady stride.

"Look at me, Seran," Caleb ordered when the demon was standing in front of him, his eyes on the floor.

The guard did as he was told.

"You'd be wise not to look upon my queen again unless you have my permission. Is that understood?"

"Yes, Sir."

Caleb motioned his head toward the others. "You may go."

Seran turned and walked away, his pace faster now.

I'd been too shocked to say anything up to that point. Apparently, I'd walked into another era where women were considered prized possessions and men were blinded for stealing a simple sidelong glance at them. I was no possession, and I sure as hell wasn't Caleb's.

"That was a bit harsh, don't you think?" I said.

"On the contrary, he got off lucky, but let's not dwell on trivial matters. Are you ready?"

"Ready for what?"

Caleb put his arms around my waist and pulled me in close. His mouth was at my ear and he whispered, "To take over the world, my queen."

He placed a kiss on my cheek, and then my world went black.

***

It was difficult to describe what it felt like to transport. At first, there was nothing for an undetermined amount of time because time didn't exist, but I still had a presence. No world around. Peaceful in the nothingness, but without time to savor it because everything changed in the blink of an eye as I became full bodied and *me* again. Realization hit and I was somewhere, and the world was there, happening, moving, being. Although my mind was trying to catch up with my body, without the peace, reality was there too.

And most of the time for me, *reality sucks*.

We'd transported back to the same room I'd awakened in when Hadraniel had brought me to Caleb. Caleb still had me in his arms, and I pulled away once I became more in control of my body. Looking around the dimly lit room, I noticed the bed was still there, shackle-less and empty. I was about to ask what we were doing back there, almost afraid I would somehow end up back on that bed and helpless, when I heard my name called from the corner of the room behind Caleb.

The voice was familiar, so very familiar, but hearing it there, in this place, changed it. Or maybe I simply wanted it to change. I didn't want to hear that person in this situation, this location. What else could it mean but not only had the trust of the angels been betrayed but my own?

As I stepped aside to see around Caleb, he turned and granted me full view. All I wanted at that moment was to un-see what was in front of me.

"I believe you two know each other already, so introductions won't be necessary," Caleb said, a smile in his voice, so very proud of his latest spin on my world.

"Braydon?" was all I could manage, too shocked to say anything else.

The room had acquired some new additions since I'd been there. A steel cage, about eight feet high and four feet wide, occupied the corner. It was bare, crass, basically an adult-sized crate meant for one purpose. Seeing Braydon in there looking back at me with relief and hope in his eyes reminded me of animals in pet shops longing for a loving family to take them home. My heart hurt to see him caged that way. At least he wasn't chained or shackled, not that there was much room in there to move around.

But my heart was confused. Braydon was here because he had made a deal with the devil, going against everything he represented... and deceiving us all. I was starting to think no good existed in this universe. And if that were the case, how would I ever fight off the darkness inside of me?

"Cassie, are you all right?" he asked, his hands gripping the bars of the cage as he peered out at me.

"What the hell are you doing, Braydon?" I cried as I approached the cage.

When I was within a few feet, Caleb warned me off. "That's close enough."

"I came to get you out."

A surge of relief flooded through my veins. I had it all wrong. He wasn't here to help Caleb. He wasn't betraying us. He was here to save me. This was obviously some elaborate plan to weed out Caleb once and for all. So, why hadn't I been told? Why, if I was supposed to play such a big role in all of this, wasn't I in the loop? And what now? Braydon didn't seem capable of doing much of anything standing in that cage like a prison inmate.

"That won't be happening," Caleb said. I didn't know if he'd read my thoughts or if he was merely addressing Braydon's statement. "You see, Cassie, your admirer, Braydon here, made me a deal. I'd give him you, and he'd give me the Sword. But as I understand it, he's not holding up his end of the bargain. I'm wondering now if he even had the balls to bring it."

"I have it," Braydon said. "I just don't trust you. I'll take you to it, but Cassie comes with and then we leave. No army. Just us three."

"Do you think I'm a fool? I've not gotten this far, this powerful, by being so naive as to walk into some trap set by a worthless angel. No. You will give me the location of the Sword if you really did accomplish stealing it, and I'll send some of my men to retrieve it. Then, and only then, will I let you go."

"No way," Braydon said, shaking his head. "I'm no fool either."

"Then you'll sit," Caleb said with a shrug of his shoulders as if he couldn't care one way or another. "Come along, Cassie." He put his arm around my waist, reaching to turn me to him. "We'll continue with that tour. I have so much more to show you."

"Wait," I said pulling away from him. I was not going to let my chance at freedom slip away. Not without a fight. "What are you afraid of, Caleb? A bunch of angels lurking in the shadows? You mean to tell me with all those fancy new powers you wouldn't be able to pick up on them the minute they poofed into the location? I thought you were almighty and invincible?"

"Two things," Caleb said. "One: I am. Two: Be careful what you're fighting for, Cassie. You're under the illusion he's come to be your hero."

When I started to argue, he cut me off.

"Don't try and deny it, I heard your thoughts moments ago. What you don't know, and what I have great pleasure in telling you, is that loverboy is here for his own selfish purposes. He won't be setting you free, silly girl. He's hoping to move you from my little corner of nowhere to his."

"What the hell are you talking about?" I asked. I glanced over at Braydon, and he quickly turned away. That wasn't a good sign. The back of my neck tensed and my skin prickled.

"He wants to run away with you, Cassie. Somewhere where no one will ever find you two. You know, like our place here. I told him I'd help him find a nice, comfy, remote home for the both of you to live happily ever after. That was the deal. I get the Sword, and he gets you... for himself."

My jaw hung open of its own accord, unable to believe what I was hearing. Braydon wouldn't do that. Yeah, he had a thing for me, that was no secret, but what Caleb was talking about was some stalker type shit. He wasn't that far gone.

I narrowed my eyes at Caleb. "You're lying."

I didn't want to look at Braydon. I couldn't because I was too afraid of what I might see in his eyes; too afraid Caleb might be telling the truth... for once.

"Nope," Caleb said nonchalantly. "I have no reason to lie about it. Isn't his silence proof enough? Ask him yourself, if you want. He can't lie. He'll never get out of that cage otherwise."

I turned to Braydon, and the way he slowly, almost timidly met my gaze was answer enough, but I demanded to know anyway. "Braydon, tell me that's not true. Tell me you weren't planning to keep me captive somewhere else like this demented animal."

"Hey, now," Caleb chuckled.

"Cassie, it's not like that," Braydon pleaded. "You wouldn't be my captive. We were meant to be together, away from all the things and people holding us back from expressing our love for each other. You'd be happy. I'd *make* you happy."

Oh, fucking hell. What was it with me and obsessed, psychotic men? Did I give off some kind of scent? Was there a huge sign somewhere above my head telling the world I took in stray psychos? Seriously. I was done. *Done.* These crazy cats needed to find another scratching post.

I couldn't help but look at Braydon with disgust. He was as bad as Caleb. Maybe he didn't want to conquer the universe, but he was just as dirty, using people, lying, stealing, all for his own selfish desires. It seemed greed was a sin that crossed all walks of life, good and evil. No prejudice there. Straight across the board. Anyone was fair game. Once it latched on, it ate away at your soul until you were left an empty shell trying desperately to fill a void, creating a vicious circle of insatiability.

"You really stole the Sword from the angels so you could be with me?" I asked.

"Yes," he said on a throaty breath.

I wanted to yell at him... scream. What a fool. But one thing held my angry words back. The Sword. He had it somewhere, and I wanted it. No, I *needed* it. My fingers twitched to feel the cold metal beneath them. The compulsion to hold it in my hands was so strong it was as if I'd become an addict in need of a fix. It ran through my blood constantly searching for that high.

Where the hell was it coming from? What had changed me so drastically that whenever it was close, I suddenly couldn't live without it? Nothing else mattered but owning that Sword.

"I need to think," I said and turned to walk away from the cage. Caleb's and Braydon's eyes focused on my back. Their concentration on me was tangible, but since the room had only one door, I made my way toward it.

"Sit tight, little bird," I heard Caleb say to Braydon.

The door clicked open when I reached it, and I continued walking and listening as Caleb followed behind me. Once we were out of the room and the door closed behind us, Caleb grabbed my arm to try and stop me, but I yanked it away from him and kept going. I had no idea where I was or where I was headed, I just needed to walk and think. Because of that, I barely noticed we'd entered a torch-lit hallway made of stone. The place was eerily familiar, reminding me of the corridors in Nergal's hell, but even that thought didn't penetrate my obsession with the Sword and new situation... new *opportunity*.

"You want it as bad as I do," Caleb said when his palm rested on my left shoulder. I stopped, and he remained where he was. His touch still burned through the material of my T-shirt, but I didn't pull away, I merely eyed him over my shoulder.

"That's good, Cassie. That's very, very good," he said with a slow, confirming nod.

I turned and faced him, looking him directly in the eyes. "Tell me why." I wouldn't deny it anymore. I just needed to know.

"Okay, my queen."

He pulled me into him, and I succumbed to the expected nothingness.

CHAPTER SEVENTEEN

Caleb and I materialized in the library he'd shown me earlier. We were standing in front of the sofa. The door was closed, and the only sound was a crackling fire still burning in the hearth.

"Have a seat, I'll get us something to drink," Caleb said as he walked over to a small wet bar to the side of the fireplace.

"I'm good," I told him, but that didn't stop him from pouring a brownish liquid into two tumblers.

"Believe me, Cassie, you're going to want this."

"Forgive me if I don't feel all that comfortable accepting a drink from you. It always seems to come with some kind of ulterior motive... or side effects."

"I promise you, this one is only to calm your nerves. Here," he said, handing the glass to me.

I took it but eyed him suspiciously. He made an X with his finger over his chest.

"If you had a heart, I might actually believe you," I said.

He laughed. "C'mon, let's sit."

I took a seat at the corner of the sofa.

Caleb sat next to me, but not close enough to make me feel intimidated. He angled his body toward me and took a sip of his drink, gazing at me through the glass. I looked back at him expectantly.

He lowered his glass, and said, "Nergal lives."

If the words had physical weight, they might have crushed me. "What?"

"He does. He lives inside of us. Both of us."

"What the hell are you talking about, Caleb? Are you talking metaphorically here, or literally?"

"Literally."

"I don't understand. How is that possible? He's dead. I was told only his essence can live on and that's only if someone uses the Sword on his dead body. That Sword has been in the hands of the angels since we killed him. Hell, that's what all this is about, isn't it? You wanting the Sword so you can embody his essence and have his ultimate power? How can he be living inside of us if neither of us has gotten the Sword anywhere near his dead body?"

Caleb smiled and took another sip of his drink. "The angels don't know as much as they think they do," he said when he was finished.

My heart rate had accelerated from the first two words of the conversation, but now it was erratic. All along, I'd believed I was prepared for the final showdown because I'd pictured it in my mind so many times. I'd already lived it one hundred times over. I was ready for deviations but wasn't naive enough to think dealing with Caleb would call for anything less. Now, I wasn't so sure. A prickly feeling deep inside was telling me I was nowhere near ready for this.

"Tell me," I said.

"You and I are the chosen ones."

"The chosen ones," I repeated, sarcasm dripping from each word.

"Yes. Nergal gave each of us some of his essence before he died. He knew he was going to be killed. He prepared for it. It's amazing, Cassie. He already lives within us. He chose us. We are the ones who will carry out his ultimate plan of domination over the universe. You and I, together."

As Caleb spoke, a fire deep in my gut grew and lapped at my insides as if his words were its accelerant. The more I heard, the more it expanded, until I was burning from the inside out. Sweat started to form above my lips and on my forehead. Had the fire in the hearth gotten hotter?

"How?"

Caleb gently put his hand on the one I was using to hold my drink and lifted it up to my mouth. "Drink, Cassie."

I did as he said, not because he told me to, but because I thought it might douse the flames. Unfortunately, the burning liquid only added to them. I choked and then asked again, "How?"

"Honestly, I don't know the exact answer to that. I guess he did it at some point down in Hell. I don't know how, but I know he's there."

Flashbacks of the time Nergal held me prisoner in Hell inundated my brain. For months I'd been tortured, half the time unaware of where I was or what was happening. I had no idea how long I'd been down there until Hunter came to my rescue. And afterward, I was too afraid to remember. My entire personality had changed, full of rage and hate, but I told myself it was from feeling so utterly victimized and helpless. I completely ignored the little hunch that was warning me it was something else.

Caleb spoke, bringing me back from my thoughts. "I feel him inside of me. I hear him talk to me, lead me. He told me to bring you here, Cassie. And now that you are, he's doing the same to you. I can tell."

I wasn't going to deny it. He was right. The voices, the feelings. Somehow I knew all along it was Nergal, but I just didn't want to believe it. He was dead. We'd killed him. I didn't want to think he was still connected to me. But somehow I knew. And now I needed to know all of it. As much as it scared the living hell out of me, I had to find out what I was up against, or more importantly, what I was becoming.

"Why here? Why now?"

"Because the rest of his essence is here, in our home. The closer we are to it, the more powerful he is within us. I knew it the moment I had his body brought to me."

I thought about the room down the hall and how something from within seemed to be drawing me in there. I knew then, without a doubt, that's where Caleb was keeping Nergal's body. It was all starting to come together, like one big, fucked up puzzle.

"This is all so unbelievable." My words came out in one exhale.

Caleb set his drink down on a table next to the sofa, then grabbed mine out of my hand and did the same with it. When he was done, he grabbed both my hands and held them in his. Ducking his head to capture my eyes and lock me into his gaze, he whispered, "But it's real, and I think you know that."

I clenched my teeth together, not wanting to say the words. Saying it, agreeing with him, that would make it too real.

"Your not saying the words, won't make it any less real, Cassie," he said, reading my mind. "It's time to face our reality and follow our destiny." He lifted one of my hands to his lips, and I merely watched as he kissed my knuckles. "We'll do it together, as Nergal intended."

I snatched my hands away and glared at him. He rolled his eyes as if my obstinacy was getting tiresome.

"What I don't understand is why Nergal would choose us. It makes no sense. I hated him. My blood is mixed with that of the angels. Hell, I'm the one who helped kill him. And *you*. You conspired with me to kill him and take over as king. Why in the hell would he choose us to carry out his plans?"

"He chose us because we're the only ones strong enough and resolute to succeed. Think about it. It makes perfect sense he'd choose me. He knew this was what I wanted all along, to rule over the entire universe, to have power over all. No one has more determination to have that than me. And you, my queen? You are an enigma, Cassie, a perfect weapon. With the power of both worlds, the angels would never know what hit them."

So, there it was. The cards were all out on the table. I knew exactly why I was there and why I'd been feeling the way I had ever since I regained consciousness from Hell. All the dreams, visions, and thoughts made sense now. I was a pawn. Again... no, still. That's what I'd been all along, since the day I was born. My fate would forever be intertwined with the mix of my blood. I was DNA. I was some*thing* instead of some*one*.

I didn't want to be someone's thing. I was powerful, more powerful than I thought, *and* more powerful than the people who wanted to use me. So, why wasn't I using that power? Why wasn't *I* the one in control?

It seemed the only obstacle in my way was me.

"Show me the body," I said. My blues glowed in their sockets as I directed them at Caleb.

When he caught a glimpse, surprise widened in his eyes for only a split second. "Why do you want to see it?"

I had a feeling he already knew and merely wanted to hear me say it, and I had no problem accommodating him this time.

"Easy. I want to find out how much power this bitch can give me."

A slow smile turned up his lips. "That's my girl," he said as he stood and held his hand out to me.

Ignoring the offer for help, I stood on my own and started toward the door.

That's exactly how I planned to keep things from here on out. On my own.

***

The power radiating from the room didn't surprise me this time. It seemed to permeate my skin and take hold of my body. I let it, whether it was an option or not. I wanted it. I *needed* it. What I would do with it, I had no clue, but that didn't matter yet.

Nothing mattered, but the power I knew was mine behind that door.

Caleb stayed a few steps behind, which surprised me. He wasn't one to let a girl lead the way. Maybe he was testing me, watching how far I'd take this, seeing if my thirst for power was as strong as I was letting on. It was. The time for false pretenses had passed.

Maybe he didn't trust me at his back.

I put my hand on the door handle and turned it, but it didn't budge.

Caleb smiled and winked.

"That's just for show," he said, and when I lost my grip on the handle, the door opened inward on its own with a quiet click.

I sighed and shook my head before entering the room, wondering if I'd ever get used to those damn mind locks.

"Wow, nice digs," I said once I was fully inside the room. It was so modern, one would think we'd just stepped into the penthouse of a newly constructed five-star hotel. We stood in a large living room with white, plush carpet and black and leather furniture. The tables and fireplace were black, highly polished and pristine with not a speck of dust on them... as far as I could see. A few statues were featured throughout the room, each about four feet tall with a stone finish. Each of them was about four feet tall stone angels in various poses, which I thought odd at first since this was Caleb's quarters. When I realized all of them were either bowing or praying, or both, it made sense. In the context of the rooms, they appeared to be pleading.

"They remind me every day of what I have to look forward to," Caleb said, confirming my thoughts, "as do the paintings."

I looked around at the paintings on some of the stark, white walls. They were all scenes of an apocalyptic war set on earth, fire in the skies, with people and white angel wings lying lifeless and scattered amongst ashes on the destroyed land.

"As if you need a reminder," I said.

"True. It's a vivid picture I carry around right here," he said, tapping his temple.

A staircase at the back of the room, with black, filigreed, wrought iron rails, wound up to a second floor. I could only make out the carpeted landing up there before it went off to the right.

"The master's chambers," Caleb said, following my gaze. "Want to go check it out?" he asked with a waggle of his eyebrows and a sinful smirk.

"I'll pass for now," I told him.

"Mmmm... for now."

He obviously missed my sarcasm, or simply ignored it, which was probably more the case.

I quickly changed the subject. "What's with that area?" I asked, motioning toward the open kitchenette off to my right. It was as pristine as the rest of the place, black marble countertops, stainless steel appliances, white stone flooring. "You haven't started eating human food now, have you?"

"Oh, hell, no. That's merely for entertaining guests."

"Guests?"

"Well, Cassie, what did you expect me to do? You've taken your time coming to your senses. A man has needs, you know. I admit, I brought a few of the ladies back to fulfill my own, but now you're here, that won't be necessary. I vow complete fidelity to my queen, so you needn't worry."

I stared at him, unsure of which was more surprising, that he'd found the need to admit he'd had a couple, or probably several, trysts, or that he thought I'd care.

"Human guests?" I asked, unable to think of any other response.

He pursed his lips to the side as if contemplating how to answer me. "Well, they were human at some point."

I squeezed my eyes shut and held up my hand to stop him from saying anything more. I'd had enough and was going into

Caleb-information-overload. In addition to the power pulsing within me, I thought I might explode any second. "I... it's... just show me the body... er... Nergal's body, I mean."

"Someday, Cassie, you're going to know all of me," he said, stepping closer and putting his hand on my back. "Every. Single. Inch."

I cringed. No amount of power radiating inside me could block that mental picture.

"This way," he said with a forward wave of his hand.

We walked toward the back of the room, to the right of the staircase, and headed down a hallway. I noticed a bathroom to the right, and then a large, steel door at the end.

"I'm surprised, Caleb."

"Surprised?"

"Yes. That you'd keep him so far away from you." He didn't need to tell me the body was in that room, the intense power radiated through the door. "I mean, what if you're upstairs *entertaining guests* and someone were to slip in down here and try and steal it."

"*No one* is allowed in my quarters," he said in a low, ominous voice. "Only two others ever step foot on this floor and that is just to guard it. They all know if they are caught anywhere near here, it would be a very painful eternity for them." His face softened, and he went from sinister to sweet in the blink of an eye. "I'm not worried. Nor should you be."

"I'm always worried," I said. "It's hard not to be when every person I've ever known has lied to me or used me. The only thing I don't worry about is trusting anyone ever again... because I'll never let that happen."

"A relationship cannot survive without trust, Cassie. You're going to have to learn to get over that with me or this will never work out."

I wanted to laugh at his delusions of us having some typical relationship as if we were a couple contemplating marriage, kids, and a white picket fence. I held back, however, because the look on his face told me he was quite serious.

"Fine," I said. "Let's start with you showing me that body then."

"What, right here?" he asked with a devious smirk and a twinkle in his eyes. "If you insist." He crossed his arms over his chest, lifting the hem of his T-shirt.

I grabbed his wrist and held it against him so he could go no farther. "You know what I meant."

The shit ass grin on his face made me want to punch him. Instead, I turned and pulled the wrist I held toward the electronic pad attached to the wall next to the door. I'd almost gotten his hand on it when he snatched it out of my grasp.

"Let's get one thing straight before we proceed," he said. "I'm still in control here. You're only here because I *brought* you. You will not force my hand... at anything, Cassie. Do we understand each other?"

Our gazes locked, a battle of wills playing out with our eyes. The urge to see how much power I really had at that moment was overwhelming. More power surged through my veins than ever before, but I didn't know if it was enough. Caleb was so strong, possibly as strong as Nergal had been. Not to mention, I had no clue how to use any newfound powers. I couldn't chance the little amount of freedom I'd already been given. I was too far in to turn back now.

I decided to use his own words against him instead. "Trust, remember?"

He studied me for a moment before his features softened. "Touché," he said with a laugh.

"All right, then." He raised his hand to the electronic device and blue neon glowed underneath his palm. "Let's go see sleeping beauty, shall we?"

The electronic lock beeped and the door in front of us clicked, but did not open.

I peered up at Caleb in question and noticed his eyes were closed, so I waited. After holding back from rushing the door for what seemed like forever, it slowly swung in.

Immediately, crisp, chilled air hit my burning skin, raising goose bumps on my arms. I crossed and rubbed my hands up and down over them to try and ward off the chill. At that point, I wondered if it wasn't so much the cool air but my sudden nerves about what I was going to encounter in the room.

"After you," Caleb announced, leaning against the doorframe. His arm stretched over the width of the open steel door.

The room was bright. Everything in the room was white— white walls, white ceiling, white furniture, although sparse, with only cabinetry along the walls. The whole setting was reminiscent of a stark, clean hospital. Well, except for the giant glass sarcophagus-looking object propped up on a huge, wide pedestal that rose up from the floor in the middle of the room. From only a few feet inside the door, I was too far away from it to see what was inside. But I knew. Even if Caleb hadn't told me the body was here, I would have known. Nergal's presence radiated everywhere in the room as if he were standing alive in front of me. It tugged at my soul like a negative and positive charge too close together. The connection was imminent. I was no longer chilled. I was energized and needed contact.

Everything in the room faded away except the glass tomb. Stillness. The only sound seemed to be the pulsing rhythm from within me, a steady droning thump, like a heartbeat in my eardrums. I stepped without falter, or hesitation, toward the body of the beast that once gave me sleepless nights filled with nightmares. When I reached the side of it and peered inside, my breath caught at the sight of the body that lay prone within. It was Nergal, looking like the last I'd seen him, lying still, eyes shut, appearing as if he were in a peaceful sleep.

It seemed a natural instinct, setting my hand on the glass and closing my eyes. The pulsing drone quieted, and I was weightless. My soul had shed my body and was floating in this space, existing on its own. The experience was incredible, making me feel... invincible.

Cassandra. I've waited long for you to come, said that all too familiar voice.

I'm here now, my mind responded.

I brought you here. I chose you. You have power within you, but with me, you'll have more than you can possibly imagine. More than any other being in this universe. More than enough to fulfill our destiny.

Our destiny, I mentally repeated. The words fit. Right, and a surge of longing, determination, and power emerged when hearing them.

The power is yours, Cassandra. You alone will rule.

But Caleb... I thought.

Caleb is a mere tool. I used him to bring you to me. His power fades in comparison to yours, to what you will have. But you must retrieve the Sword to complete your transformation. Only with the Sword will you retain the ultimate power I have to give you. Find the Sword, Cassandra. Find it and take your destiny.

And Caleb? I asked the voice.

Once you have the Sword, kill him.

His words gave me extreme pleasure. I could practically feel the blade of the Sword entering Caleb's flesh and taking his essence, and I would smile down on him as the glow of his eyes faded to black.

The Sword will be mine, I assured him, or maybe it was me I was reassuring.

Good. Now go before another finds it.

Inch by inch, the weight of my body lifted as my head began to take in my surroundings again. The room returned to focus, and the pulsing throb faded to nothing. I sensed Caleb behind me, behind my left shoulder, but he was silent. For a moment, I panicked, wondering if he might have heard us. Somehow, I knew my conversation with Nergal had been private, so I brushed the thought away.

I withdrew my hand from the glass and stared at Nergal's body for a moment longer, not wanting to turn around and face Caleb yet.

Much too soon, Caleb leaned in and wrapped an arm around my waist. "He spoke to you?" he whispered.

"Yes," I answered.

"What did he say?"

I paused for a moment, wanting to choose my words carefully. "He showed me our destiny." I knew Caleb would think I meant his and mine, together.

"You know how long I've waited so long to hear you say that?"

"I only needed to be shown the way."

I sensed him nodding behind me, his head lightly brushing against the side of mine. Then he leaned down and placed a kiss on my temple. I let him.

Nergal had used him as a tool. Now, he'd be *my* tool.

CHAPTER EIGHTEEN

Caleb and I ended up back in the library. Who led whom, I couldn't remember. We both knew where we were going and what needed to be done. Only I knew our goals were completely different. Or so I hoped.

The room had become warmer than before. I looked at the fire still burning in the hearth. *Was it bigger, hotter, or was it the anticipatory state I seemed to be in?*

Caleb handed me a drink, and I took it without hesitation. I gulped the fiery liquid, the burn down my throat and belly almost imperceptible, seemingly matching my body's temperature. It did nothing to dull my senses as the others had, but I didn't expect it to, didn't *want* it to. I had a mission now and nothing would cloud my vision toward it.

"You need to let me go with Braydon to get the Sword," I said bluntly. I couldn't risk Caleb reading any thoughts of my deception. The less time I spent talking with him, the better. This had to happen fast.

His eyebrows shot up. "Look at you," he said with a stupid grin. "So eager now." He was standing at the side of the fireplace, his elbow resting on the mantle, drink in hand.

"I am." I set my glass down on the table next to the sofa. "I've had a taste of the power I can have, and now I want all of it."

"*We* can have."

"What?"

"The power *we* can have, Cassie. Together."

"Yes, of course," I said, mentally slapping myself for the blunder.

Caleb eyed me, the way he does when he's trying to read me from the inside out.

"Why can't I hear your thoughts anymore?" he asked.

He couldn't? Not at all? Interesting.

"Why can't I read yours?" I countered.

"Because I don't want you to. I don't let anyone in my head."

"Well, I don't want anyone in my head either."

"So, you've learned how to block it."

Had I? I hadn't put any effort into blocking thoughts. I'd only hoped he couldn't hear them. It couldn't be that easy. I'd wished that a gazillion times before.

He was still studying me as if I'd become a new specimen he was trying to identify, and it was starting to make me edgy.

"I don't know." I shrugged. "I didn't know I was even doing it."

"Your powers are growing faster than I anticipated. Being in Nergal's presence has obviously made you stronger." His eyes took on a lustful gaze. Caleb set his drink on the mantle and sauntered toward me. "I like it," he said with a growl. "I don't, however, like the fact that I can't hear your thoughts." When he stood directly in front of me, forcing me to look up to meet his gaze, I didn't dare look away for fear he would see that as an admission of guilt over the deception.

"Why, because you don't trust me?" I accused.

His hand came up, and he cupped his fingers around my neck as he stroked my cheek. "I want to, Cassie. I really do."

"Then let me prove it to you. Let me go to Braydon, on my own. He'll take me to the Sword, and I'll bring it back to you. I promise. You can trust me now."

I wasn't lying. I would bring it back to Caleb, but not on the terms he had planned. I remembered him telling me *the devil was in the details*, but there was no need to remind him of that now—not before I had him exactly where I wanted him—with the hilt of that Sword sticking out of his neck.

Shit. I needed to be careful with those mental images. I wasn't certain how this mental blocking was working or how long it would continue. If he knew...

"Too risky," he said. "But I can think of a way." His thumb moved to my lips and he brushed it over them, back and forth, while his glowing gaze locked onto mine. "You want to prove your loyalty to me, Cassie?"

Oh, God. I didn't need to be a mind reader to know what he was implying.

"You think me being in your bed will prove my loyalty to you?"

His eyes lowered to my lips, and he put pressure on the bottom one with his thumb, causing my mouth to open slightly. His tongue darted out, and he wet his bottom lip as he stared.

"I think you in my bed is definitely a step in the right direction, a step I will thoroughly enjoy." He angled his head and leaned in until his lips were a mere whisper from mine. I sucked a breath in anticipation. "You'll enjoy it too, Cassie. Immensely. I'll make sure of it."

This was going to kill me, but I didn't have much choice if I was going to get him to trust me enough to let me get at the Sword. At one time, I would have refused to sacrifice my body to such a vile creature as Caleb. Now, with ultimate power over everything and everyone, I'd sacrifice almost anything. My body was mere flesh. Ultimate power thrived on the soul, paying no heed to the flesh. The soul could live with or without the penetrable shell. Ultimate power survived only on will and determination, and I was oozing with them both.

I thought his lips had been too close before, but now, when I asked, "So if I give you my body, you'll trust me to go get the Sword?" my lips brushed his with each word.

"Our coming together will be so much more than you giving me your body, Cassie," Caleb whispered against my lips. "You will give me your soul and its commitment to be mine."

With that, he urged the back of my head forward with his hand, forcing my lips into his hard, needy kiss. He ravaged my mouth, wasting no time on a sweet, tender buildup. No, he devoured me instantly, his tongue plunging in and invading my mouth. He tasted of whiskey and desperation, smelled of it too. The desperation claimed me, something he'd been declaring to do for a long time.

His frenzied hands frantically slid down my back and stopped on my ass, where he squeezed my cheeks hard in his palms while pulling me toward him. I crashed into his body and instantly felt how eager he was for me. His large, hard shaft dug into my pelvis and stomach, causing me to move my mouth away to take a breath. I wanted to be disgusted, but my body hadn't caught up to my mind, and a wave of pleasure shot up from my core, a sigh escaping my lips along with it.

Caleb stilled his movements, and I opened my eyes. He was fixated on me, his eyes so clouded with passion, even the glow that normally happened in this aroused state appeared glazed.

"You like that, baby?" he asked, his voice low and husky.

When I didn't answer, he circled his hips into mine, creating a new wave within me. Reflexively, I moaned again.

The corner of his mouth slid up into a self-assured smirk. "Yeah, you like that." He moved to my neck and began suckling the side of it, making a trail with his tongue and lips from the sweet spot under my ear to the top of my collarbone. When he worked his way back up the other side, his hands found my breasts, his thumbs circling my nipples through the material of my shirt.

I was lost in the sensations of my body until his lips stopped at my ear and said, "I bet you're drenched for me, aren't you? I bet you can't wait to feel me inside you. I can't wait for it either, baby. I'm going to make you scream my name all night long. Lie back on the couch, Cassie."

He pushed, urging me backward to the couch, but I dug my heels in and put my hands on his chest to stop him. "Wait, what? Here?"

"Yes. Here. I want you now. I can't wait."

I knew I'd gone too far in this game to be able to stop it without a fight to the death. But I wasn't ready. My body was out of control, and I needed my mind to lead this show. I needed to slow him down, slow *me* down.

"And after, I can go with Braydon to get the Sword?" I asked.

It had worked. I saw his mind working around my question, trying to wrap itself around my game, as he studied me. While trying to catch my breath, I kept my gaze fixed on his, showing him he could read me all he wanted. I had nothing to hide. Nothing he would know about until I was ready, anyway.

Finally, he smiled back, rubbing my arms from shoulders to elbows. "You're so persistent, Cassie. That's hot. Really hot. But I'm persistent, too." He tugged me against his chest and locked his arms around me. Hovering over my lips again, he said, "You prove to me you truly want to be my queen in every way, and you can have anything you want."

He kissed me and slid his hands down to my ass again. With a small squeeze pushing me into his hard length, he sent my body back to the sensual charge, my mind once again losing the battle with my body. His hands inched lower, to the backs of my thighs. He grasped them in each of his hands and, all of a sudden, I was wrapped around him, legs around his waist, arms around his neck, clinging to him. He lifted me and started carrying me backward toward the couch.

This was it. He was going to take me. Right there and then. Was I ready for this?

Almost out of breath, I pulled my lips away from his and asked, "Would you really take your queen for the first time on a couch like some hormonal teenage boy?"

It stopped him, and I applauded myself once again. The ego was an easy target to manipulate, and Caleb was all ego, all the time.

Grabbing me under my arms, he pulled me off him to set me back on my feet. With an apologetic glance, he stroked my cheek. "I'm sorry, baby. You're right. You deserve to be treated like the queen you are." He bent forward and picked me up like a husband would his bride before carrying her across the threshold of a new home.

I let out a whoop of surprise, but he placed a tender kiss on my temple to settle me. Then he whispered in my ear, "Let's go back to our quarters so I can ravish and worship you good and proper."

I barely had a chance to catch my breath when everything went black.

***

The smell of vanilla and lavender hit me. I was still in Caleb's arms and when I opened my eyes, the first thing I saw was a super-sized bed taking up a quarter of one wall. Candles surrounded it, on tables at each side and in elaborate wall sconces above, as if outlining the bed with a flickering glow, causing the dark, satin bedding to shine with their reflections. It was a vision of seduction. Instead of making me feel all warm and cozy, as it was most certainly intended, the scene gave me chills.

"Someone is sure of themselves," I said, without looking back at him.

"I may have been a little hopeful. One can never be unprepared for momentous occasions such as this."

"Wow. You must have gone through a lot of candles."

His chest rumbled against me. "It'll be worth it." He nuzzled his nose near my ear. "You like?" he whispered.

"It's definitely more romantic than the couch. Set me down so I can see everything."

He did as I asked, albeit very slowly after turning me to face him so my body slid down the length of his. It didn't go unnoticed that he hadn't lost his... *enthusiasm* for what he anticipated was about to take place in this room. As if he read my thoughts, the corner of his lips lifted into a sinister smirk when I looked up at him.

"Easy, cowboy," I said before turning out of his arms and putting some distance between us.

The bed was undoubtedly representative of the room itself, bigger than it needed to be and covered in luxurious extravagance. Mirrored walls, armoires, wet bars, vanities, sofas, chairs, desks, wall-mounted televisions, and a token fireplace, were the most obvious items I spotted as I did a three sixty in the middle of it all. Surprisingly, the fireplace wasn't blazing. All the others had been. It probably had to do with the number of lit candles around the room and the heat they were already giving off.

Three of the four walls included doors. Through one, I could faintly see a marbled countertop housing a porcelain sink. The bathroom. The other door was closed. I approached it and stopped in front. Eyeing the door handle, I didn't grab it, curious to see how far my new powers extended. I closed my eyes and mentally willed the door to open. With barely a thought, and much easier than I'd expected, it worked. I opened my eyes to see the door slightly ajar and couldn't help the satisfied grin from lighting my face.

Taking a step inside, I couldn't see anything except the plush, light-colored carpeting that continued from the main room. When reaching the wall behind me, near the entrance, I felt nothing. I was just about to turn to see if I could spot a light switch when the room suddenly lit up around me, causing me to jump in surprise.

"They're basically on the same frequency as the doors," Caleb's deep voice resounded from behind me.

I glanced back at him and nodded. The room was the size of my apartment, and every wall was covered with racks and racks of clothing, only spaced enough for a long vertical tube light to be attached to the walls around them. Clothes hung on racks or were folded neatly in piles on top of them. The room held more clothes than I'd seen in some clothing boutiques. Hundreds of pairs of shoes lined small cubbies underneath the racks near the floor. The place was a woman's wet dream closet. Well, most women.

"I only have this wall," Caleb said, breaking my trance. When I looked his way, he was motioning toward the right side. That section was all men's clothes. "The other two are yours. If you require more room, more closets are located in the rooms down the hall."

More room? How could I possibly need more room? I barely had enough clothing to fit one corner of this closet. Hell, I only really had the clothes on my back if we were being technical.

"Whose clothes are all these?" I asked waving a hand toward the dresses and other items hanging on the left side of the room.

"They're yours, Cassie. I had them brought in for you. My queen won't do without, I assure you. Anything you want is yours. If you find something that doesn't suit you, or you need something else, you only need to tell me, and I'll take care of it."

The reality of the extent of Caleb's obsession hit me. He saw us living as if we were some super couple, together in this otherworldly mansion, doling out death and destruction over the universe and then lying together at night in our bed of triumph. I knew he wanted me, heard everything he'd said about me being his queen, but until that moment, seeing his fucked up *his and hers* idea of our life, I hadn't realized the enormity of his psychotic fixation.

Why me? Why was he so intent on having me as his queen? Caleb was impulsive, without a doubt, but he wasn't out of his mind. He was methodical, cunning, and always had an end game, a method behind his madness. When he'd sought me out, I thought it was merely an unhealthy obsession. He was a stalker, and I was his target. I attached normal though deranged, qualities onto this highly intellectual, supernatural being, a being who manipulated others to fit precisely into his big-picture plans.

So, why me? It wasn't my beauty or glowing personality. Caleb was base, but he wasn't some hormonal male who thought with his penis. No, he was too smart for that, as much as I would have liked to think it was all that simple.

Then it hit me. He didn't want *me*. It was my power he wanted. He knew what I'd become, what Nergal told me I'd become, and he wanted a piece of that.

Seems the only person who didn't know what I'd become was me.

But I knew now.

And he couldn't have it.

"That was very thoughtful of you, Caleb," I said while turning to look at him.

His eyes locked on mine, and he took a predatory step toward me, bringing us only inches apart. "It was," he said, his voice deep and rumbling, "but I'm only thinking about one thing right now, and it has nothing to do with you in any clothes."

The ginormous closet suddenly became too small, closing in on me, but I stayed my ground. It was time to get this over with.

I licked my lips. He watched the movement of my tongue like a hawk watches its prey from above before it attacks.

"Then let's not wait any longer," I said.

I barely heard the growl he let out before he was on me, his lips crashing into mine, his tongue plunging in violently, as if it had been caged for too long and finally released. His hands were at my waist, at the back of my head, on my ass. They were everywhere, and I was so wrapped up in his crazy hungered movements, I hadn't even realized he was working us toward the bed. In fact, I hadn't noticed how much I was doing the same to him until I'd fallen back on the bed. Without realizing what happened, I was staring up at Caleb's bare torso. I faintly remembered helping remove his shirt.

The monster had a great body. I couldn't deny it. Also difficult denying how hot I'd become, and not in the kind of way I wanted. Not from him. My deepest desire was to cringe from him, break out in hives, something other than wanting more. I might not have been able to control my body's reactions to him, but I could definitely take control in other ways.

I sat up and reached for the button on his jeans, but he snatched my hands and pushed them back.

"Oh, no, baby, your turn," he said with a smirk. Leaning in, he grabbed the bottom of my T-shirt. He lifted it up over my head, and before I had the chance to acknowledge what was happening, my arms raised to aid in the process as if they were on autopilot.

I sat in my bra, the heat of the room doing nothing to help my nipples from straining against the material. Caleb noticed too, his eyes glowing and fixated on them.

"Take it off," he hissed as if he were straining to keep his focus long enough to form words. I knew how he felt. I could barely breathe from the rate my heart was pounding and wasn't sure how much longer I could keep it together. But I had to. I needed to make sure he was past the point of no return, so drugged on the lust of the moment he couldn't think straight. The hardest part would be not falling into it myself.

Easing one arm behind me, I reached back and unclasped the bra, letting the straps slip down my arms. They hadn't reached my elbows before Caleb let out a guttural sound and ripped it the rest of the way off me. And then I was on my back, Caleb covering me with his body, grinding his mouth against mine, in the same way his hips were between my legs. His hands were mashing and squeezing my breasts as if he couldn't get enough of them in his hands.

His loud, long moans vibrated against my lips. I think they were all his, but I couldn't be sure. He was hitting the right spots, and this power I seemed to have now heightened every single sense of mine tenfold. I was losing control.

"Lift up," I said on a heavy breath as I struggled to move my hands between our bodies, trying to get at the button on his pants again.

He lowered his mouth to my neck, sending shivers down my body, but he did raise up, and I quickly undid the jean button and lowered the zipper, unsure how I was even working my fingers. As he trailed kisses down my neck toward my chest, I pushed down on his jeans enough to feel the heavy drop of his erection land between my thighs.

I took him in my hand and heard his intake of breath when he froze over me. Being honest, I had to admit, he was... *impressive*, his shaft thick, smooth, and very hard in my palm. I slowly stroked up and down his long length while Caleb let out his breath with an extended low groan. I knew he was almost in my control.

"Cassie," he growled, slowly pumping himself into my hand. "Oh, yes, Cassie."

I pulled my hand away from his erection and pushed against his waist. "Lie back on the bed," I whispered, almost out of breath.

He looked at me, a smirk on his face. "Why? What are you going to do to me?"

I locked my gaze on his and said with a smirk of my own, "Do as I ask and you'll find out."

A rumble echoed from deep within his throat as he smashed his lips against mine, shed his pants, and launched himself away from me and toward the head of the bed. "I *really* like this new Cassie."

Turning and facing him, on all fours, my breasts hung there for his viewing pleasure. "Then you're going to love the new Cassie very soon, my king."

He narrowed his eyes at me, and for a moment I was afraid I might have laid it on a bit thick, but then he gave me a lusty smile and said, "Fuck, you're sexy. I could look at you like that for eternity."

I could have said the same about him as he lay there in all his naked glory. I almost regretted not allowing myself to take advantage of the situation for my own pleasure.

Almost.

But something more pleasurable was headed my way.

I crawled over him, letting my eyes drink him in as I inched closer. When we were face to face, I leaned down and kissed him, pushing my tongue into his mouth and swirling it around, playing with his.

His hands went to my waist where he began pulling at the top of my jeans. "Take these off. I want to feel all of you."

I grabbed his wrists and sat up, straddling his hips. *God, how could he be even harder between my legs than before?* My breathing rate increased. I didn't know if it was from having to restrain myself from my exploding hormones or from what I was about to do, but it didn't matter. Complete control was so close. Locking eyes with him, I pulled his hands from my waist and methodically raised them up and over him. "Not yet. First, I want to service my king properly," I said, making sure my breasts brushed against his chest.

"Mmmm," he groaned as I nibbled the skin near his ear and trailed my tongue down his neck. "As you wish, my queen. Service me."

I was making my way down his chest when he said, "You better hurry it up, baby, because I'm close to throwing you beneath me and fucking the memory of Hunter out of you for good."

The mention of Hunter froze me, sweet memories of us together invading my head. So long ago, in another lifetime.

But that's all it was... a memory. Nothing more. I shook it away.

As I peered at Caleb from down by his waist, he looked back at me, his eyes glowing with bright possibilities. With a smile, I said, "Oh, don't you worry about Hunter. I'll deal with him after I'm done with you."

I closed my eyes and heard the sweet sound of metal clanking.

"What the fuck?" Caleb yelled.

When my eyes opened, the shackles I'd conjured up around Caleb's wrists, and the chains accompanying them, kept him prisoner on the wall. I knew without looking I'd find the same at his ankles, those chains attached to the floor.

"That's right, Caleb. You're fucked. Just not in the way you had hoped. I'd love to stay and gloat over your predicament, but I have to go see an angel about a Sword. You see, I really *don't* trust you. Oh, but don't worry... I'll come back with it... let you see it. Up close and very, very personal."

I only caught a few of Caleb's raging words as I grabbed my clothes, closed my eyes, and let the darkness come over me.

A darkness I chose... all by myself.

CHAPTER NINETEEN

Solid ground was beneath my feet, not the lush carpeting of the bedroom, but I tapped my foot to confirm it. I'd done it. I'd transported myself. No help from any damned angels or demons. Wow. Good. Liberating.

Don't start celebrating just yet, I told myself. I hadn't even opened my eyes to make sure I'd poofed to the right place. No sense patting my own back if I had only moved to the bathroom of Caleb's love lair.

"Cassie?"

Braydon's voice hit me like the opening sonata of a melodious symphony.

Upon opening my eyes, I was standing in the middle of the same cold, dimly-lit room Caleb had brought me to earlier to witness Braydon's caged prison. While facing that very cage now, Braydon stood against the steel bars staring back at me wide-eyed and open-mouthed. He appeared as surprised about me popping in, as I was about performing the action on my own.

He called my name again, snapping me into action. Without having time to ponder all of my newfound skills, I had to free him and get the Sword. Besides, I had no idea if or when Caleb would find a means to escape, or if he even needed to in order to thwart my plan. For all I knew he could summon his minions by using telepathy. I was strong but didn't know if I was capable of taking on an army.

Not until I had the Sword.

I put a finger to my lips as I approached the cage, gesturing for Braydon to keep quiet. "I'm getting you out of here," I whispered, "but we don't have much time."

"Where's Caleb? Cassie, what have you done?"

"I have him... detained, but I don't know how long that will last, so we have to hurry. You're going to take me to the Sword, Braydon, and then we're going to get it back to the Sanctuary where it'll be safe. We'll be safe."

I eyed the bars of his cage, contemplating how to free him. Without visible locks or switches, I couldn't see a way to break him out.

"Wait, Cassie, no," Braydon cried out in a hurried breath.

I snapped my head up at his worried tone and spun around, thinking he was warning me of something in particular. Maybe some had joined us in the room. But the door was still closed. I looked back at him, confused.

"If we do that, we're right back where we started. I had a deal with Caleb, one that would help us be together, lost somewhere, away from everyone. We'd finally be away from all of the distractions keeping us apart."

"Are you delusional?" I squawked in a harsh whisper. It was all I could do not to scream at him. If I'd been in that cage with him, I might have punched him into reality. Or worse. "Did you not hear a word Caleb said before?"

"I know we still have to work out the details of how to go about this, but—"

"Dammit, Braydon. He has no intention of letting us run off into the sunset together. He's using you to get the Sword and then he's going to kill you with it. Are you really that naive?"

I didn't realize I'd flushed myself up against the cage, until he came nose-to-nose with me, wrapping his fingers around mine on the bars I clenched. "No, Cassie. I would just do anything to be with you."

His reality was clouded with love, or lust, or whatever the hell it was he had for me. He wasn't processing right. The subtle way he'd expressed his feelings from the beginning had been replaced with deranged delusion. *Jesus, he was almost as bad as Caleb.* The only difference... Caleb wasn't stupid. Sure, calculating, methodical, and patient. Braydon, on the other hand, was reactionary and reckless. That combination would only get him one thing... dead.

"That's not going to happen," I told him. "Not like that. Caleb wants me as his queen, Braydon. He never had any intention of letting us go after he got the Sword. He's going to kill you and make me his queen while he plays Master of the universe. If he gets the Sword, he'll have the power to do whatever he wants, with whomever he wants. We can't let that happen. That's why we have to get it first."

"And then what? You said we'd take it back to the Sanctuary. I don't want to go back there, Cassie. Not if it means we can't be together."

I was seriously considering killing him myself at that point but still needed to know where the Sword was. So, I decided the only way we were going to get anywhere anytime soon was if I played a different angle.

"Braydon," I said. Calm and sweet gushed in my tone of voice "We'll figure it all out when we get the Sword. I'll find a way for us to be together, I promise. It's you I want. I realize that now. After everything you've done for me, for us, how could I not?" I put my lips to his through the bars and held them there for a moment. "I'll find a way. Trust me."

He rubbed his fingers over mine and looked me in the eyes, all the depth of emotion he was feeling had become obvious in his green ones. "That's all I want."

"Then let's do this," I urged.

"Okay," he said and stepped back from the bars. "But you have to get me out of here first. I can't transport us to it unless I'm out of this cage."

"Right." I stepped back too and check again for a lock or mechanism. After a moment or two of searching, I realized how much of an idiot I was being. Of course, Braydon's cage would have a mental lock on it. Everything else in this mind-fuck realm did. I closed my eyes and concentrated on seeing the door opening. When I did, I heard a pop and a clicking sound. When I opened my eyes, a portion of the cage had sprung forward and was now moving to the side, creating an opening in the cage.

I let out the breath I'd been holding and watched Braydon, realizing he hadn't stepped out even though he was obviously free.

"How did you do that?" he asked from within the cage.

"Long story," I replied. "C'mon, let's go. They might catch us any minute."

He eyed me warily for a moment. I was about to grab him out, but he finally rushed toward me. Without a word of warning, I was locked in his arms, his lips crashing into mine. Completely taken off guard by the motion, if he hadn't pinned me to him, I think I would have fallen from the impact. The shock of the situation caused me to lose my breath when his mouth smothered mine.

"Braydon, please," I gasped, trying to wedge my hands between us and push him back. "We have to go."

"I'm sorry, I just—"

"Let's get out of here," I yelled.

His hands went up on either side of my face, and his eyes locked on mine.

I softened my gaze, guessing he was asking for some kind of reassurance we were doing the right thing. "Once we get the Sword, we'll have all the time in the world for this."

He slowly nodded. "Okay," he whispered. His head angled down, placing a sweet, tender kiss on my lips, before pulling back and leaving a vacuum from the wind of his words.

"Let's go," he said, pulling me to his chest.

**

It was as if I'd been transported back through time. I was in a familiar forest, night was upon us with only a sliver of moonlight on the huge stone slab of wall in front of us. Vines snaked up and down the sides as if they fed upon the concrete for their nourishment to survive. I'd stood on this very spot, possibly eons ago, in a time where I knew nothing of who I was or what I would become. It had been a time when my nightmares began to blur into reality. I knew exactly what lay beyond the concrete door in front of me. Back then, it had seemed I had somehow come home. Now, I *knew* I was home. Hell was where I belonged.

"Here?" I asked Braydon, confusion obvious in my tone. "The Sword is *here?*"

"Yes," he said. "It's inside. I figured the angels wiped this place clean after Nergal was killed, so no one ever thinks of looking here anymore, and the demons won't step foot around here either after being driven out. I checked it out several times in the last few weeks to make sure."

I didn't know what surprised me more, that he'd pick Hell, the devil's original lair for the Sword's hiding place, or that he and Caleb had been planning this for so long.

It didn't matter. The Sword was here, so it was where I needed to be.

"Okay, well let's hope no one decided to re-think that theory since we've been gone," I said. It was a valid concern. I'd have checked here if only to make sure Caleb wasn't trying to live out some sick fantasy of being Nergal and torturing me in Hell.

And so would Hunter, I thought to myself.

His name rang like a song in my head and gave my heart pause. Or was it a warning? I couldn't tell. I closed my eyes. Images of him chained to one of the walls beyond the massive stone door flashed in my head. Then I saw myself running down the corridor, desperately searching, the Sword painfully held in my grip. I knew it was my memory of the last time we'd been here. Back then I was desperately running for love.

A sharp pain in my chest doubled me over, and I gulped in a breath. Reaching out to stable my balance, I pressed my hand against the cold stone in front of me.

"Cassie," Braydon called out. His hands were on my back. "What's wrong? What happened?"

I was still sucking in air when the stone heated beneath my hand and the giant slab moved to the side.

Braydon grabbed me from behind and pulled me back.

I straightened and watched as the doorway to Hell opened and welcomed me inside. The pain in my chest had quelled; however, my heart was beating a mile a minute.

"Did you do that?" Braydon asked.

I assumed he was referring to the door opening up. "I... I guess. I mean, yes. Of course. How else would we get in?"

"Every time I've come here... I've had to transport directly inside. I could never get that wall to open for me. I only brought you out here to make sure you were ready instead of just throwing you right in. How'd you do that?" Confusion crossed his face.

"Need I remind you of who I am, who you want to spend the rest of eternity with?" I asked with narrowed eyes. "Or rather, *what* you want to spend eternity with?"

A pained expression had replaced the confusion before he scrubbed his hand over his face. After letting out a heavy sigh, he grasped my upper arms and said, "Cassie, I know exactly who you are. As I've already mentioned, I don't care, because I know

I can bring out the light in you. Once we're together, my love for you won't ever let the darkness overshadow it. I promise you."

I wanted to laugh in his face at the irony. No. I wanted to yell that he was too late because the illumination was gone. My light wasn't as simple as a burned bulb that could be replaced. A huge power surge had taken it out and completely annihilated the circuitry, never allowing another connection. I *was* darkness.

He would see that soon enough, but not before I got my hands on the Sword.

"Cassie?"

Braydon was waiting for me to say something. His head had tilted slightly to the side and his eyebrows furrowed down as he peered at me.

"I'm sorry," I said, shaking my head as if to clear it. "I know you'll try, Braydon, and I'm so thankful for your faith in me. It means so much to know someone sees the good in me. Being in Hell, being around Caleb, I'd started thinking maybe my fate was to remain in the darkness."

One of his hands came up and rested against my cheek. "Never think that, Cassie. Never again."

I pulled away from his hand and focused on the doorway, now open to the view of stone steps leading down into the depths of Hell. "Let's do this, so I can put the darkness behind me for good."

"Okay," he said and held my hand in his. "Follow me."

He led me through the doorway and down the steps. The minute our feet hit the floor of the long, shadowed corridor, the door behind us slid closed, blanketing us in darkness. That image only lasted a second before all of the torches hanging on the walls magically lit with bright flames, lighting the path in front of us. Just as magically, a surge of energy hit me, like a strong gust of wind in a powerful storm. The torch flames continued their slow, steady flicker, making me realize the rush of energy was only impacting me. Before I had a second to rationalize it, the force beckoned me forward.

Braydon had given pause from the torch flames appearing, so I found myself pulling his hand, urging him to follow me. I had no idea where I was going but knew I was being led exactly where I needed to be. The Sword was calling me.

My steps quickened, and eventually our pace became a steady jog, turning corners, following one corridor, then another. Braydon's hand had dropped as he trailed a few steps behind. A few times, he asked how I knew where I was going, but I didn't bother to answer. The power within me grew with each step. I followed it like a lifeline until finally reaching a cell door. I was familiar with this one.

Peering through the bars at the top of the door into the chamber beyond, I thought of the irony of our location. It had been my prison... for however long... I'd never know. I'd been chained and tortured at the very pillars where I now longed to be. Fate had become a very witty and poetic bitch. I couldn't help but laugh out loud.

Braydon grabbed my wrist and spun me around to face him, forcing me out of my thoughts. "Cassie? What's going on?"

I couldn't let him know how strong the Sword's pull was to me. I didn't want him to question my motives. Not now, not when I was this close. "I'm sorry. I just... this is where Nergal kept me prisoner. I... I had to see it again. I had to see that it was empty, and I was free of him. I can't explain it. I just... I..."

"It's okay," he said, pulling me close. "You don't have to explain it." I laid my head on his shoulder and let him hold me.

"Did I take us too far off course?" I asked, trying to sound innocent.

He pushed me away from him and gazed down at me with wide eyes. "No. You're not going to believe this..." He paused and glanced into the room before checking my reaction. "This is where I hid the Sword, Cassie. Jesus, I'm so sorry. If I'd known..."

I put my hand on his cheek to soothe him with mock sincerity. "It's all right. You couldn't have known."

His eyes held so much sympathy, I almost felt bad.

"I'll go in and get it. You stay out here."

I nodded, letting him play the hero.

He disappeared, and I knew without turning around that he had transported inside the cell. A faint shuffling sound came from within, but that wasn't what proved to me he'd located and taken hold of the Sword. It was the overwhelming urge I had in the depths of my soul to rush into that cell, tackle him, and take back what belonged to me.

The Sword was mine and mine alone.

I was so close to ultimate power and could practically feel the thrumming energy in every molecule of my body, but I had to stay patient for a while longer. Soon enough, I'd be in total control of everything. Of everyone.

Afraid of losing my resolve, I didn't turn around to see what Braydon was doing in the cell with my Sword. Instead, I'd follow through with my visions of annihilating anything keeping me from my destiny. Luckily, Braydon reappeared in the corridor with me before I lost control.

I knew, while staring at the Sword in his hands, my gleaming eyes and parted lips, I'd probably revealed too much of my adoration for a material thing. He couldn't know how much it meant to me, how much it was a part of me, but it was difficult to conceal when it was this damn close and pulling me closer.

The blade, pointing down, radiated with an iridescent glow when Braydon held the beautifully jeweled hilt in both hands. It had become a beacon of light filling my darkness, and I craved it.

Knowing from experience the weight of the Sword was much heavier to others than to me was evidence enough of its rightful, natural home. My fingers brushed over Braydon's hands instinctively, an act of longing to feel a direct connection without showing my true desperation to have it in my own hands.

"Okay," he said, breaking my trance, "what now?"

"We get out of here," I answered, concentrating on the Sword in his hands.

"You said you wanted to take it back to the Sanctuary, right? Are you sure? We can take it with us, Cassie. Go somewhere now, search out someplace where no one will find us. We don't have to go back at all."

The love and innocence in his soul were real. He truly believed we could live out some *happily ever after*, and for a moment, I even wanted it too. The truth of what I was, what I planned to do and become, would crush him and put out his shiny light like wind to a candle flame.

I could make it easier for him by killing him now. I'd figure out a way to get into the Sanctuary without him once it was all done. Using him would be less challenging, but not exactly necessary.

My hands squeezed over his at the hilt of the Sword. The power radiating through my palms from underneath was fierce. It would be so easy to snatch it from his grasp and slice the blade through his neck. Without any apprehension, I knew he wouldn't stand a chance.

Take it, Cassandra.

As much as I wanted to, as much as I was compelled to, I just couldn't bring myself to act.

"Cassie?" he said with puzzled eyes.

"Ahhh." A shout rang from down the corridor. "By the angels, I think you've found it."

Caleb sauntered toward us, followed by at least a dozen of his minions.

My window of opportunity had just expired.

CHAPTER TWENTY

"Give me the Sword, Braydon," I said through clenched teeth.

His eyes were wide with panic. I couldn't blame him. The numbers were not in our favor, and he knew how powerful Caleb had become. "Let's just transport out of here, Cassie. We have what we came for. Let's just go."

"No," I said, determination in my voice and in the grip of my fingers over his. "We can end this now. I can end this. With the Sword, I'm more powerful than any of them, even Caleb."

"Cassie, no. I can't let you—"

"This is the only way." I stared directly into his eyes, softening mine, pleading with him to see. "If I don't do this, we will always be running, forever looking over our shoulders. Let me do this so we can be together. Give me the Sword, Braydon. Trust me."

Caleb let out a loud, low laugh that bounced, echoing off the stone walls. We both looked in his direction. He was approaching too fast, getting too close. "Oh, you are good, you little devil," he said with an evil smirk. "My dear, love-stricken angel, why don't you ask her how she was envisioning you moments ago. I promise you, it was not together. As a matter of fact, it was very much in pieces. Don't worry, boy, the first cut is the deepest."

I snapped my head back to Braydon. His eyes had narrowed, and I couldn't tell if he was contemplating what Caleb was telling him or if it was pure hatred aimed at the monster ambling down the corridor toward us.

Grabbing Braydon's forearms, I forced him to face me. "Don't listen to him. He's only trying to trick you. Give me the Sword and transport back to the Sanctuary. I'll come as soon as I finish this here."

"What? No. I'm not leaving you here."

"Goddamit. I can't beat them all if I have to protect you too. Now go." I snatched the Sword and pushed him with enough force to send him down the corridor in the opposite direction of Caleb and his demons. He stumbled to the ground and pulled himself back up. He started running back toward me, but I aimed my glowing eyes his direction and watched as he hit an invisible wall, the one I placed there. "Go, Braydon," I shouted. "Trust me."

I quickly turned to face the approaching army. I couldn't worry about Braydon anymore. My fate pressed upon me step by measured step. This was it. My ultimate life, Caleb's ultimate death. Or maybe it would be the other way around. We were about to find out who held the most power.

Caleb stopped about twenty feet ahead of me. His army continued to walk around him as if Caleb were parting a sea of evil slowly rolling toward me.

"I'll be back, Cassie," I heard Braydon shout from behind me. "I'll bring help."

"Don't bother." Caleb sneered without taking his eyes off me. "This will be over soon."

I held up the Sword, brandishing it as a warning to the demons, who were now only a few feet away, flanking the sides of the corridor. They all stopped and glared at me.

"Cassie, I must admit, I'm quite impressed with you," Caleb said, keeping his distance. He was either scared, or biding his time. If I were to guess, I would choose the latter. I'd never seen Caleb scared. Regardless of the weapon I held, I probably didn't appear as foreboding as I felt, especially when the odds were about twenty to one. "You've come a long way from the sweet little guardian angel I met back at that bar. Not so angelic anymore, are you? It's such a shame. You really would have been the perfect queen, if only you would have realized your place, serving your king. Me, Cassie. I'm the king."

"See, that's your downfall, Caleb. You're still stuck in the dark ages where only men can rule. Well, welcome to the new age where the queen reigns supreme. If you fall to your knees and bow down before me, I may not make you suffer too long before your Final Death."

He laughed, a loud hearty one, which shook every nerve in my body and set me on high alert. My body had been humming with energy, feeling so light on my feet I might have believed I'd been floating had it not been for seeing them touching the stone floor with my own eyes.

"I really am going to miss you," Caleb said in typical high-handed tone. "Give me the Sword, sweetheart, and maybe I'll reconsider killing you. I could make you my pet, but, of course, you'd require a permanent collar."

My lips curled back at his suggestion, baring my teeth, like the dog he alluded to, albeit a feral one.

"The only way you'll get your hands on this Sword is if you pry it from my stiff, dead fingers."

Caleb shook his head as he stared back at me, a forlorn look on his face, but a glow in his eyes. "What a waste. Sadly, the time has come then." With a nod of his head, his voice matching the calm demeanor, he called out, "Men."

The army of demons descended upon me, but I knew they were hesitant, not of a fight with me, rather of what I held in my hands. They eyed the blade cautiously, knowing its power, but they were loyal to their leader and would die trying to carry out his orders. They stopped a few feet in front of me, and we seemed to be at a stalemate, none of us willing to make a move for fear it would be the wrong one.

I needed to get this over with, be done with it, not only because the anticipation of a life or death situation was one of the worst feelings in the world, but because if Braydon were bringing back the angels, I'd have to contend with them too. That situation was on my list of plans, but on my terms, when I was ready. And I would be ready if I survived this.

How did one go about fighting off an army? I had very little experience with any kind of physical altercations, aside from beating the hell out of the bags in the gym and fending off Caleb a time or two. Now, I was facing a freaking army, emboldened with evil sneers and really shiny, sharp swords. They weren't as deadly as the Sword of Final Death, but they could take me down and give Caleb the opportunity to change the hands of power in an instant if I weren't careful. Did I take the risk of striking out at one in hopes I was quick enough to fend off an attack from another? I honestly had no idea what the hell I was doing.

The darkness within me called my name. Pure instinct caused me to close my eyes. A burning sensation ignited in my chest and radiated throughout my body, heating my blood and loosening my muscles. My heart rate slowed, as my breaths became long and deep. Sound silenced around me and my mind cleared. All anxiety faded away. I no longer worried how this battle would play out because I knew the only outcome for me was victory. I had the ultimate power. No, I *was* the ultimate power, and there was nothing or no one who could defeat me.

With eyes still closed, my arms raised the Sword horizontal above my head, pointing behind me. I inhaled once, and then exhaled, long and slow. Swinging the Sword left to right, spinning with the action, I felt no need to open my eyes. My body was on autopilot, and I let it take over. I was cognizant of each movement, each breath, but at the same time I stood in my protected shell, waiting for whatever was happening to play out until I could open my eyes and claim my conquest.

All sense of time had disappeared before I finally opened my eyes. When reality returned, I was standing in the middle of a black tarry mess, a bloodbath all around me. Pieces of demon, or what I assumed was demon, lay among the dark, gooey mess, bits of black stained flesh stuck on the walls and ceiling of the corridor. Not a demon was in sight. I'd defeated them all without a drop of sweat.

All but one.

Frozen and standing in the exact same spot he'd been before I'd closed my eyes, Caleb stared back at me, his face devoid of emotion. No glaring eyes. No sinister smirk. He was blank, unreadable.

"You must be feeling pretty powerful right now, little girl," he said.

"And you, Caleb? How about you?" I asked. I was enjoying the power, but experiencing the nervous side too. This was it. The final moment. A fight for ultimate power. Do or die. Would my power be enough to defeat Caleb once and for all?

"Oh, no, my dear. You see, all those new powers you've recently stumbled upon, I've had months to perfect. You're no more than an adolescent trying to control all those raging, chaotic hormones. Me? I'm a full grown man."

He disappeared before my eyes, and without an instant to react, I felt his length behind me. His arms had wrapped around mine, and his hands clamped my wrists, preventing me from swinging the Sword. Squeezing me into his body, he ground his hips close to my ass, smashed his face into the side of mine, and whispered in my ear, "And I know exactly what to do with them."

I gasped. While involuntary, it was a sure sign to Caleb that he'd gotten an edge on me. And he had. I couldn't move. I couldn't even try, his grip was stronger than a solid, metal vice.

He spun me toward the wall, and we launched forward until I slammed against it. The Sword jerked toward me. If I hadn't moved in time, it would have sliced my head in half. It did, however, manage to nick my cheek as it swung over my shoulder. A small trail of blood dripped down my face.

"I'm afraid it's time, my queen," he said, his lips still close to my ear. "I want you to know, Cassie, this really does pain me to have to do this, but believe me when I tell you, this is going to hurt you way more than it will me."

He pulled me away from the wall enough so he could maneuver my hands.

Mind racing, I searched for a means to escape the death hold. While I did, Caleb managed to get the Sword pressed against my neck. My heart beat too fast, and I was out of air from the breath I'd been holding, but I didn't dare exhale. Energy assaulted me from within, and I thought I might explode with it.

"Don't you love the irony of it all?" Caleb asked, with a snicker. "I mean, who'd have guessed you'd die by your very own hands?"

Everything stopped. The pulsing energy, my wild heartbeat... it all leveled out as if a calming switch had been flicked. I knew exactly what I needed to do.

Turning my face to his, I whispered, "You want irony? I'll give you irony."

He released me so fast, I almost fell back and dropped the Sword. His painful cries and groans confirmed I was in complete control. He was wrong. I was no adolescent, and my new powers were fully operational.

"Hurts to be on the receiving end of that one, doesn't it, Caleb?" I said with a curl of my lip as I glared at his bent form. He was doubled over, holding the sides of his head, shaking it from side to side, but I knew from experience no amount of shaking would release him from the searing pain slicing through his skull.

"You should have killed me when you had the chance," I said as I walked up to him, dragging the Sword over the concrete behind me, sparks flying from the tip. When I leaned over, my lips practically brushed the outside of his ear, I didn't worry he would take advantage of our close proximity because no way was I letting up on my power over him. "Oh, how the tables have turned," I added.

"Bitch," he hissed, spit dripping from his mouth onto the floor. Veins popped out on his forehead as if they might burst from his head at any second. I almost wanted to continue the torture in hopes of seeing black blood spew from his ugly skull. But there wasn't time.

I lifted the Sword and positioned the blade across the back of his neck. "Actually, I prefer the sound of Queen Bitch, don't you? It's too bad you're so weak, Caleb. I might have made you my king if you were strong enough to keep up with me." I inched closer, my lips touching his ear. "But you're just a soft wannabe, and it's time for your delusion to end."

"No," he cried, struggling to stand, only to be met with pressure I placed on the blade at his neck.

"Yes, Caleb. Oh, and I almost forgot—this is going to hurt you way more than it will me."

With that, I lifted the Sword and let gravity bring it down through his neck, the blade cut through flesh and vertebrae like a tender piece of meat.

***

Caleb's head hit the concrete floor with a thud and rolled a few feet until it stopped at the wall. Blank eyes stared back at me while black blood oozed from his severed stem. It was a grisly sight, but to me it was picture perfect. If I hadn't known the angels were on their way and might wonder where Caleb's head was after seeing this gruesome scene, I might have taken it to mount on a wall somewhere for my own sick pleasure.

For as long as I could remember, I'd been haunted by the person, or thing, attached to that head, and now, it was over. I was triumphant, but I could hardly believe Caleb was gone. It had happened so fast. The power had come easily. Too easily. That was when doubt crept in about the possibility of some twisted scenario yet to play out. The battle between Caleb and I should have been epic, long and hard, exhausting to the point we would both be near death before one of us finally won out. At least that was how I'd always imagined it would be. But my powers soared far above anything my imagination could conjure up. The quickness with which I ended him solidified my true destiny.

I was the ultimate ruler. I was *born* to reign supreme. I no longer cared whether good or evil was my calling. Those were simple thoughts for the weak-minded. The strong only thought about what made them more so. I had more strength and stamina than all of them now, but I needed to do one last thing to cement that fact. And to do that, I needed to get out of Hell fast.

With one quick look at Caleb's severed head, I squeezed hard on the hilt of the Sword, closed my eyes and allowed the blackness to whisk me away.

CHAPTER TWENTY-ONE

I transported back to the castle... Caleb's *ex*-domain. Still not sold on residing there once this was all over. The place was big, roomy, palatial, plenty of room for me. I'd have other options soon too, residences as spacious, but that decision could wait until after the final phase of my plan was complete. Only a few more loose ends to tie.

In the room where Braydon had been imprisoned, I figured it would be the safest location for the time being because some demons had been left at the castle. Caleb always covered his bases and wouldn't have left his possessions unattended, although I was sure he expected to return to them. They were my possessions now, or they would be as soon as I did away with the remaining demons. I wasn't worried, though. Demons were merely pesky mosquitoes to me, irritating insects that would disappear with a simple swat of my hand, unlike the angels, who were now my biggest threat. I'd get to them soon enough. Only one more important thing to do.

Using utmost caution, I exited the room and headed down the long corridor. I could have simply transported where I needed to go, but I wanted to catch any demons lurking in the castle along the way. None appeared around the dining hall or any of the hallways, but when I came to the main staircase leading to Caleb's chambers, I spotted six of them. Three were positioned on the second floor, two mid-staircase, and one in the center of the foyer. They were all guarding the path to my destination.

When they saw me approach, their armored bodies stiffened in place. I stopped in my tracks, regarding them, making sure I had them all in my sights. They glared back at me, and even if I couldn't see how tense they were, the suffocating energy emanated from them. They were ready to pounce.

I knew I could kill them as easily as I had the others, but this time I had other plans.

"Your king is dead," I announced, holding the Sword upright in front of me so they could see the blood-stained blade. "You can join him, or you can join me." I paused and studied each one of them in turn. Glances skittered back and forth between the Sword and me. "I'm giving you a choice, but do not falter in your decision. You're either with me or dead. There is no in between."

I heard the thoughts of a demon sneaking up behind me before I heard its movements, so I spun, swinging the Sword about eye level, easily slicing off his head. Being stealthy hadn't mattered. Without faltering a fraction of a second, I returned to face the demon from the middle of the foyer. He'd taken the opportunity to step closer but stopped in his tracks when the tip of the blade was inches from his neck.

"I'd give you the chance to re-think that decision, but I honestly don't care enough," I said with a shrug of my shoulders. I jumped forward, shoving the Sword into his throat, swiftly cutting off whatever he was attempting to say.

Another one's thoughts contemplated jumping over the railing above, believing the element of surprise was a good opportunity to strike. I gazed up at the three demons leaning against the rail on the second floor, and zoned in, his pensive eyes giving him away.

"It won't work," I said with an exasperated sigh as if the whole situation was starting to bore me, which it was. "But I dare you to try," I added with a wink. He glared at me, and I waited for him to finish his relenting thoughts. Once I was sure he'd abandoned his idea of heroism, I switched my gaze to each and every one of them, reading their thoughts as I went. They all now accepted the power I'd gained and the stupidity of going against it. I was surprised. I had expected more of a fight but decided they were weaker than I thought... or smarter. Either way, it seemed I had gained my first army. Granted, it was only an army of five, but it was a start.

To be honest, I didn't feel the need to have an army, and gaining their support was more about doing away with obstacles than it was having others to back me up. Although, I had to admit, having someone watch my back while I might be busy doing other things, like ruling over the universe, could come in handy. But since they'd been Caleb's protégés, I couldn't completely trust their loyalty.

"Good," I said. "I'm glad we could all come to a quick agreement. But just in case any of you has thoughts about changing your minds..." I shot a blast of searing pain into their heads and they all sank to their knees, ten hands instantly raised and trying to ease the torture. I let them suffer for a few intense minutes before I backed off. *Damn, I liked this trick.* They remained on their knees but slowly raised their eyes to mine. That image burned into my memory. It was where they were meant to be.

"That was a sampling of what your previous boss endured for attempting to cross me. Let it be a reminder of what you could experience if you so much as think about defying me. Is that understood?"

They all nodded, some more enthusiastically than others. I made a mental note of the less enthusiastic ones.

"Good, then we shall proceed with your first test. All of you are going to let me pass as I go into the room upstairs. Once I'm in, you will continue to guard this area. If anyone tries to gain entry, you are to restrain them by whatever means necessary until I return. Got it?"

They all nodded again. It wasn't good enough for me.

"And I'd like you all to address me as *my queen*."

A pause, as if they were processing, and then another nod from all of them.

"Yes, my queen," I prompted.

They mumbled their acquiescence to my liking, so I grinned and climbed the stairs.

This all seemed way too easy, but I liked it.

***

My first stop was the room where Nergal's body lay imprisoned in glass. He was in the same prone position, looking as dead as ever. But something was different. The first time I'd walked into this room, I was hit with a tidal wave of power. It had called me to Nergal's lifeless form, magnetized me to it as if my very essence depended on reaching him. His presence had been alive, huge, *so*, so powerful then. Now, he appeared small, old, and decrepit in his glass case, similar to an ancient unwrapped mummy on display. I knew then I was doing the right thing.

I know why you're here, his voice said inside my head.

I moved toward him.

You're making a mistake.

I stared down at him through the glass.

It's unnecessary. You already have all the power you need.

"I know," I said, with a smile. "I thank you for that, and for helping me see my rightful place. You taught me well, Nergal. And I know ultimate power isn't merely about being stronger than all others. That's only part of it. To maintain that power, you have to continue to be stronger than others, constantly ensuring no one can ever gain the same mastery over you. There's only one way someone else would have that chance."

But you have the Sword. Without the Sword, no one can ever steal my essence and match your power. You know this.

"Yes, I do, but I also know even the best can falter once in a while, you know, like when *you* lost the Sword."

I pressed a button on the side panel of the case and the glass opened with a hiss. A putrid smell overpowered my senses, but I breathed through my mouth to avoid vomiting. This would soon be over. I grabbed the hilt of the Sword with both hands and held it up above my head, the blade aimed down toward Nergal's throat.

You need me to guide you, Cassandra. You know nothing of the power you hold, nor how to rule over such a vast, rebellious universe. Without me, you will fail.

I glared down at him. Even though his eyes remained closed, I imagined looking right through his glowing blue orbs. "You're the one who failed, Nergal. It's *my* destiny now to finish what you weren't capable of. Perhaps that was Fate's plan all along."

Perhaps you're just an ignorant little bitch.

I imagined his features blazing, and I chuckled knowing he lay before me vulnerable and lifeless.

"That's Queen Bitch to you," I said.

I never gave him the chance to address me as such because I slammed the Sword into his throat. It went through his flesh, the bottom of the coffin, and even through the stone podium before I finally stopped my thrust. The hilt lay against his throat, and I took my hands from it. For a long time, I stood there, looking at him, relishing in the sight of his Final Death.

It was a momentous occasion and I wanted to remember the image forever. Ingrain the scene in my memory so I could view it again and again. I had sealed my final fate. Nergal was gone. The king was dead.

All hail the queen.

After dislodging the Sword from Nergal's neck, I closed the case and stared through it one last time. Final Death already seemed to be affecting his body, hardening and cracking the skin as if his essence had been the moisture it needed to give it life but was now slowly dissipating. I wondered if I came back later, would I only find ash where a full six-foot-plus of flesh once lay? How fitting that would be.

I wiped the Sword on a nearby tapestry. His body had long been dead, and I only wiped the blade as a useless precaution of any essence being transferred to it. Doubting it could be that simple, I was anything but careless given current circumstances.

Upon leaving the room, the demons turned toward me from the same positions where I'd left them. They contemplated me with questioning eyes, whether wondering what I'd done in the room, or what was going to be required of them now, I didn't know. As far as I was concerned, their business wasn't about what I was doing, but what they would do for me. My first order... "Search the castle for more demons and either recruit them or imprison them until I return."

I assumed Caleb had other cages with which to hold many, and I was sure these goons knew where they were. When they answered, "Yes, queen," I knew I didn't need to waste any of my time confirming it.

Once they all left the area, I stood at the railing and looked out over the large, empty room. The castle was quiet, but a soundless echo seemed to fill the silence, pulsing with a foreboding symphony of sound, urging me to embrace my fate and continue on with my mission. I closed my eyes and breathed deep, filling my lungs with strength and determination, repeating a mantra in my head—*I am indestructible*—until the power of it billed every molecule in my body.

I was ready to face them... ready for them to bow down before me. And if they didn't, I'd destroy them all.

Nothing else mattered.

The universe was mine to control.

Angel of Fate

CHAPTER TWENTY-TWO

I knocked on the Sanctuary doors, stepped back, and half-turned to see the open courtyard and keep an eye on the door. I could have transported inside, but figured I had a much better chance of not being ambushed out in the open where I had a better vantage point. The interior included too many rooms where angels could hide. Not that they'd succeed even if they tried.

One door of the double entry opened, and Michael, a high-ranking angel, peered out at me.

His eyes scanned me up and down, and then they grew wide when he realized I carried the Sword.

"Hello, Michael," I said, hoping the gleam in my eye wasn't too obvious, or at least interpreted as excitement for obtaining the Sword. I needed to play it cool long enough to have the right people in the right places. "Get your boss. We've got a few things to discuss."

In a similar manner to the demons, Michael's gaze juggled between my eyes and the Sword, as if contemplating my motives with it.

He finally caught my gaze and said, "He's not here."

I knew exactly where Hadraniel was—scouting through the remains of slaughtered demons in Hell in the hopes of finding me.

The other door opened and a few more angels appeared beside and behind Michael. I recognized some of them but didn't acknowledge them more than a glance.

"Well, I suggest you go and get him. I believe I have something he wants." I held up the Sword and the angels flinched back in response. "Don't you think?"

Michael leaned over and whispered in one of the angels' ear.

I rolled my eyes. "Yes, Detri. And please hurry. I'm getting quite bored out here."

A few of them glared, but I returned their animosity with a smile.

Detri disappeared, along with two or three others, leaving me standing out there with Michael and about four other angels. Each of them wore armor and carried weapons. They'd either recently been out fighting, or were preparing to. Or maybe they'd all been instructed to stay on alert due to the recent events in Hell. I expected Braydon had informed the leaders.

"Would you care to wait inside, Cassandra?" Michael asked.

"And what?" I replied with a knowing look. "Get a bite to eat or a drink? No, thanks."

Any normal guilt-filled person would have cast their eyes down, knowing they'd just been exposed, but not Michael. No, his eyes sparked with conceit. One might think he was proud of being one of the backstabbing bastards who signed, sealed and delivered me to Caleb by drugging me. I shot him a smug look of my own, telling him he'd failed miserably.

"I thought you might want to visit with your parents," he said. "You know, catch up and whatnot. If you follow me, I can take you to them."

My heart pumped harder for a brief moment at the mention of them, but I took a deep breath and sealed up that wall. "Why don't you go get them and bring them out here. I'm sure they're dying to see me. Or wait, do they even know I'm alive?"

He pursed his lips to the side, scrunched his eyebrows, and rubbed his finger over his chin with an exaggerated flair as if thinking. "Hmmm. You have a point. I'm not quite sure what their guards have told them."

"So, they're under guard?"

"Not all the time. Their cells keep them in line so we don't worry as much about having to guard them. Your boyfriend, however, turned out to—"

"Cassandra. What a pleasant surprise."

I stepped away from the door and turned to see Hadraniel making his way across the courtyard with at least fifteen or twenty angels in his wake, Braydon among them. Hadraniel held a welcoming smile as if seeing a long, lost friend. It burned my blood, and I gripped the Sword tighter. I wanted to carve that smile right off his face. Braydon's, on the other hand, appeared more heartfelt, relieved even. I had conflicting emotions about that but couldn't deal with them at the moment.

"Which surprised you more, Hadraniel?" I asked. "The fact that I'm not dead or that I have the Sword?"

"You have it all wrong, Cassandra," he said flashing his trademark smile. "I fully expected you back. It's the reason I sent you."

"You're a liar," I hissed as I clenched the Sword so hard my knuckles were white. It took an ounce of willpower not to stab him in his lying face, cut out his tongue and mount it to wear around my neck. Watching that smug face brought out my primal instincts, like an animal wanting to fulfill nature's revenge on its enemy. "You sent me there to rot or die. I'm sure it made no difference which."

"I can see how you might think that, but that was the whole reason why I couldn't tell you what I planned. Caleb was too instinctive. He would have easily sensed a trap if you were to merely play the part. It had to be this way, Cassandra."

I pursed my lips and shook my head. I'm not sure what I expected from the Holiest of the Holy. As far as I was concerned he was every bit as evil as Caleb and Nergal. Angels and demons were no different. They both used others for their own purpose. Everything was all about power. It's what they all wanted, what they would kill for regardless of whether they were supposed to be saviors or not.

"You're a fool if you expect me to believe anything you say," I said. "But you're right, it did have to be this way." I held up the Sword between us, the blade angled slightly toward Hadraniel.

The angels all grabbed their weapons and slowly circled me. If they only knew how similar to the demons they really were. Hadraniel merely stared back at me, his glowing green eyes slamming into my blue ones.

"Cassie," Braydon called out, coming up beside Hadraniel. His features were panicked. "What are you doing? Stop this. He's telling the truth. It was all a ploy to bring Caleb out and get Nergal's body. Just... just hand over the Sword and this will all be over. Like we talked about."

I kept my eyes on Hadraniel. One slight and I might be overtaken. "Don't be so naive, Braydon. Did he tell you that when you came back and told him I had the Sword?" When he didn't answer, I knew I was right. "Tell me Braydon, you stealing the Sword and hiding it in Hell, was that part of the plan too? How about my family and friends being locked up? And Anael? Where is she? Surely if this were just some elaborate scheme to kill Caleb and get Nergal's body, she'd be out here right now to assuage my doubts."

I stuck the Sword closer to Hadraniel, making sure he didn't move but chancing a glance at Braydon. He appeared confused, maybe he believed me but didn't want to accept the truth.

"He sacrificed me, Braydon, just like he'd sacrifice any of you to get what he wants. He's no different than Caleb, for chrissakes. Hell, he's no different than you or me. Halos, horns, it doesn't matter. Our souls may look different, but they're all greedy little bastards who will stop at nothing to get what they think they deserve. You, of all people, can't argue with that. It's why you stole the Sword and came for me."

His eyes narrowed, and his jaw clenched while staring back at me. I knew he didn't like hearing it, but he couldn't deny it either.

When a niggling sensation invaded my skull, trying to get inside of it, I closed my eyes for a second to figure out the source. The second I did, huge pressure bore down on my brain and I hunched over, dropping the Sword to reach my hands up to my head. I heard movement around me and realized the angels were coming after me.

"No." I shouted and launched myself back upright, sending shockwaves of mind-numbing energy in all directions. All of the angels went down, grabbing their heads, some in fetal positions on the ground. Hadraniel was the only one left standing, not unlike Caleb amongst his demons. The only difference being Hadraniel couldn't contain his surprise at my powers the way Caleb had. If I read the expression on his face, he might have even been... scared. *Hadraniel*... scared. I never thought I'd see the day, but there it was, and I wanted to savor it. The moment was a fleeting, however, because before I had the chance, his eyes swept the ground next to me, and then he lunged.

I looked down where he was headed and saw the Sword lying there. I kicked him, catching him in the ribs, and then bent to grab the hilt by my feet. He was only able to reach the tip of the blade as I pulled it up and away from him. He cried out in pain and fell back, holding his bloody palms out away from his body.

Seeing Hadraniel like that, sitting on the ground, defeated and bloody, his face clenched in agony, he seemed smaller than I always knew him to be. In a way, it was sad. Watching someone so big fall so far, while necessary for my advancement, was almost like watching a plane fall out of the sky right before you were about to board.

But it couldn't happen to me. Not anymore. I had Nergal's essence and the Sword. I'd single-handedly taken down the three most powerful beings in the universe. Nothing left to stop me.

"How far you've fallen, Cassandra," Hadraniel croaked out. The irony almost made me laugh when he looked up at me with complete disdain.

"How far *I've* fallen?" I couldn't hold it back any longer, and I laughed as I stood over him. "Seems you're the one down, old man."

"Why'd you do it?" he asked. "Why'd you choose to let your darkness take over? You could have been so good, Cassandra. More power is available when the darkness doesn't shadow over the light of your soul."

"What makes you think I had a choice?"

"Everyone has a choice. You, me. Nergal even had the choice."

"Are you trying to tell me you're any better than he was? You sacrificed me, your own blood, for selfish gain. I'd say that's as black a heart as any demon in Hell. Don't pretend to be better than any of us."

"You're wrong, Cassandra. Our motives are quite different. While my means were far from ideal, the end goal was for the greater good. I would do anything to ensure evil does not fall into the wrong hands. At the time, it meant keeping the Sword and Nergal's corpse out of the hands of those who would use it against the world. I had to prevent that by all means necessary. You were my only leverage, and I'm sorry for the circumstances, but I'm not sorry for what I needed to do. I would do it again if given the chance, but it seems that chance has been taken away. After Nergal had you in Hell, I had my doubts about you, but I must admit I held out hope you'd fight it. Did you even try to fight it, Cassandra? Or did you just take the coward's way out and let the darkness overtake you before you stole Nergal's essence?"

"You're wrong, Hadraniel. Not all of us have a choice. Some of us have our decisions made for us. I didn't *steal* Nergal's essence. He implanted me with it when he was doing god knows what else to me down in Hell. Seems he had been one step ahead of you. As always, I was simply a pawn in your little chess game of life."

"So, his corpse still remains?" he asked, hope sparking from that mere possibility.

"Oh, no," I said with a shake of my head. "I made sure no one else would have the chance to overpower me ever again. He's nothing but a dried up *has been* now."

Hadraniel stared at the ground, his features falling along with his gaze. "What are you going to do?" he asked, his head still bowed. When his head returned level, he looked around at all of the fallen angels, still writhing on the ground around us. "Will you kill them all?"

I peered around me, at first unfeeling, until my eyes fell on Braydon. He was on his side, hunched over, his face contorted in pain. I had caused that pain. It shouldn't have bothered me, but it did. Maybe it was because I still had some feelings for him deep down in my blackened heart, but I couldn't handle seeing him in pain.

"The light is still within you," Hadraniel said, breaking my focus on Braydon. "It's there. I can feel it."

"Maybe, but then all I have to do is think of you and what you've done, and that light shuts off completely."

"Then do what you need to do to me, Cassandra, but don't punish them," he said, motioning toward the rest of the angels. "They've done nothing but follow orders."

"Do you think I'm stupid enough to believe they'll allow me to waltz away from here after killing you? They're no match for me, but why deal with that when I can just be done with it all now?"

"You'll never be done with it. There will always be someone looking to take what you have. Don't you see that? With power comes enemies, Cassandra. Even those you probably wouldn't even dream could be your adversaries. Nergal wasn't always mine. For a long, long time, he was my confidante until he began to covet the power I had. Enemies are born from greed, and greed is not a trait found only in demons. It transforms good into evil if left to grow. That's how darkness was born and how it continues to feed. You'll never be safe."

He was right. I knew he was absolutely correct, but I couldn't just let them all go. I'd deal with whatever came after, but at least my biggest threat would be gone for the time being.

Again, I caught Braydon in my peripheral vision, still writhing in pain. I choked up. Dammit, why did it bother me so much? I wasn't supposed to feel anything. Not for these high-handed pricks.

But he was different.

Hadraniel glanced over at Braydon and then back at me again. He knew.

"Do it, Cassandra. Let him go."

I jabbed the Sword toward him, so close that when he raised his chin, the blade almost pierced it. "Shut up. Just... shut up."

He came for you. Not to use you, only to save you. But he was an angel, my sworn enemy. The argument in my head carried on for long moments before I finally gave up.

Shit.

I concentrated on Braydon only and saw his body go limp against the ground. I checked around to make sure none of the other angels had been released. They were all still in obvious pain.

Braydon slowly turned his head from the ground and looked up at me. "Cassie?" he croaked, confused or surprised. He wasn't the only one.

"Go, Braydon. Get out of here before I change my mind," I said, turning back to face Hadraniel, tightening my grip on the Sword, as if punctuating my intentions were imminent.

I saw Braydon pull himself into a sitting position out of the corner of my eye.

"Cassie, please don't do this. Let them go."

"Dammit, Braydon," I screeched. "Just get the fuck out of here, or I'll kill you too." My tone was harsh, monster-like. I barely recognized it. My head hurt from straining so hard keeping all of the rest of the angels down, and my heart raced causing a throbbing in my neck. I didn't know how long I could keep it together.

Braydon hadn't moved. *Why wouldn't he go?*

I turned my head and stared directly into his eyes. My eyes glowed. "Go, Braydon," I said through clenched teeth.

He stared back at me, his features sad. "No, Cassie. If you're going to do this, then you might as well kill me too. If you do this, you're not the person I thought you were." He studied me for a few moments before he said, "But I know it's not you. Fight it, Cassie. Don't do this."

I narrowed my eyes at him. "Who the fuck do you think you are? You think you *know* me? You don't know me." Spittle flew from my mouth with my words because I was so pissed. I was that feral dog, foaming at the mouth, rage-crazed and losing control.

"No, but I do."

That voice caused my skin to prickle and I tensed at the sound of his it behind me—*Hunter.*

How had I forgotten about him?

My heartbeat quickened, but it was different now. It wasn't the rage-infused drumming, it was nerves and... something else. Maybe fear? I couldn't think straight. I needed him to go away so I could think. No, so I could complete my mission.

"You don't know me anymore either." My voice sounded way too soft. I didn't dare look behind me. Keeping my focus on Hadraniel, the Sword still aimed at his head, I said, "No one does."

"I know you more now than I ever did. Look at me, Cassandra."

God, why did the mere mention of my name from him cause me to tremble inside and out? How could he still have an effect on me? I checked my hands, still clenched around the hilt of the Sword. They appeared steady, but the Sword was growing heavier in my grasp.

"No," I said. "You need to leave, Hunter. You can't stop me."

"*Look* at me, Cassandra."

He didn't raise his voice. It was low and smooth but guttural, dominantly male, and it commanded total compliance. His was the same voice that melted me so many times in the past.

I wanted to close my eyes and catch my breath, but I couldn't. If I gave one inch, everything would fall apart. Hunter might not be able to see the weakness since he was at my back, but Hadraniel was staring straight at me, and he would use any slight to overtake me. More pressure built in my head. I was losing control of my hold on the angels. It became harder to keep them down.

"Don't make me kill you too," I said, desperately trying to maintain control.

My hands trembled, and I almost dropped the Sword when Hunter's heavy hand grabbed my bicep, and he swung me around. He jumped back when the blade swiped out in front of me. I heard the faint sound of gasps behind me.

"If you're going to kill me," Hunter said, his eyes narrowed but practically iridescent, "you better damn well look me in the eyes when you do it."

My chest heaved as I breathed heavily in and out, in and out. Jesus, as dark and raging as I'd become, he was still beautiful to me. So gorgeous, it froze me. I couldn't think. I couldn't speak. For all the control I had, I might as well have been a victim in shock after witnessing something horrifying, or having seen something absolutely beautiful beyond words. Like seeing an... *angel.*

Hunter couldn't be here. He had to leave, one way or another. I had plans, and dammit, I was so close. But the love in his eyes when he stared back at me told me I was going to have to kill him before he'd ever let me go through with them.

"I'll do it," I said, shaking the Sword in front of me. I didn't know who I was trying to convince, him or me. Somehow, even with my heart as dead as stone, it still beat for him.

He raised his arms to his sides while his gaze penetrated what was left of my soul, and said, "Then do it, Cassandra. I have no weapon, and even if I did, you're more powerful than any of us. Do it, because if I mean nothing to you now, I don't want to live in this world anymore. I told you once before, you are everything to me. I lived for you and only you. And I would still die for you."

A battle raged within me, tearing me apart from the inside out. I craved the power like a starved mortal craved food, but to get it, I needed to kill the one thing that had once driven my very life force. I thought it was gone the second I plunged the Sword into Nergal. I thought there was nothing left of my heart to feel, but I was wrong. A tiny speck of light remained, and looking at Hunter, standing there so close, it pulsed with life. The spark was familiar and warm, but at the same time like poison.

I lunged at him but stopped as the tip of the blade touched his chest. He didn't move... hadn't flinched while continuing to hold my entire being with his penetrating gaze.

A memory flashed back of my dream, a nightmare back then. The time had come. This was my fate. Every single moment of my life had led up to this. My dreams had been glimpses of the destiny that awaited me. For so long, I was the one changing fate for others so they could have life. How ironic I never thought to change my own before it was too late.

"I know you're still in there," Hunter said, breaking me from my thoughts. "The woman I lived for, she's still there. If she weren't, you would have already plunged that blade into my chest. I love you, Cassandra."

My heart thumped even harder at his words, and my mind slipped, releasing its hold on the angels. I heard them moaning and scuffling around on the ground but didn't have the energy to try and claim hold of them again. Within a few moments, some of them rose slowly from the ground.

Hunter held his palms out, warding them off, and to my surprise, they stayed back. I didn't know whether I was relieved or not. In a way, I wanted them to overtake me so I wouldn't have to fight anymore, but the craving for power still warred within me.

"I'm going to give you five seconds," Hunter said, bringing my full attention back to him. The silence around us made his voice boom. "If you don't kill me in that time, I'm going to take the Sword from you."

"You think you can?"

"You're wasting time."

His cockiness irked me. I pressed the tip of the blade to penetrate his flesh. At the same time, an image of him lying on the ground, a pool of blood seeping from his chest flashed in my mind, and it was as if a lightning bolt struck my heart. A gasping cry hurt my ears, and I realized it was me. Then, my arms gave out.

Before I even knew what was happening, Hunter grabbed my wrists and peeled the Sword from my hands. He pulled me in and wrapped me in a steel embrace. I was aware of footsteps all around me, but I couldn't see anything with my face buried in his chest. Raised voices, angry words, and more commotion were happening behind me, but I didn't have the energy to do anything but let Hunter hold me.

"Don't even think about it," Hunter's said, his deep voice vibrating through his chest. "You touch her, you die. The Sword will stay with us until we come to an agreement. Now, back the fuck off."

More shouts and commotion. Hunter moved us back, not letting up on his hold of me. "Hadraniel, call them off now. Or I swear to you, I'll give her back the Sword and let her finish you all off."

A voice inside me cheered his words, wanting the Sword back in my hands to do just as he said, but another warned me of what else I'd need to do with it. I was a mess with no idea who or what I was anymore. My resolve and purpose, all seemed to have blurred into a hazy unknown the minute I heard Hunter's voice. I was lost... no direction, broken.

Hunter lowered his head against the side of mine and whispered, "I'm going to take you out of here, Cassandra. Everything is going to be all right now. You ready?"

I was numb, confused, so... lifeless. Was I ready? Yes... no. I had no idea, so I just nodded against his chest.

"I'm taking her away from here, and the Sword is coming with us," Hunter announced. "You will not come after us. Once she's stable, we'll come back and talk about what we're all going to do. If I see one halo anywhere near us, all bets are off. Is that understood?"

"No, it's not." The shout had come from Braydon. "I need to talk to her. I need to know she's okay."

"You're lucky I didn't kill you already." Hunter's voice was low, calm, but deadly. "I still might, but if you come anywhere near her, I'm going to make your death as painful as possible."

"She's filled with Nergal's essence, Hunter," Hadraniel said. "She was going to kill us all. She declared herself our enemy now. We can't just let her leave."

"We're all your enemy," Hunter retorted. "You don't have a choice here. We're leaving. Your only choice is whether you want to pursue us now and die, or wait for us to come to you when we're ready." He paused for a moment. "Eric, I'm taking her home. Gather with the others nearby and take the Sword with you."

"Okay, baby," he said into my hair. "Let's go."

And then I disappeared into sweet nothingness.

CHAPTER TWENTY-THREE

Hunter continued to hold me close, but eventually I lifted my head from his chest so I could see where we were. We had reappeared in a living room of some huge mansion I'd never seen. All the furnishings were modern, rich in comfort while the structure of the place seemed to come from medieval times. Incredibly high ceilings, arched doorways, and rooms as far as my eyes could see.

"Where are we?" I asked, my throat feeling gritty, my voice small and cracked.

He pulled me away from his chest and lifted my chin until our eyes locked. "Home," he said.

"Since when?"

"Since we escaped Hadraniel's jail after he betrayed us. It's always been my home, however. I only stayed in the apartment next to yours to be close to you. Eric and the others live here, as well. This has been our headquarters while searching for you." He rubbed both my cheeks with his thumbs as he stared into my eyes. "But you're here now. You're home, with me, where you belong."

It was all too much. After everything that had happened in the last few months, hell, in the last few days, for me to feel like I belonged... *anywhere*... was unreal. One minute I was hell-bent on a mission to take over the universe and the next I was back in the arms of the man I had once planned to spend the rest of my days with. I didn't know where I belonged, or which fate was true. How could I, when they both felt so... so me?

"I'm not sure where I belong anymore, Hunter."

His hands clamped the sides of my head, and he forced me to look back up at him. "You belong with me, Cassandra. Only with me. I will pledge the rest of eternity to get you to remember that if I have to, but you will remember. I promise you that."

"The evil, it's inside of me now. I mean, it always was, but Nergal he... you don't understand." He couldn't possibly.

"I don't understand?" he said, his eyes narrowed, his jaw tense. "I live it, Cassandra. Every damn day. Have you forgotten what I am? Where I came from? I was the right hand of Nergal, for fuck's sake. I was made for evil, but I chose you. Every day since I met you, I've chosen you over that pull to do what I was meant to do. Every day I fight it. There are times it took every bit of strength I had, but it got easier the more I fell in love with you. I know what Nergal did. I can sense it in you, but it doesn't mean you have to be like him. What runs through your veins, Cassandra, it doesn't matter. What your heart beats for is what matters."

He did know. How could I think he wouldn't? He was a demon, a seeker, someone who drained the life of guardians and brought them over to evil. In the beginning, that's all I could see, but once I'd fallen for him, he'd become like an angel, my guardian, and I forgot all about his past.

Maybe *this* was my fate, to come to a point where I completely lost my soul, and he'd be here to put me back on the right path. Was it possible I was meant to fall so far down to appreciate the goodness I had in my life and realize how easy it was to be that person? Evil had drained the life out of me. I'd never been so exhausted. I also knew if I continued down that path, it would always be that way, constantly fighting for power. And I'd be alone.

Looking back at Hunter now, seeing the unconditional love in his eyes, my heart beat again. And it didn't want to me to be alone. I knew at that moment that it wanted to grow stronger every day with the love I saw in those eyes. I wanted him to make it beat and keep it beating. I wanted him to be the guardian of my beating heart. I wanted him to be the guardian of my fate.

Tears slowly made their way down my cheeks as I gave in to this man before me and let him take the control I'd tried so hard to maintain during the last few days, or weeks, however long it had been. It felt so incredibly good to let it all go.

Hunter lowered his head and kissed the tears when my emotional dam crumbled. He continued to rain kisses on my cheeks, trailing them down to my jaw and softly brushing his lips against my quivering mouth.

"Just let go, baby," he whispered against my lips. "I'm here now. I'll always be here. I love you, Cassandra."

He kissed me. One kiss, then another, and another, until I had to have more, and pressed my mouth firmly against his. I wrapped my arms around his neck and held his head against me.

"I love you," I cried against his mouth. "I love you so much," I said while pressing my lips hard against his. He needed to know exactly how much.

When he tilted his head, we both opened up, allowing our tongues access into each other's bodies, encompassing each other's souls. They thrashed together, seeking, exploring, relearning the depths of emotions we once had for each another, our moans vibrating in a frantic, erotic symphony.

"You need to remember *us*," he said as his hands slid down over my ass, and then farther, until he lifted me up, urging me to wrap my legs around his waist, not once breaking our lips apart. Once my ankles were locked around his lower back, he carried me, to where, I had no idea because I didn't want to miss his mouth on mine to find out. At some point, however, I knew we were climbing from the rise and fall of his thighs against my backside.

Finally, he leaned me over and my back hit something soft. When he lifted me up and I released my hold on him, we were in a large, luxurious bed. As I lay there, my legs still parted, bent at the knees, I looked past them at my beautiful god, standing at the foot of the bed, admiring me as if I were the only thing on this earth.

He leaned over and placed his hands on my knees. "You've been gone for too long from me, Cassandra. I'm going to have to reclaim every inch of you." Upon saying it, he slid his hands down my thighs, toward the very place that throbbed longingly for him.

His thumbs came together over my core, and he applied the right amount of pressure to shoot a wave of pleasure up my body. No sooner had it subsided, than he slid them over it again. I was amidst another wave when he scooted up and unbuttoned my jeans. I lifted up as if on automatic and let him slide my pants down, taking the panties with them. I was gloriously bared to him, and his eyes filled with pleasure as he soaked up the sight. My hips moved of their own accord while I watched him send another wave of pleasure through me. The anticipation of his touch was almost unbearable.

"Lift up," he said, hoarse and demanding.

I did, and he grabbed my T-shirt by the collar with both fists and ripped it with ease down the center. Letting out a moan of appreciation, he leaned over me, grabbed the back of my head, and slammed his mouth into mine. I was lost in his kiss, completely, utterly absorbed in the delicious taste of him. His other hand eased down over my breast, and I pushed into his hand as he molded his palm to it.

A groan and a deep growl vibrated from my throat. His touch was magic, consuming, but teasing because he knew I needed more.

"Hunter," I breathed into his mouth, pleading.

His hand shifted in between my breasts, and then his fingers latched on to the bra there. I knew what was coming, but I reached behind me and undid the latch before he could rip the lace garment from my body. When the straps slipped down my arms, he pulled it off, sending it across the room.

He leaned back, breaking our kiss, and hovered over me, his hands planted on either side of my hips, his eyes heating my body as he studied every single inch of me. "You're the most beautiful thing I've ever seen," he whispered, and then his eyes locked onto mine. "Don't ever leave me again."

"I didn't leave—" I started, wanting to explain how it hadn't been my choice, but he shook his head and raised his hand to my forehead.

"You did, Cassandra. You left me long before you were physically gone from the Sanctuary. Here," he said and brushed his fingers across my forehead. "And here," he moved his hand down and covered my chest with his palm.

He was telling me he knew I'd begun to barricade him from my thoughts and my heart in the days before Hadraniel had taken me. I couldn't argue with him. At the time, I'd become so self-absorbed in my own thoughts and needs, I built a wall around my heart and allowed it to rot until it was so black and hard, I didn't feel anything.

Could it be by doing that, I'd made it easier for Hadraniel to take me and throw me to the wolves?

I reached my hand up to his face and brushed my thumb over his cheek, his lips. "I'm sorry." It was all I could say. No words seemed good enough, really. "Never again."

"I'm going to spend every second of every day making sure," he said. That was when he stood and started undoing his pants.

The image was hot, but his words made me chuckle. "So, I'm never leaving this bed?"

He winked at me with a sexy little smirk. "If I could get away with that, I would, but no." Dropping pants, I watched as his hard, beautiful manhood bobbed out and settled straight ahead. "I thought this would be a great way to start, though."

I couldn't keep my eyes off him, all of him. He was a gift, an undeniably gorgeous gift the universe bestowed upon me. Better than any piece of metal could ever be. With him, I had all the power I would ever need.

"God, I love your plans," I said with a grin of my own.

He crawled between my legs and then on top of me until his face was over mine, his forearms planted on the bed at either side of my head. "I love you," he told me, and then placed his lips on mine for a long, sweet kiss.

"I love you," I said back, hoping he could see how much I meant it when he lifted his head and gazed down at me.

He smiled, and I returned the expression, reveling in the sight of him being happy.

We stayed that way for a while, savoring the moment, looking into each other's eyes, feeling the unbelievable amount of love and adoration we felt for each other.

How could I ever have thought anything was better than this... than being with him like this? No power had ever been greater than the love we had for each other. Neither of us had to fight for it, it just... existed. We were always meant to be that way and always would be. That was the greatest emotion possible. I knew now, it was all I ever wanted.

Hunter pulled back and sat up on his knees between my legs. Placing his hands on either side of my neck and caressing his thumbs against my lips, I teased them with my tongue. His eyes clouded with even more desire, and he slid his palms down until his hands cupped both my breasts. His damp thumbs teased my nipples, sending a direct bolt of desire between my legs. I arched my back against his hands, filling them, encouraging him to pinch my nipples between his thumbs and forefingers. The pain came quick and I cried out, but he leaned over and suckled each one until it subsided into such an intense erotic sensation, it resonated throughout my entire body.

Hunter leaned back again and let his hands slide down my body with the movement until they were hovering over my most sensitive spot. My breathing became heavier, and I swore if he didn't move I'd pass out from lack of oxygen. Thankfully, I didn't have to wait long. With his eyes on mine, he shifted the thumb over my entrance, and I moaned with the pleasure it created. After a few torturous strokes, he finally used a thick finger to enter me, and then another. My hips launched up, wanting deeper, oh so much deeper. Plunge after plunge I rode his touch, the burning in my core getting hotter and hotter until I thought I might self-combust.

When his lips met my sensitive nub, I lost it. Sparks lit up behind my eyes from the most intense orgasm I'd ever had. My body had elevated to some other plane, one made of pure, senseless, erotic pleasure. I was floating in another realm, fully aware of the sensations of my body, but unable to control them or bring them down from their sensual high. I wasn't sure I ever wanted to come down.

Before I could get my bearings, Hunter grabbed my boneless body, lifted me up, and spun us around until he was lying where I'd been, and I was straddling his waist. His incredibly hard, unrequited desire was flush up against my sensitive core, sending new waves of longing through me.

My hands went to his chest. His eyes were equally hard and lustful as his erection beneath me.

"You're mine," he said, his voice low and gravelly, "but you have all the control right now."

"Do I?"

"Yes, but if you wait much longer, that could easily change. I've been without you for far too long, Cassandra."

"Hmmm," I teased, and slowly fluttered my fingers over his hard chest, down his defined abs. Gyrating my hips ever so slowly, I watched as his eyes took on a glow I'd never seen before. His chin raised causing his head to push back into the pillow behind him, and he let out a long, low moan. I *was* in control. Complete control. He surrendered everything to me, not only his body but his entire being. I witnessed what his body was feeling, but my soul knew what he was giving me much more than my eyes could ever see.

The now familiar power within me began to pulse. It was like a beacon, reminding me of where to go and what I needed to do to get there. That old nightmare vision of me in this very position, holding the Sword of Death up above Hunter, ready to plunge it into his heart, flashed in my head. I reached across the bed and over the side of the mattress. My movements were robotic as if on autopilot.

A hand clamped over my wrist and stopped my movement.

"What are you looking for?" he asked, his eyes no longer glowing, only curious.

I couldn't speak, I could only stare back at him, trying to bring myself back to reality. My chest heaved up and down as though I'd been running and couldn't catch my breath. What the hell was I doing?

"Cassandra, talk to me. What's happening?"

I still couldn't find the words to answer him. How could I tell him what I thought I was doing, what I was feeling? What *was* I feeling? Guilt? Regret? Disappointment? I didn't even know. A moment ago I wanted nothing more than to touch the Sword, have it in my hands. Killing him wouldn't have caused me to blink. But now, I was so relieved the Sword wasn't within reach.

Hunter shot up to a sitting position and grabbed the sides of my face. "Dammit, tell me what the hell is going on. I am not letting you go again. You can forget about blowing this off. We'll stay here like this until you talk to me."

Tears streamed down my cheeks as I stared back at him. "I... oh, god, I'm so broken," I sputtered as I cried.

He pulled my face forward and kissed me. "Tell me, baby," he said against my lips. "Tell me so we can fix you."

"I don't know if it's possible," I said. I was crying all out now, ugly crying. "It's a part of me now, he's a part of me."

He pulled back and watched me, so sincere and full of love. "That doesn't have to change who you are, Cassandra. You're strong enough to be whatever or whoever you want to be. *You* decide. *You* control how it beats your heart. *You* control your fate."

"But how? How do I let go of the spontaneous impulses? Jesus, Hunter, if the Sword had been here, I would have killed you."

"No, you wouldn't have."

He sounded so sure. How could he know?

I cast my eyes down, ashamed. The confidence he had in me was undeserved. He obviously didn't see how weak I'd really become.

He lifted my chin to look him in the eyes. "I know because you had that chance and you chose not to. That blade was almost an inch in my chest, but you pulled back. You've already proven you're strong enough to overcome the urges." He rubbed my cheek with his thumb. "It'll get easier, I promise."

"How do you know?"

"I know because I've been fighting those urges ever since I met you. The urges barely register now. I don't know why. Maybe my love for you has grown so much there's no more room in there for anything else. I don't care why because I couldn't change it if I tried. I love you more than my own existence." The love in his eyes held mine. "It's your turn, Cassandra. Choose me. Let me be the love that fills your heart and leaves no room for anything else. Let me be the guardian who saves your soul from the shadows that chase it. Choose. Me."

Looking back at him, his naked soul bared to me, the love and promise in his eyes confirmed every single word he said, scattering my doubts to the far corners of my mind. They disappeared far enough away to ease the weight on my heart and allow me to remember how to let him in completely once again. I knew those doubts would always linger, but I also knew I could trust this man to keep them where they belonged, tucked away in the recesses of my mind, only there to remind me of how much I needed him with me.

He was my everything. The love of my life, my hero, my savior, my angel. And I knew he'd watch over me the way all angels were meant to do. With Hunter, my fate seemed filled with light. It would be suicide to live any other way.

I looked deep into his eyes and remembered the way it had always been there between us. It was so familiar and filled me with all the love I needed.

"You've always been my choice, Hunter," I said as I wrapped my hands around his neck and breathed him in. "I just needed to open my eyes and let the light back in. Your light." I kissed him for as long as my lungs could take it. "I love you." The whisper tickled against his lips.

He backed his head up ever so slightly and watched me. His sexy little smirk made an appearance, and I realized how much I had missed it.

"Yeah?" he asked with a spark in his eyes.

"Yeah," I chuckled back.

"Then prove it," he said and ground another gorgeous part of his body against my core.

I moaned in absolute bliss, and then I did prove it... over and over... and over again. All the while vowing to never let either of us ever doubt it.

CHAPTER TWENTY-FOUR

As much as I wanted to stay in the safe cocoon that was Hunter, I knew I couldn't put off reality forever. Even if I tried, it would find me one way or another. I was reminded of that when Hunter left the bedroom after several hours of lovemaking and I heard conversations coming from downstairs. I sat up and listened, recognizing the familiar voices of Eric and Nora.

I didn't want to face them after all I'd done, especially since they knew what had become of me, but I knew I had to. At the very least they deserved an explanation. Nora especially, along with my most humble apology and gratitude, which probably wouldn't even begin to repair the damage I'd done to our friendship. I didn't know if we could re-tie the severed bonds we'd once had, but I needed to try. Whether I deserved it or not, I needed the support of my family and friends to survive this. Without them, I was as cold and empty as before and couldn't go back to that black place again. I'd rather die than be that person.

I stood up and put on the robe Hunter had laid out on a nearby chair.

"It's safe," I heard Eric say. He was talking in a low voice, but I could hear him as clearly as if he were in the room with me.

"Here?" Hunter asked.

"Yes, it's—"

Silence filled the house, and I knew they had been referring to the Sword. Hunter had somehow warned Eric off mentioning where it was. He knew I would hear them, and he didn't trust me to know where the object of my evil ways was located. I didn't blame him. If I were being honest, I didn't really want to know either. It was bad enough I knew it was in the same building. I didn't want to feel that pull any more than I already did. I couldn't trust myself.

I found my way to the staircase when Nora said, "Her parents are begging to see her, but he won't let them go."

"My parents?" I asked from the top of the staircase. "Handraniel's still keeping them prisoner?" I didn't know why I was so surprised. Nothing had changed. We still had what Hadraniel wanted, and they were his only leverage now on getting it, other than the threat of war.

They all turned and stared at me. My name crossed Nora's lips.

"Of course, he is," I said, making my way down the stairs. "We need to get them out of there."

"Cassandra," Hunter said, meeting me at the bottom of the stairs and cupping my elbow as we walked over to join Nora and Eric. "We'll get them out."

I greeted Nora and Eric with a nod of my head, then turned to look at Hunter. "I know, and I know how. I'd like to do that as soon as possible, please. They don't deserve to be there." I glanced at all of them, settling my gaze on Nora. "None of you deserved any of this."

Her features softened as she turned back to me. "No, but neither did you, Cassie."

"I'm not convinced of that, but thank you," I told her. "I'm so sorry about what happened, Nora. I know it's not much, just words, but if I could take it all back, somehow take back everything I did, I would. To be honest, I don't know how you can even look at me." I dropped my gaze to the floor hoping to make it easier to turn away. Easier for her or me, I wasn't so sure.

"I couldn't for awhile," she said. "You were so different, so…"

"Evil?" I said, finishing the thought for her.

"Yes, but that wasn't you. Not the real you, anyway. I knew that, but I didn't know how to get through to you. I'm just glad someone was able to. Welcome back, Cassie. I missed you more than you know."

She pulled me into a hug, and I had to stop myself from squeezing as hard as I wanted for fear of crushing her. Nora had to be the best friend anyone could ever have. I wasn't sure I was even worthy of her in my life anymore, but I wasn't going to let her go. I needed her now more than ever.

"Thank you," I breathed out as we pulled apart.

"We're all happy you're back," Eric said, reaching his arm around Nora.

I smiled at them both, so thankful they had each other. I hoped it would always be that way with them.

"Okay, so what's the plan to get the Sword to the angels and get my parents out?" I asked.

***

We showed up at the gates of the Sanctuary, Eric, Nora, Hunter and I, leading our group of loyal demons. We'd agreed not to transport any farther than the gates, so as not to appear threatening. The four of us weren't welcome guests anymore, not that we ever really had been. Now approaching as enemies, again for some of us, we'd come to call a truce.

Hunter was in charge of the Sword, not physically, only how it was being transported, and I hadn't seen it yet. They all decided it was best that way, the least amount of time I was tempted by it, the better. I knew it was physically with us in our group because it called to me as if we were long lost soul mates, but I fought it. Hunter's arm never once left my waist, and I had my family to save from a prison they didn't belong in to keep my mind focused on something other than universal destruction.

Six angels appeared on the other side of the gate, Michael, Detri, and Aviar among them. They all stayed at least a foot back, glaring at us through the wrought iron bars.

"Where's the Sword?" Michael asked with a bite to his words.

"What, no, welcome to the Gates of Paradise?" Hunter snapped back.

"Demons don't warrant welcomes," Aviar spit out, grouping us all in the category.

Yep, still hated him.

"Get Hadraniel, you asshat," Nora blurted. "Or we may just use the Sword to shut that mouth of yours up for good."

I stared at her, surprised by her outburst but was so very proud to call her my friend.

"Asshat?" I whispered.

"What? He is *so* an asshat." She beamed with her special smile.

I laughed, but it was short-lived.

"Do you have the Sword with you or not?" Michael said, his tone revealing irritation.

"We do," Hunter said.

"Then hand it over."

"No way," I said. "Not until my parents are free and we speak with Hadraniel."

"You think you have the power to order—" Michael started.

"I think you know firsthand the power I have, Michael," I said, my narrowed gaze piercing his. "How's the head, or do you need a reminder?"

Hadraniel appeared out of nowhere, standing in front of his angels on the other side of the gate. "There's no need for that, Cassandra. I assume since you're standing outside of the gates and not inside the Sanctuary shedding blood you would like to discuss some kind of agreement. If it has to do with you giving over that Sword, I'm listening, but I'm not promising."

"Release my parents, and we'll give you the Sword," I said.

"How about, you hand over the Sword now, and I'll send them out to you," Hadraniel countered.

"Not happening," Hunter said through clenched teeth.

"Oh, for the love of God, Hadraniel, just open the damn gates." Anael appeared next to Hadraniel, hands on hips, glaring at him.

"Anael, this is not your place," Hadraniel said. I could tell he was trying his damnedest not to lose his cool. It was actually quite fun to witness. Not as much fun as Anael putting him in his place, but damn close.

"The hell it is. If they wanted to kill us with the Sword, they would have already done it. They're here to make a truce, and we're going to listen. They've been through enough, we all have, so let's put this to rest once and for all, okay?" She put her hand on his arm and added, "Please," in a much softer tone.

Hadraniel stared back at her. I couldn't see his eyes well enough from our vantage point, but from the way they were staring at one another, I guessed there were a lot of emotions passing between the two.

Eventually, he said, "Fine." Turning to the angels, he nodded. "Set them free and bring them out."

Within seconds, my parents were approaching the walkway toward the gate. The angels hadn't even left yet, so someone else had to have released them. From the look Hadraniel gave Anael, I knew exactly who that someone else was.

Anael broke her gaze from his and focused on me.

"Thank you, Anael," I said.

The gates opened and she walked over to me. Before I knew it, she had me in her arms. "I'm so sorry for what you've been through, Cassie. I know how hard it is to break the hold Nergal has over you. He may not have been in my blood, but for awhile, he had a hold over me in another powerful way."

"Love," I said as she pulled back to look at me.

"Yes, or what I thought was love. The heart is the strongest, but it's also the hardest to let go. It took me awhile to learn that." She glanced at Hunter then. "I'm so glad those who hold your heart have captured it for the right reasons."

He nodded her direction and then his eyes latched on to mine. "I am too," I whispered.

My parents had reached us then, and they practically flew at me. I barely had a chance to smile before I was locked in an embrace between them. My mom cried, and they both told me how thankful they were I was okay, how they were so worried, how much they loved me.

The love in my heart swelled, and I could barely feel the call of the Sword. Anael was right—the heart *was* the strongest. As long as it was filled with love, it was much stronger than the deadened pull of power. I knew that now.

"I believe you have something to give me," Hadraniel interrupted our moment, killing the whole love-vibe thing we had going on.

"Not just yet," Hunter said.

"I knew you would—"

"You'll get the damn Sword," I shouted, his hypocritical mistrust in us grating on my nerves. "But we have terms."

"You have terms?" he repeated, his face showing disdain for the idea.

"Yes," I said.

Hunter approached Hadraniel so they were only a foot apart. "We'll give you the Sword as long as you guarantee to keep it locked away. And I suggest somewhere other than the Sanctuary. No one else can know of its location but you, and maybe Anael. None of your angels, no one who may decide to turn on you again and steal it from under your nose."

"That was one—"

"And you never know when there may be another. You and I both know anyone is capable of turning into something else. Trust no one."

This was a stipulation we came up with for both the angels, the demons in our group, and me especially. I didn't want to know where it was. If I knew, the draw to go to it, possess it, by whatever means, would be too great.

"This is for the good of all of us," Hunter added.

I don't know if Hunter motioned toward me with his eyes or Hadraniel just got the drift, but he glanced at me and then agreed.

"Where is Braydon, by the way?" I asked, the talk of him stealing the Sword reminding me I wanted to talk to him, tell him how much I appreciated what he did for me. Console him if I needed to. He did claim to love me, and I had taken advantage of that. It was an awful thing to do, and while he wasn't the most innocent party in this, I still had the need to defend him.

Hunter growled. He was glowering at me. Could he read my thoughts or was he just angry I even asked?

"He's locked up for his crimes as a traitor," Hadraniel answered.

"I want to talk to him."

"Not a chance, Cassandra," Hunter said.

"I won't allow it anyway," Hadraniel said. "He's being punished for what he did. He's not permitted visitors."

"For how long?" I asked.

"A year, perhaps. I haven't decided."

"But—"

Hunter grumbled again at my protest, but it was Anael who stopped me. "He'll be okay, Cassie. I'll talk to him. He won't be treated unfairly. *I* won't allow it." She aimed the last part at Hadraniel.

He rolled his eyes, shook his head, and took a breath as he turned from her to me and asked, "Anything else?" in a way that told me he was nearing his breaking point from this conversation.

"Yes, you are never to use the Sword against any of us, or anyone in our group. I know it's in your nature not to trust demons, but you know us now. You know we're different. And I ask that you consider that fact when you come across any other demon. Unless you see them doing harm to mortals or another angel, I want you to find out if they might be something more than just evil blood in a mortal body."

"That's asking a lot," he said. "We're angels, it's what we do. We fight evil."

"Your perspective of evil is distorted, Hadraniel. You know it, as well as I do. There is evil in every form of being. It's in demons, mortals, and even the angels. We're all capable of it. What makes the difference is how we choose to act on it."

"Like you?" Hadraniel asked.

Hunter stood up a little straighter in front of Hadraniel, a silent threat permeating from him.

"Like you," I retorted.

He narrowed his eyes at me, but I knew I'd gotten to him.

"Fine," he said. "Now is that all, or do you have a list for me to read through?"

"That's all," I said.

"Great, then give me the Sword."

"We'll have your word," Hunter, his voice low, but demanding.

They stared at each other for a few moments, before Hadraniel said, "I agree to all of your terms. You have my word."

I breathed a sigh of relief, but that feeling of respite ended quickly when Hunter turned and strolled over to one of the demons in the back of our group. I knew what he was doing. I knew what was coming, and my pulse raced with anticipation. The call for power was back, and it was strong, so strong... I was trembling where I stood. I turned away, facing my loved ones, hoping their faces would drown it all out again, but the sensation was only dulled.

Within a blink, Hunter was next to me, the Sword in his hands, the hilt facing down. I could barely breathe. I wanted to run, disappear, touch it, grab it in my palms again and feel the heat pulse through my body from its power.

I was close to breaking again, Hunter put his arm around my waist, leaned over, and whispered, "I love you, Cassandra. You can do this. I'm right here with you."

"You want me to..."

At the same time, I heard Hadraniel say, "I don't think that's a good idea, Hunter. It's obvious she can't fight it."

I don't know if it was Hadraniel's lack of faith in me, or Hunter's trust and warmth wrapped around me, but I knew at that moment that I had to do this. I needed to prove to all of them I was strong enough. I was *good* enough.

I took the hilt of the Sword from Hunter's hands, and when I did, that familiar heat shot through me. My hands shook, but I held it as steady as possible. Hunter leaned in and planted a soft kiss on the cheek, and whispered against my skin, "I love you, baby."

The heat remained, but my resolve strengthened against it. Hunter's love was the light of protection that wrapped around me and numbed me from the force I held within my hands.

I turned the Sword up and laid it out horizontally on my outstretched arms. When I took the focus off the placement of the Sword, I realized the angels had begun to spread themselves around Hadraniel and Anael. Hadraniel put his hand out to stop them from closing in.

Taking careful steps, one foot in front of the other, I looked Hadraniel in the eyes and extended my arms and the Sword to him. "May this truce bring peace among us, even if we can't stand to live amongst each other. I trust you with this,

Hadraniel. I know in my heart you want to do good. Someday you'll trust that we do too."

He took the Sword from me and placed it blade down between us. "Believe it or not, Cassandra, I've learned a lot through all of this. You're quite unique and have shown me things I've never known were possible in all of my existence. Sometimes it takes more for an old dog like me to come around, but we can change. I'm learning. May you find peace in your world now. God knows you've been through enough to deserve some. Keep fighting the good fight, and we'll see each other again. Thank you for this."

With that, he disappeared. Gone in an instant. And one by one, all of the angels left the area too. Anael gave me one more hug and made me promise to keep in touch, but I knew that wouldn't be possible, not for a long time anyway. The wounds were deep and slow to heal. But the angels and demons, who had a long history of bad blood, now had a mix, one who connected the two, possibly one who could bring them together and bring peace among us... once and for all.

The potential existed. Anything was possible. Fate was an open field of opportunities now, and I couldn't be happier for it.

After more hugs from my parents and Nora, Hunter wrapped me up in his arms and kissed the top of my head. I smiled into his chest, feeling freer than I've ever felt before.

"I knew you could do it," he said when I raised my head to see his face.

"You did? How could you be so sure?"

"Because you're mine and I wouldn't have it any other way," he said with a smirk.

I pushed at his chest playfully, but my demeanor changed to serious. Eyes locked on his, my soul reaching out to touch him, I said, "I chose you."

He smiled at me. "You chose me." Then he leaned down and placed a sweet, tender kiss on my lips. "Ready to go home?" he asked.

I smiled back. "I'm ready to live."

THE END

Reviews help readers decide if a book is right for them. If this story worked for you, please consider leaving an honest review. Just a few words make a real difference.

Thank you!

More books by L.J. Kentowski

Fate Trilogy:

Guardian of Fate (Book 1)
Seeker of Fate (Book 2)
Angel of Fate (Book 3)

Lexie Pearce Series:
Descended in Vengeance (Book 1)

Heart of Seeton Series:
Love Owned (Book 1)
Full Potential (Book 2)

Learn more about these books at
http://www.laurakentowski.com/

<u>Get a FREE Urban Fantasy Short Story!</u>
When you sign up for my VIP Newsletter, you'll receive access to release news, upcoming events, and exclusive content and giveaways!
As a thank you for joining, you'll also receive a FREE bonus short story companion to the Lexie Pearce Series!
Get started here:
https://preview.mailerlite.io/forms/1675703/160480288834586588/share

About The Author

L.J. Kentowski lives with her husband and son in the Midwest, where to keep from freezing her tail off for nine months out of the year, she bundles up in front of a fire, writes stories, eats Twizzlers, and tries to ignore the Great Dane on her lap while she types.

Her first series is an Adult Urban Fantasy/Paranormal Romance trilogy, *The Fate Series*, filled with Angels, Demons, and the In-Betweens.

To learn more about L.J.'s books, visit her at the following places:

Newsletter (free newsletter announcing book releases and special contests)
Website
Facebook
Pinterest
Instagram

www.ingramcontent.com/pod-product-compliance
Lightning Source LLC
Chambersburg PA
CBHW070857180626
46817CB00003B/808